One Man's Quest for Righteousness

Robert J Cottle

Copyright © 2023 by the **Bellbird Trust**

Published by: **Bellbird Books,**
2 Sabine Drive,
Richmond, Nelson, 7020,
New Zealand.

ISBN 978-1-7386151-0-0 (Paperback)
ISBN 978-1-7386151-1-7 (Hardback)

Special thanks:

To: my new friend Bruce for his time-consuming efforts in editing this book.

To: my Bible study life group leader and Church elder who also diligently reviewed this book.

To: my brother, David Nation for his incredible work of checking my theology within this book

Revelation 19:7-8 tells us, *"For the marriage of the Lamb is come, and his wife hath made herself ready. And to her was granted that she should be arrayed in fine linen, clean and white: for the fine linen is the righteousness of saints."* [KJV] This book explores the question; whom will attend the marriage supper of the Lamb?

*"Pursue peace with all men, and the sanctification **without which no one will see the Lord**."* Hebrews 12:14 (ASV)

A Prayer for David

He was but born in God's own time

His little body just so fine

At six months old he fell quite still

My daughter fret, he sure was ill

The seizures came more frequent now

Though doctors clearly knew not how

The tests, they always came back clear

His little life we held so dear

The medications, oh so abundant

The seizures still were not redundant

So bright and happy he did keep

And seldom did we see him weep

Oh how he's grown, it's now nine years

We give to God, the many cares

His body, fully formed and blessed

What happens in his brain is guessed

There is so much that we could ask

But to walk and talk, that is the task

Please pray to God, for this big need

As on his goodness, we do feed

Jesus heals, we know he can

We ask it, Lord, for this young man

And he, no more, will lie upon the floor

But like his peers, in life will soar

In your Name Lord Jesus.

Dedicated to my Grandson David – please lift him up in your prayers and give all Glory to God.

Table of Contents

Introduction – Why Fifty Shades of White?

Let's deal upfront with the elephant in the room. Yes, this is a Christian book and yes, I am aware that there is a very earthly book with a similar title relating to a different color. And no, I've never read the Grey book, and nor do I intend to, but I have reviewed the plot – an innocent young woman is drawn into an ever deeper complexity of sexual depravity under the adept manipulation of a certain Mr. Grey. The only true similarity between that book and this is the title and in our case an increasing level of relationship with God.

While researching for another Christian book I had planned to write, the Holy Spirit revealed to me that there is often a substantial gap between God's standard of righteousness and that of many Christians and, dare I say it, whole Christian churches. Why is it, for instance, that some Christians are accepting of aborting infant babies or having an openly gay pastor while others abhor the very thought? Now those are extreme illustrations, for sure, but at the other end of the scale, we find those who, under the guise of being righteous, forbid any contact with unbelievers and essentially live their earthly lives in communal isolation. Meditating on these examples led me to ask the following questions:

- What exactly is Righteousness?
- What is God's standard of Righteousness?
- Are there really varying degrees of Righteousness?
- How is it that we have so many have different ideas of what Righteousness is?
- Is it just individuals affected or does it affect whole churches too?
- Does it actually matter that there are so many human variations of Righteousness?
- Why is there confusion regarding Righteousness, are the scriptures ambiguous on this subject?
- What's the long-term (eternal) effect of a varying standard of Righteousness?

The list could go on but I guess you get it – it's all about Righteousness. Clearly, some Christians fully understand true Righteousness but from God's level to the bottom rung of the ladder there are at least fifty different shades of white (as in righteousness) and perhaps many more. Again why should this be? The risk is that unless we clearly understand the real standard we become self-guided. In the same way that Mr. Grey led innocence to a very depraved level, self-guided righteousness will not lead us towards God but far away from him.

Unfortunately man in his natural cunning, in attempting to live by an acceptable standard of righteousness, creates religion. Religion is essentially a set of rules which, if strictly adhered to, may demonstrate the resemblance of righteousness but in reality be anything but. Religion in its fullest extent frequently reverts backward plunging into the lowest shades of so-called white or perhaps even grey.

This book sets out to explore exactly what righteousness really is and why and if it's important. It is not intended as a how-to, self-help guide to obtaining righteousness. Nor is it a religious description to help us achieve understanding. My goal is to inspire Christians to understand and seek God's righteousness and allow that to show through in their lives.

The scriptures are very vocal on the subject of righteousness – right standing with God – and from them, we see that the consequence of not being clothed in righteousness will completely exclude us from living in eternity with God. Since our eternal destiny is at stake, clearly this is not a subject to be taken lightly. The Bible provides an excellent portrayal of God and exactly what His standard is. The scriptures are the only place to go to when seeking an understanding of such an important subject.

Writing 90,000 words on the theology of righteousness based on biblical foundations is relatively straightforward. However to retain the interest of most readers, without the sudden onset of rigor mortise, is an entirely different challenge. To counter this I invented Maxwell White and followed his life and discovery of righteousness and where that led him. While Maxwell is a figment of my imagination he is loosely based around someone I know well who has gained a little experiential knowledge of what it is to be in right standing with God.

In this book, my intention is to allow the Word to speak for itself and not instill personal bias. Please read carefully and ask the Holy Spirit for understanding. Also, don't take my word for it. Please personally check out all the Bible references given.

Finally, I believe that God has a sense of humor so again I've incorporated well-meaning but ambiguous quotes from various church signs around the world at the start of each chapter.

*"God made Adam and Eve
not Adam and Steve"*

Chapter 1
The Foundation

"Get a move on Maxwell, your school bus leaves in fifteen minutes; it'll take you that long to bike to the factory in this wind." Maxwell heard his mother but ignored her. Firstly, he reckoned, it does not take fifteen minutes to get to the bus stop, besides, he is eight now and can do it fast on his new bike. "Do I really have to go to school on my birthday, Mum?" Maxwell asked, hopefully. No motherly answer was forthcoming except that Maxwell suddenly found a large school satchel thrust in his face and felt himself being ushered speedily towards the bike shed.

The year was 1958 and for all of his eight years Maxwell's parents had worked a busy dairy farm with his three sisters. The delight of his father was obvious, three daughters were great but to produce a son was a crowning achievement. This fact was never lost on Maxwell and while we would never call him privileged, he certainly knew how to milk the favour of his doting father at any opportunity. This day his father was busy milking the herd therefore his plea to his mother for a birthday recreation were ignored and before he knew it, he was peddling the two miles down the country road to the bus stop at the milk processing factory.

Maxwell enjoyed the ride, he always liked to think and despite the essential task of racing his sisters, the ride was a time to smell the country air and ponder. He was becoming a man now, eight is a major birthday milestone – "in 13 years, Maxwell considered, I'll be 21 and then I'll know everything, just like my Dad!"

As the wind swept against his face, Maxwell reflected on the past few weeks. A feeling of smugness welled up within him – he was now permitted to "break bread", the youngest ever at his fellowship to do so. Normally one had to wait until at least 16 or 17 before they could possibly be responsible enough to understand the vast implications of partaking of the Lord's Supper. No, not Maxwell, the international leadership said kids his age could, so he was up for it. He loved Jesus and breaking bread was the next logical step in following Him. That was the easy bit, he reflected, getting there was sure a bit scary though.

Maxwell's parents together with their wider family attended a local fellowship in their rural community that was part of an international movement of several thousand devoted subjects led by a spiritual authority based "overseas." The movement had no name; it was just "The Assembly" as in the only true Assembly and followers of Jesus our Lord and Saviour. The Leader, well let's just say he was very close to God and

Chapter 1
The Foundation

what he said and what God said were actually pretty much one and the same – or so Maxwell's Assembly believed.

Fellowship life consisted of meetings, meetings and more meetings. Sunday was a special day; first there was the breaking of bread service at around 11am (to allow the attending farmers time to milk their cows) followed by a lunch break then a one hour bible study discussion, off home to milk the cows again then straight back for a fiery preaching of the Gospel at 7.30pm. For a young man with few farming responsibilities the fellowship lunch was the pinnacle of the day. It was time to hang out with a friend or grandparents and enjoy their cut sandwiches, which naturally were always several levels better than anything his mother could create.

Attendance on Sunday was compulsory even for young families but Maxwell didn't mind. All his friends came and there was always plenty of fellowship time, not to mention the twenty acres of bush that adjoined the country hall. Monday night was prayer meeting, Wednesday night another Bible discussion night and once a month on a Saturday evening there was a "Care meeting" when the Assembly's business and finances were discussed and agreed. Only those who had officially been accepted to "break bread" were allowed to participate in communion on Sunday or take any part in the service. Prayer meeting and care meeting attendances were only for those who broke bread on Sundays. Maxwell felt a small lump in his throat – truly he was a responsible believer now, his life had been elevated to almost adult status.

A decree had come from overseas, or was it from on high, or was there a difference. Seventeen's too old to deign church attendees to "break bread." It was said that if they were accepted as a part of the Assembly then they might be less likely to frequent the "Picture Palaces". Movie theatres were becoming common place and the pictures on Saturday night was no place for a believer to be found before coming to meet the Lord on Sunday morning. No, it was much better to bind them in as fellowship members at a younger age, and let guilt lock them there. Since few ever joined the church from the outside holding on to the many bred within was the simplest solution for increase.

None of this reasoning was ever conveyed to Maxwell and neither did he care. He had attended the Gospel meetings since he was first able to sit in a chair by himself and he knew full well what sin was and that Jesus had died in payment for his sins. That seemed like a good thing to Maxwell and if he was allowed then he wanted to be a formal part of His fellowship.

It's fair to say that not every Assembly member was totally on board with a twelve year old – let alone, heaven forbid a seven year old – taking part in the Lord's Supper! What if they addressed God incorrectly? It would bring the church into disrepute. Maxwell drank in the conversation with interest but

Chapter 1
The Foundation

in truth he only heard the bit about there being on real age limit on who could or could not "break bread." Maxwell was in.

At the dinner table that night he brought up the subject, questioning not so much on the fact if he could but on the how it was done. Maxwell's dad, while a little hesitant at having his young son to be the first of the local fledglings scrutinised and initiated into the believer club, sensed the eagerness in Maxwell's questioning and gave the explanation. "First you have to ask someone, they will discuss it with one or two other brothers and then the Assembly elders. The elders will select two or three brothers to make a time and come and visit with you to ask you why, to be sure you're genuine. The whole Assembly will then meet, but you'll have to stay home, and they'll discuss the report of the brothers and consider if you should be allowed to 'break bread.' Once that's done the same brothers as first met with you will come back and report the answer to you." "No sweat," thought Maxwell, "that'll be a breeze I'll do it next Sunday."

Later in bed Maxwell assessed who was best to ask. He went through the twenty or so men he thought would be worthy to receive his request. No, too old, too strict, funny laugh, horrible kids etc. Finally he decided on the father of one of his best friends. He liked the way he preached the gospel as he made it interesting, not such a guilt trip like some. Decision made, Maxwell fell in to a satisfied sleep and couldn't wait until Sunday.

Sunday finally arrived and much to his surprise Maxwell felt a little nervous but not the least bit apprehensive. After the meeting, seeing his man by himself, he approached. "Hello Mr Honeycutt," Maxwell stated nonchalantly, and then abandoning any further attempt at small talk blurted out, "I would like to ask if I could please break bread." Honeycutt was a kindly man about the same age as Maxwell's own father and if he was taken aback he certainly never let it show. "Oh, I see," he answered. To Maxwell the pause seemed like hours but Mr Honeycutt wasn't known for his speedy vocabulary and eventually he smiled knowingly, and said "Ok, I'll have a talk with the brothers."

How that conversation went Maxwell never found out but judging by what he later heard, not so well. "How old – NOT YET EIGHT – and he asked you if he could break bread!" "What were you thinking Honeycutt?" Fortunately the international leader's words held precedence and two of the most staunch and spiritual brothers in Maxwell's little fellowship where dispatched to "visit" with Maxwell after School on Thursday.

Mr Truman and Mr Belmont arrived and were ushered into the lounge room and seated with a cup of tea. Maxwell was summoned and given last minute counsel by his concerned mother. "Don't be scared, just try and answer their questions best you can," she advised.

Maxwell, just a few weeks short of eight years, sat on the couch. Truman and Belmont sat in the armchairs opposite, the clock on the mantelpiece obliviously chimed for quarter past the hour. Belmont had poured half of his cup of tea into his saucer to let it cool. Maxwell had seen his grandfather do that when he was in a hurry, could be a good sign he thought. Truman wasn't in any rush; he sat stony-faced alternating between surveying Maxwell and dunking of his ginger-nut biscuit into his cup of tea. "Only way I can eat these things," Truman blurted, to no one in particular, "They'll shatter my false-teeth otherwise," he continued, following which he quickly threw the whole thing into his mouth with a slurp before the sloppy residue fell apart completely.

The local assembly didn't have an official leadership as technically everything was agreed collectively at fellowship level. However in practice, the older one became the more spiritual he must be, as he'd walked with God that much longer. If you were 'spiritual' then your voice carried considerably more influence than those not so blessed. Truman and Belmont were in their late 60's which in the 1950's was unquestionably twilight years. Both had been dairy farmers all their lives and showed the effects of a tough life. They saw no reason to use twenty words when five would do and as for the choice of words anything would do provided it wasn't a designated swear-word or a blasphemy. Conveying the message clearly and forcefully took strong precedence over charm, wit and compassion. Maxwell sat in silence wondering if he'd perhaps been a little rash, these two were going to fry him alive, he thought, "but too late to back out now."

After what seemed like the whole of eternity, Truman spoke first. "Honeycutt tells us you want to break bread. Why?" Truman left his sentence hanging as if there couldn't possibly be an appropriate answer – least none he could think of. Without waiting for Maxwell to speak Truman continued, "Do you know what a sinner is son?" His tone and the deliberate pause made it very clear to Maxwell that a definitive answer was mandatory.

"Yes Mr Truman," Maxwell replied hesitantly.

Truman didn't acknowledge Maxwell's answer but continued with his own thoughts on the subject. "The world is full of sinners; they are not like us as they don't have the value of our leader, 'the man of God.' We are the blessed ones, they're all sinners, every one of them, especially the Catholics!"

Maxwell didn't know how to reply to that and nor did he dare, the last thing he wanted was an angry Mr Truman. For reasons unknown to Maxwell the Catholics were a pet hate of Mr Truman. "Do you know what righteousness is, boy?" Truman asked gruffly.

Crikey we're all in trouble if Mr Truman doesn't know what righteousness is Maxwell reflected. "Yes" replied Maxwell. He'd been to many gospel preaching's and knew too well that if he did wrong, he was unrighteous and had to repent. "If we repent of our sins we're righteous," Maxwell added almost as an afterthought.

Chapter 1
The Foundation

Even though he didn't show it Truman was taken aback at Maxwell's answer, the lad had been well coached, he thought. A change of tact was necessary if he was to find the true colours of this young whippersnapper. He is not even eight, for goodness sake he thought; nobody can be spiritual at that age. "So why do you want to Break Bread?" Truman asked after a consider pause.

That one's easy thought Maxwell, relief flooding his little body at finally getting to the real subject at last. "Because Jesus died for my sins," he answered confidently; he knew that was the right answer and Mr Truman couldn't frown this time.

"Are you sure about that, Boy," Truman snapped back.

"Absolutely, Mr Truman," Maxwell replied confidently. At that very moment something clicked within Maxwell, he just knew that he knew that Jesus was his Saviour. He was only seven years old but he'd done enough to know that some things you did, you got into trouble for, like kicking your sister (whatever the reason), or telling a lie; they were sins. The only way a sin could be removed was to confess it to Jesus and because Jesus had died for sin then the penalty of what was done was paid in full. His father had explained to him once that there were consequences for our sins sometimes, whatever that meant. Probably that was why he still got a hiding for doing some things and not for others, even if he had confessed it to Jesus.

Right at that moment a milestone was established in Maxwell's young soul. He was saved and was going to go to Heaven, because Jesus had died for his sins, and yes if he was truthful he had committed some. There was no penalty anymore. There was, however, still Mr Truman.

The questioning went on for a full hour and a half and strangely Belmont never said a word. Truman frequently referenced him, asking him if he agreed with this or that but never gave him time to answer. Belmont wasn't bothered, he was only there as a witness and he would back-up whatever conclusion Truman came to. It's all about witness he thought, as he recited Matthew 18:16 in his mind, *"But if he do not hear [thee], take with thee one or two besides, that every matter may stand upon the word of two witnesses or of three."* According to the translation he used. [DBT]

Finally the clock on the mantelpiece struck three quarters past the hour – it was 4.45pm. Truman looked up as if woken from a trance, "Getting near dinner time, we'll leave it there Boy, and have a talk to the Assembly about it." With that the two got up said their pleasantries to Maxwell's mother and were gone.

Maxwell's Mum wanted all the details, but Maxwell wasn't interested. It was still light outside and he had wasted enough valuable playing time.

It was three weeks until the next Care Meeting and Maxwell's case, as it had become known, was on the agenda.

Chapter 1
The Foundation

During the preceding weeks nobody had asked Maxwell any further questions and neither was the matter discussed by anyone, it was as if he'd never raised it. Maxwell had expected a few words of congratulations or encouragement, but zilch. All his friends, however, were very eager to proffer their advice. Na, Truman will never allow it, seemed to be the popular opinion. Maxwell though was quietly confident. The overseas leader had said people his age could and he had asked, so the outcome was obvious, wasn't it?

Finally the Care Meeting arrived. It was held as usual after milking at 7.30pm Saturday. Only those that already broke bread and therefore 'in Fellowship' were allowed to attend. Maxwell's mother stayed home to mind him and his sisters and he quickly found himself bathed and into bed.

It was never reported to Maxwell precisely what had transpired at that evening meeting but it's suffice to say his father didn't get home until 10.30pm that night and Maxwell was already sound asleep. Next morning Maxwell begged his father for information as he hurriedly ate his breakfast, ready for the Sunday meeting schedule. "Sorry Maxwell," his father replied, "you know the rules, I'm not allowed to talk about anything that happens in the care meeting. Mr Truman will have a talk to you soon" Stupid rule, Maxwell thought, but he knew better than to say that aloud as that would be a sin and he better not sin any more. Those that broke bread had to be righteous.

After the morning 'breaking of bread' as everyone mingled, Maxwell made his way in the general direction of Mr Truman, without making it obvious, or so he thought. Next thing he found himself right beside Mr Truman, who up close today really didn't look in a good mood. Maxwell flirted with the idea of making a run for it but it was too late. "What is it son," Truman grunted. I do have a name, was what Maxwell wanted to say but instead opted for the direct approach. "Am I allowed to break bread?" Maxwell asked. "It seems so," Truman retorted and abruptly walked away. "Yesssss," said Maxwell quietly to himself.

Later, after ecstatically sharing the news with his friends and anyone else that would listen, he was heading back into the meeting room ready for the start of the Bible reading meeting when he caught sight of Mr Honeycutt striding towards him, he hadn't talked to him since asking to break bread. "Did Mr Truman give you the good news?" he asked. "Yes" replied Maxwell excitedly, "what happens now, when do I start to have communion?" "Not so fast," Honeycutt replied, "first you have to be announced. During the notices part in the breaking of bread service it will be announced that the assembly has accepted you to break bread. That has to be announced for the next three Sundays to make sure everybody knows. The week following, you will be handed the emblems, the cup and the bread, like the rest of us."

"Oh, thanks Mr Honeycutt," Maxwell replied a little subdued. He didn't know about those rules but he did know about the notices even though he'd never really listened to them. He'll have to pay attention from now on. One small fact did escape Maxwell thoughts though; how could it be, in such a small fellowship, that someone would not have already heard of Maxwell's case and outcome. Clearly 'Rules' were paramount.

The next three Sundays seemed like an eternity but on each one Maxwell sat proudly as he heard the words, "Maxwell White had been accepted into fellowship and would begin to break bread on the Lord's Day of 20th September." Eventually the 20th arrived, this was the big day. Just as if he'd been allowed all his life, when the bread was broken and passed around it was very deliberately handed to him by his father who sat next to him. Maxwell broke off a chunk, as his mother had coached him – not too big, not too small. His three sisters and his friends watched on enviously but secretly hoping for some catastrophic failure – surely he's going to drop it!

Partaking of the bread was easy enough Maxwell thought, therefore it was with much newly assumed confidence that he grasped the large glass cup which everyone shared containing the emblem of the Lord's blood. Before Maxwell could restrain himself he had inhaled a substantial mouthful of the finest sherry money could buy in a country village in the 1950's. Unable to breathe or swallow Maxwell fortunately had the quick presence of mind to pass the cup on. He had never tasted alcohol before and despite his mothers' coaching nothing had prepared him for this.

Option one: Spit it out.

Option two: do anything else.

Even through the watery eyes Maxwell emphatically dismissed option one, while probably the most logical and easiest solution that could never happen. He was almost eight, he had pride. The powerful sherry could have made a great paint remover, or perhaps it really was, Maxwell pondered. The burning up his nose, unbearable but somehow he had to breath. Maxwell made a quick grab for his handkerchief (provided clean by his mother that morning) and surprisingly the motion created a swallow, the mouthful of fine sherry slid gracefully down his throat, burning as it went. With an empty mouth and hanky in hand Maxwell was free to cough, splutter and dry his watery eyes. Disaster avoided and nobody had even noticed Maxwell told himself. This self-generated myth was however eagerly shattered later at lunch when his sisters loudly told him that they all saw him crying when he took the wine. Such shame he thought, but at least he was allowed to break bread!

To say the first time Maxwell partook of communion was indeed a spiritual experience would be a gross overstatement but the whole encounter gave him a great peace. He was now 'saved' and part of God's Assembly and would be going to

Chapter 1
The Foundation

Heaven. His underlying anchor was firmly reinforced – he thanked Jesus for dying for his sins. He was fully righteous.

Maxwell's little fellowship was a regimented affair with a precise set of rules. It ran to a strict schedule like a well-oiled machine. While there was no official leadership everyone knew their place and peace prevailed. That is until the hymn incident, one Sunday morning. It's a little known fact that long before the Nixon era and the Watergate scandal that the Hymngate incident occurred in a small rural corner of our world.

The Sunday morning order of service was strictly observed. It was a solemn occasion and absolute reverence was paramount, it was an assembly before the Lord. Best clothes were compulsory without exception, men (and boys) in suits and ties, women in smart dresses, hats and coats. Service start time was exactly on the stroke of 11am. The Assembly had its own printed international hymn book consisting of about 250 clearly numbered 'spiritual songs' that had been personally approved by the overseas leader – the man of God! Every attendee on a Sunday morning was required to bring along their own hymn book and Bible in readiness to worship. There was no roster of hymns and any male member that broke bread could announce a hymn number at an appropriate time. All the members would quickly find that hymn and anyone who knew a referenced tune (and sometimes a reasonable voice) would lead the singing with everyone joining him as they recognised the tune. No musical instruments allowed. God apparently frowned heavily on such contraptions in a meeting – so the man of God stipulated.

The hymn book itself was a labyrinth of hidden significances. There was no particular layout that defined the types of hymns but if one read them carefully he could skilfully suggest a number that would encapsulate a moment in the service. There were Worship songs to Jesus, to the Father and to the triune God. There was even one or two that acknowledged the work of the Holy Spirit, some were songs of encouragement, wedding songs, funeral songs, songs for solemn occasions and general gratification songs. And then there were the gospel hymns – heart felt, bellicose response songs that loudly proclaimed the greatness of all that Jesus had done for us – as sinners.

The seating at all meetings was also strictly adhered to. Men and women were seated separately – there will be no marriage in Heaven so why should a man sit with his wife when meeting with God in His Assembly, was the edict. Since there was no leadership no pulpit was necessary, therefore the seating was generally arranged in a large oval shape with several receding rows as the shape of the building allowed. The men and boys sat on the front rows, the women sat behind – in silence. Only males, who had been accepted by the Assembly to break bread, could give out hymns or speak in any meeting. There were no exceptions.

Chapter 1
The Foundation

At the breaking of bread meeting on Sunday morning, a table with a white tablecloth was placed in the centre of the oval. On it, in a small basket, sat a whole loaf of bread – the emblem of the body of Christ, and a large stemmed glass containing the sherry – the emblem of the blood of Christ. Finally there was a covered basket to take up the collection.

All meetings followed a standard format and the members knew the order well. The Sunday service was no exception but since it was such a solemn occasion it was 'spiritually' inspired. The service started with a general welcoming hymn followed by the notices. These recounted the meetings for the coming week (even though they were exactly the same every week), declared the names of any visitors from other assemblies or a newly accepted member. Fully prepared the service could now begin.

A brother, usually someone very spiritual, would, after an appropriate pause, approach the table containing the bread and cup. For centuries all of Christendom had called this communion but the 'Man of God' frowned heavily on such a term and it was simply named 'the breaking of bread.' This brother would in his own worded way give thanks to Jesus for giving His body for us. Following which he would break the home-baked loaf into several parts, arrange it on the basket and pass it to the brother at the start of the oval who would rip off a small piece for himself and pass it on and in turn each would partake. He would then repeat the procedure for the cup, each drinking dutifully from the same fount. Once this was completed the same brother would pass the collection basket around and each would add their weekly contribution.

After the Lord's Table there would be two or three hymns each followed by a brother standing to his feet to give a short worship account to Jesus. Only hymns giving praise to Jesus were allowed at this time. The next part of the service was a short acknowledgement of the Holy Spirit; usually just a hymn was enough. Praise to the Father was next again with hymns interspersed with various brothers standing giving a short worship. Occasionally at any random part of the service a brother, who was moved by the Spirit, could stand to his feet and read a relevant Bible verse followed by a short talk. The final part of the service was always worship to God, as in the Trinity. The whole meeting would always miraculously finish exactly one hour after the start. The order was strictly followed; the Breaking of Bread, worship to Jesus, the Holy Spirit, the Father then God - any other format was demonic. If one was very spiritual he could pick up a theme running through the service as the Lord manifested Himself to the Assembly. Discerning such a theme was very important as that determined the topic of the afternoon Bible study meeting.

So was the order of Sunday meetings that Maxwell had grown up in. He knew of nothing else and his fashioned belief was that he was privileged to be righteous and a part of the true worship of God that so few on this earth obtained to. He was also very privileged, to not only break bread, but to give

Chapter 1
The Foundation

out hymns during the service – such were the spiritual heights he had conquered, and at such a young age too. After several weeks of breaking bread Maxwell determined he was ready for the next stage. Today he would give out a hymn!

Maxwell knew of the order of service and had studied his hymn book well during the past few days and had selected one or two that he thought would complement a suitable spiritual experience. The breaking of bread was over and Mr Belmont had just completed a very moving worship account to Jesus and a subdued presence filled the gathering. There was a small break in the service and Maxwell saw his chance. The hymn he had chosen was Hymn 5 but for some reason Hymn 4 kept coming to mind. Maxwell had been quietly going over it in his mind, sounding out how he would say it, "Can we sing Hymn 5?" No, too formal, perhaps just, "Hymn 5." Annoyingly every time he said Hymn 5 the number 4 would pop into his mind and he found himself rehearsing Hymn 5 quickly followed by no, I mean 4. Whatever he did he couldn't shake it, every time he thought 5, 4 would follow immediately. I can do it he thought collecting himself together for the big occasion. The waiting silence screamed into Maxwell's mind, now, now before anyone else gets in. "Hymn 5 … 4" blurted Maxwell. Suddenly what he had said echoed in his brain, not 5 not 4 but he had just given out hymn 54. What was that one even about, Maxwell had no idea. The whole assembly obediently thumbed through their little books to number 54 – as did Maxwell. Should he just say, no sorry, I meant number 5. No, never can things like that be uttered at the height of such a sacred service, number 54 it was. Quickly Maxwell flicked the pages and found hymn 54. Immediately he got there his heart froze. Dear Jesus, it's a full blown gospel song, what could be worse, right in the middle of worship time. Maxwell wanted to die!

The little gathering however duly broke out in such a heartfelt rendition of "Count your many blessings" as ever had been heard in the middle of a breaking of bread service. "Name them one by one and it will surprise you what the Lord has done," the song continued. Maxwell sang along but his heart wasn't in it, then he happened to glance across to Mr Truman. There he sat, hymn book open, no doubt at number 54, ashen faced, lips welded shut, his eyes piecing the distant nothingness. Maxwell had no idea what was going on in Mr Truman's mind but that face was certainly screaming profanities.

The remainder of the meeting seemed to Maxwell to last about a year and a half and immediately it was over Maxwell slipped from his seat ready for outdoor play with friends. Very shortly after hitting the outside air, Maxwell's mother arrived commanding him to quickly find his sisters as they were going home for lunch that day as his father had to move the cows from the turnip patch. Maxwell was a bit surprised as nobody had mentioned that on the way to the meeting but he dutifully headed off to round up his sisters. Moving the cows took longer than usual for some reason and Maxwell was disappointed they couldn't go back for the Bible reading meeting but nobody else seemed bothered so he never gave it another thought.

Years later after Mr Truman's funeral someone filled Maxwell in on the details of that afternoon. Mr Truman was livid, insisting that the devil himself had invaded the body of an eight year old to deliberately devastate the Assembly's sacred time of true worship of the Lord himself. Others joined him and a schism of the little assembly almost occurred that day. The climax came when Truman suggested the words of the 'Man of God' the international leader were plain wrong. Such language invoked collective shock and condemnation. It was suggested to Mr Truman in no uncertain terms that he back off and after a few days he did and by the next Sunday he reluctantly accepted young Maxwell's presence at the breaking of bread and fortunately for all no further incidences were forthcoming.

Maxwell's thoughts were jerked to the present as he neared the bus stop. He had left his sisters in his dust, again, and he could see the Clarke kids there. They all went to his little fellowship and there were eight of them although the three oldest now attended high school in town. He needed the support of the Clarke kids if he was ever to carry out his long term plan to toss the youngest snotty nosed Mitchell kid out of his prized front row seat. Maxwell didn't want to sit there, it was just that this Mitchell kid didn't go to his fellowship therefore and as a sinner he needed to be taught a lesson.

Besides he never shared anything, especially his cricket bat. Obviously he's a true son of the devil, Maxwell thought.

Such was the spiritual base that formed Maxwell's early life. He knew of God and knew of righteousness and the little gathering he was born into had determined their own rules which they proudly portrayed as the true colour of white. Maxwell had a real relationship with Jesus but knew only one thing; that Jesus had died for his sins. While this did allow him to have right standing with God his single focus skewed his knowledge of the love of God toward all others. The concept had moulded Maxwell's life, affirming that he was somewhat privileged to have the knowledge of forgiveness that others in this world would never obtain unless they too joined his small group of God fearing warriors. Because of his privileged position he presumed he had obtained righteousness.

Maxwell had begun a personal relationship with Jesus and a definite shade of white now coloured his life. However, like drops of black ink into clear liquid so had Maxwell's foundation of self-righteousness severely coloured his life. While he did have a vivid white understanding of Jesus, the limiting nature of that relationship severely diminished the clarity.

Fortunately God wasn't through with Maxwell and as he developed in life, God led him along a very unusual pathway.

*"Forget Google
God has all the Answers"*

Chapter 2
The Law

"See if you can take it out a little deeper this time," Maxwell's father advised. They had borrowed a fishing net from a friend at his father's work and the two of them, along with Maxwell's pal from their Assembly, had driven to a nearby surf beach in the hope of snaring a few snapper. It was a warm evening, the breakers were only a metre or so and the water looked appealing.

Maxwell and his friend Niles were commissioned to take the end of the net out into the surf in a large circular sweep while his father held the other end secure on the beach. The theory being, the multitudes of fish feeding in the breakers would be trapped and end up on The White's dinner table. The first couple of sweeps however had identified a few flaws in that theory, one being; multitudes may well be a myth. The second being dragging a large net through the breaking surf was a Herculean task and no match for two seventeen year old men unaccustomed to unsuccessful challenges.

After a short consultation between the three hunter-gatherers Maxwell's fathers advice held sway. Clearly the fish must be just a little further out.

The next four attempts achieved the same result. Not a single fish made its presence felt let-alone landing one on the shore. Disheartened, the trio abandoned the idea of a meal of fresh fish and while Maxwell's father retrieved and folded the net on-shore Maxwell and Niles decided to take on the breaking waves and have some well-earned fun.

The beach was a sandy cove arching round to a rocky outcrop at the far end. Never a popular swimming beach because of the notorious surf it was however frequented by a few ardent fishermen, particularly after a storm. Today the beach was deserted and in relative terms the surf was low. "Perfect for dolphin dives through the waves," Maxwell declared.

Niles and Maxwell endeavoured to outdo the other with various wave dives or having it break over them or allowing themselves to be rolled in the surf towards the shore. It was fun and even better there were no Assembly rules disallowing it.

During the past ten years of 'breaking bread,' much had changed in Maxwell's life. His siblings had grown from three sisters to two more sisters and, finally, two brothers. His next brother however was fifteen years his junior therefore more a mentor relationship than a brotherly companion. Nevertheless his brothers were a welcome respite from his five protective sisters and he felt a masculine balance in his life.

Rules had also become a major focal point of Maxwell's busy Assembly. The ageing 'Man of God' had finally gone to be with the Lord and the torch had passed to another very spiritual brother, also based 'overseas.' So spiritual was this one that in reverence he was named the 'Elect Vessel' as in the Lord's words about the apostle Paul, Acts 9:15 *"for this [man] is an elect vessel to me"* (DBT). Most other translations used the term 'chosen instrument' but somehow that didn't quite have the right ring to it, so Elect Vessel it was.

Of all the 'spiritual' characteristics of the Elect Vessel, one in particular stood out - whiskey. It seemed the amber liquid was necessary to fully appreciate the teachings of the Elect Vessel and every brother and sister of the Assembly around the globe were 'encouraged' to partake. While some stick-in-the-mud oldies had balked at the concept initially, objecting to the word of the leader resembled contradicting God himself and so the message was drink up or get out. Maxwell however had no objections and despite his seventeen years had learned how to manage the potent liquid without appearing drunk, or worse, throwing up.

The elect vessel had also made a declaration of purity in the assembly. The sexual revolution of the 60's abounding in the world around his saints was intolerable. The world had become absolutely detestable and the words of 2 Timothy 2:19 became the foundation of the teaching of this Elect Vessel. *"Yet the firm foundation of God stands, having this seal, [The] Lord knows those that are his; and, let every one who names the name of [the] Lord withdraw from iniquity."* (DBT)

His insistence was that this verse be lived literally, in every sense, and in order to complete the mandate substantial expansion of the words 'withdraw' and 'iniquity' became necessary – terms the Elect Vessel embellished with gusto.

The assembly had to be a place of righteousness if it was to be the shrine of Godly holiness. After all, it was the only true church on the earth. All other so-called churches had fallen so far from the truth, or so the Assembly members were instructed. Every person who wasn't approved to break bread in the Assembly was surely destined to be punished in hell for all eternity regardless of their relationship with Jesus. The indoctrination of the 'truth' of the Assembly was compelling and fiercely defended and upheld. For Maxwell, a position in the Assembly was a privilege. He was so fortunate to have been born into a family that had the direct guidance of the Elect Vessel that had allowed him to become fully righteous.

In order for holiness to be enshrined in the Assembly the nature of iniquity had to be clearly defined. Fortunately the Elect Vessel was able to provide a complete list for his faithful followers. Essentially, it entailed everything that the 'Assembly' was not. There were only two camps, the World or the Assembly. The World had a population of a few billion and the

Assembly of a few thousand, but numbers didn't matter to God, so the Elect Vessel said, it was true righteousness He was looking for. Such understanding strongly reinforced the natural status of privilege a place in the Assembly bestowed.

The functioning of the Assembly had to be transformed if the Elect Vessel's holiness was to be instilled in every member. Meetings were necessary every day and at least three times on a Sunday. Since the scripture stated that Jesus was put on the cross at the 6th hour and died at the 9th hour then these were important times for gatherings. The fact that these times were translated literally from the 12 hour day and 12 hour night observed at the time of Christ was never considered. The Bible said 6th hour so that was obviously 6am! All local weekend meetings were to start at 6am and attendance was compulsory. It was amazing how enlivened a 6am breaking of bread was compared to 9am, or so it was reported. What incredible understanding the Elect Vessel had!

Maxwell was okay with the additional meetings and he observed every word, fully confident he now lived in a sphere of righteousness. Many physical changes were also necessary too, in order to achieve holiness. Living in rural areas was ungodly, how can you be a witness to your neighbour when he was miles away. Milking cows, something Maxwell's father had done all his life, was no-longer allowed as it involved working on the Lord's Day. Women serving meals and caring for the saints was not work but duty. Maxwell and his family had moved from the peaceful farmlands into the local town (population 7,250) along with his entire farming fellowship and a new assembly building had been built. Maxwell missed the country life immensely but what was that to being faithful to the Elect Vessel.

Education was necessary to a point but higher learning at a university was forbidden as every such place was a natural breeding ground for every kind of demonic revelation. How could a righteous Assembly person enter its gates and return untainted. Qualification as a doctor, lawyer, engineer etc. weren't an option for Maxwell so he settled for a motor trade apprenticeship; there would always be a need for panel-beaters he reckoned.

The other mainstay of the Elect Vessel's creed was withdrawal. 2 Timothy 2:19 *"let every one who names the name of [the] Lord withdraw from iniquity."* (DBT) Identifying iniquity was one thing, what to do next was a whole new level. Fortunately the Elect Vessel had heard from God and knew precisely what that involved. Withdraw meant completely separating from, as in isolating oneself from, any possible iniquitous contamination.

A verse in 1 Corinthians 5:11 made the Elect Vessel's teaching beyond doubt; *"But now I have written to you, if any one called brother be fornicator, or avaricious, or idolater, or abusive, or a drunkard, or rapacious, not to mix with [him]; with such a one not even to eat."* (DBT) This verse was enforced with a passion. Obviously this was the method to become holy, particularly when combined with the term withdraw.

If one couldn't eat with a person tainted by iniquity then surely that meant having no associations with that person on any level. Of course one had to work and usually that meant being employed by a worldly enterprise, but that was okay as it was essential in order to obtain the necessaries to function in life. Employment, however, was strictly a working encounter. No socialising with workmates was permitted nor was eating and drinking of any kind. Having a morning coffee could not be a sit down affair with your workmates even if the pretence was to discuss business. Any tea or coffee must be consumed in isolation – how else can one maintain holiness?

The fact the Corinthians verse specifically related to a brother who had turned their back on Jesus and returned to a deliberate sinful life meant nothing. The list of iniquities specified in that verse cover every person not breaking bread in the Assembly, the Elect Vessel decreed. Maxwell understood completely and carried out the edict to the letter. Every morning at tea break he would make his cup of tea then take his seat outside the lunchroom and pass not a word to any man. The ridicule and jibes from his workmates subsided over time and, as the Elect Vessel taught, such suffering must be endured if we are to remain holy and continue in our privileged position in the Assembly. Maxwell knew nothing of his workmates except they were all doomed to hell, his only friends were his fellowship contemporaries. Fortunately these were numerous as most families in his Assembly were large with eight to ten children being the norm. The elect vessel encouraged large families as it was the way to maintain growth. Given the strict position on iniquity and the means of cleansing from contamination it was exceptionally rare for any outsider to meet the standard required to partake of the breaking of bread at the Lord's Table. Maxwell had only heard of one such case in his entire seventeen years. Salvation was not for everyone – or so it was believed. It was indeed an honour to be so righteous.

There were of course some in Maxwell's Assembly who were not so enthusiastic in carrying out the Elect Vessel's orders and considered forbidding fraternisation with their workmates over a morning cup of tea a step to far. Some of these had worked at the same place for decades and they were genuine friends with their fellow workers. They deeply struggled to understand how their friends had suddenly become so vile that they should barely speak with them let alone drink a cup of tea while together in the same room. A few of these continued to disregard the decree but now did so ever-so discretely. Others however openly rebelled.

Rebellion was not tolerated at any level. What the Elect Vessel spoke was the word of God Himself so disregarding it was a very serious matter. Fortunately the Elect Vessel knew of another verse that covered this. 2 Thessalonians 3:6 says *"Now we enjoin you, brethren, in the name of our Lord Jesus Christ, that ye withdraw from every brother walking disorderly and not according to the instruction which he received from us."* [DBT] This verse clearly provided direct Biblical guidance on how to deal with any person who did not accept his teachings. The only solution was that they be withdrawn from – excommunication.

Being ejected from the Assembly was a very serious matter as without that association Hell was the only eternal destination. In order to demonstrate his true compassionate heart the Elect Vessel reverted to the Law of Moses. Leviticus 13:50 provides a scriptural example although the practice is referenced several times in the book of Leviticus. *"And the priest shall look on the sore, and shall shut up [that which hath] the sore seven days."* [DBT] Even though the only High priestly position defined in the New Testament is that of Jesus, the Elect Vessel considered the Law of Moses definitive and appointed priests in every Assembly. Their role was to coordinate the process of withdrawal or restoration of a brother (or sister).

Should someone be found to openly disobey the teachings of the Elect Vessel then the Assembly would, usually immediately after one of their regular meetings, 'move into assembly.' Maxwell was never quite sure what 'moving into assembly' really was, except it was a very serious matter. The case of the disobeying person would be discussed, sometimes briefly, and the announcement would be made that the person would be shut up for seven days and the priests would review things and report back to the Assembly. Immediately after the shutting up decision was made that person would be asked to leave the meeting.

The shut up person was considered contagious and no family contact on any level was allowed. Husbands or wives couldn't share the same bed and meals were to be eaten separately. At the end of the seven days the priest would visit to vigorously gauge the level of repentance. They would report back to the rest of the fellowship but the infected person was to remain absent. Should the priest consider true repentance was definitely present then they would recommend the brother be restored and, upon Assembly agreement, he would be allowed to again break-bread. Should they detect some movement but perhaps another week would deepen it, then that was the recommendation. In some cases this position of being shut up could extend for weeks or months. It was never considered a form of punishment but so astounding was the reversal of acceptance of the Elect Vessel's teachings by some brothers after just a few days of isolation.

Unfortunately, if the condemned person did not express the correct manifestation of repentance from the level of the iniquity the poor brother was caught in, then the priests would recommend the person be 'withdrawn from'. The Assembly almost always accepted the priest's guidance and, just like that, the statement was made, and then brother or sister x was 'withdrawn from'.

The consequence for the 'withdrawn from' person was dramatic. As soon as practical they had to vacate the family home leaving behind their wife and children. If they worked for another Assembly brother they had to leave their job, effective immediately. The result was identical to a real-life death of the person. No Assembly person could speak, eat or have any contact with them. They had turned their back on the Elect Vessel and, hence, the work of Jesus; therefore they were to be despised. The fact that homes were broken up and children deprived of a parent was irrelevant; it was a matter of holiness. The Assembly was a righteous place and no deviation from the standard was permissible.

Maxwell understood the reasons well and firmly stood by every Assembly judgement. Compassion and empathy simply were not relative when it came to righteousness regardless whether the evil person was a close friend or blood relative. Besides, dissention would only transfer the same fate directly onto the dissenter.

Maxwell's thoughts reflected back to his Grandfather's recent case. In the 1960's hair came to symbolise a manly statement of fashion. Long hair, beards and moustaches represented a rebellion against the status quo. The Elect Vessel was very vocal in proclaiming that such extreme worldliness held no part in God's Assembly. Maxwell's grandfather (known by most just as Gersh) unfortunately supported a magnificent version of upper lip maturity and had done so for many decades, long before it symbolised any such rebellious fashion icon. Gersh was a kindly man but also very definite with his opinions. He had done well in business after selling his farm and was selectively generous, particularly to male members of his family. Maxwell enjoyed spending time with him as he was full of interesting stories of various life events. Never-the-less rules were rules and after consultations with the Elect Vessel by phone the priests approached Gersh and demanded he remove his upper lip's hairy growth.

To say that Gersh was a stubborn man may be a slight understatement. He had lived out his seventy years serving God very well with his grand moustache and saw no reason why he should shave it off at this late stage of his life just because the rest of the world had caught up with his fashion sense. Shock and disbelief unnerved the priests. Here was an elder of their Assembly who dared to openly decry a direct order of the Elect Vessel. They quickly conferred with their peers on the question if he should be allowed to break bread the following day in such a rebellious condition. The assembly must be consulted, they agreed, but there were no more meetings scheduled as it was Saturday morning and the 6am meeting that day had already passed. The phone lines got busy immediately and a meeting was called for 3pm that afternoon, attendance was compulsory – this was a very serious matter that must be dealt with immediately.

Maxwell and his family arrived early, as had most, so they could informally discuss the matter with each other before the meeting started. Almost to a man everyone agreed with Maxwell's thoughts, Grandfather or not, he had disobeyed the Elect Vessel and it was right he should be withdrawn from, immediately.

Everyone was seated early and just before 3pm Gersh arrived. Supported by his walking stick he slowly waddled across the hall and sat down in his usual front row seat. Every eye in the room followed his every move and as he sat down an audible gasp ensued. Maxwell looked up quickly to account for the noise and for the first time in his life he witnessed his Grandfather's clean shaven upper lip. The image of what he saw never left him. Instead of a usual assured presence here sat an old man dejected, embarrassed and ashamed as in someone caught naked in a crowd. For the first time in his life Maxwell felt a fleeting spark of empathy.

The meeting started as usual with a hymn followed by a prayer which included particular thankfulness to the Lord for the teachings of the Elect Vessel. After a short pause Gersh picked up a microphone. "I'm very sorry Brethren," he began in exceptionally remorseful tones, "I have sinned, please forgive me," he continued. "I have belittled the words of the Elect Vessel and brought the Assembly into disrepute." His words came out slowly through a faintly breaking voice, as much as a man of his era could allow. Clearly he was fighting back tears that could never be permitted to make an appearance. He spoke on for at least five minutes in the most heart-inspired repentance speech that little Assembly had ever heard. By the time he finished there was hardly a dry eye in the room and even several hardened priests had large lumps in their throats.

Whether the repentance was the result of his true awe of the Elect Vessel or perhaps the thought of living out his remaining few years completely isolated and alone deprived of all his family and twenty plus grandchildren will be never known for sure and nor did it really matter. Clearly he was remorseful and it was plain for all to see. In this case a report from the priests was immaterial.

Gersh finished up and replaced the microphone. For several minutes nobody spoke and finally one of the priests picked up his microphone and said "Thank you Gersh for your humble repentance and obvious acknowledgement by removing that worldly symbol from your upper lip. I speak for all the Assembly in saying we forgive you for your actions and you may break bread as usual tomorrow."

With that the formal part of the meeting was over and, not to allow an opportunity to go begging, the local leader, Mr Dave, gave a short rousing sermon on the importance of following and appreciating guidance. Not once did he mention the Elect Vessel but little doubt was left on where the guidance to obtain righteousness was derived.

Suddenly Maxwell was jerked back into the present. Niles was shouting, "Your father is waving from the shore, I think he wants us to go in." Maxwell replied in the affirmative and attempted to obey but something was wrong. He couldn't touch the bottom anymore, and, between the breaking waves, it seemed that the beach was much further off. He called out to warn Niles but he was nowhere to be seen. With the breakers now between him and the beach, on the crest of one of them he saw Niles swimming strongly toward the shore. Maxwell tried to do the same but no matter how hard he swam he made no progress. "Oh NO," he thought, "I'm caught in a rip and being swept out to sea."

The shoreline quickly became distant and panic invaded every part of Maxwell's youthful frame. Swimming produced nothing; the only option was to tread water and go with the flow. The waves were much bigger out there, wherever there was. Some waves broke over him while others lifted him high as if mocking him about the distance to shoreline. Maxwell was surprised how quickly he tired. He'd only been in the rip a few minutes but already his legs felt exhausted. He tried to float but that only served to roll him in any breaking waves and fill his lungs with water. "Crikey," he thought, "this is dire, I don't want to die." In desperation he cried out "Jesus, please save me." Jesus never answered.

Time wore on and little changed except Maxwell's lungs now were filled with water and gasping for air only seemed to exasperate the problem in this choppy area of the sea. Strangely the panic had gone from his body and he felt unexplainably calm for someone facing imminent death. Now in a trough between two waves Maxwell looked up to seaward and caught a glimpse of the incoming wave, it was massive, and it was going to break over him. Totally at peace Maxwell watched it approach and knew it would break over him, "but not to worry," he thought as in some sort of surreal dream, "I'll just drift beneath it and let the waters take me." All fear of death had completely abated, fighting anymore was pointless.

Right at that moment, while watching the impending breaker, a very vivid picture of his father standing on the shore shouting his name flashed into his mind. Suddenly Maxwell was jerked into reality; he couldn't leave his family like this. In desperation Maxwell shouted out as loud as his impeded lungs would allow him to splutter, "Lord Jesus, Please save me? Jesus if you do I commit myself to serve you wholeheartedly, for the rest of my days." With the prayer out and gasping for air, Maxwell considered tactics for the approaching wall of water. It was definitely going to break, but this one was shaped dramatically different from the previous ones. It was like two waves had joined with the smaller one in front creating a kind of ramp. Something screamed into Maxwell's foggy brain, swim! Without a thought he mustered all his remaining strength and began swimming in front of the approaching deluge, all the while waiting to be inundated by the watery monster.

Chapter 2
The Law

Miraculously the imminent wave never broke; instead it buoyed Maxwell's swimming body like a surfboard and thrust him on towards the beach. Had the situation not been so serious, Maxwell may have enjoyed it. On and on it went jetting him like a cannon ball until, just like it started, the ride ended. Much smaller now the wave swept past him and diffused among the rocks ahead. At that same moment Maxwell felt something hard under his feet and realised he'd been deposited on a rocky outcrop, within paddling distance to the beach. Looking back out to sea there was not a wave in sight. Breakers were still pounding further over but on his rock it was dead calm.

Confused, coughing profusely and still gasping for air he clambered higher on the rock. "What the heck just happened," he said aloud. Then he remembered his last-gasp prayer. Maxwell spontaneously broke out into the most thankful prayer he had ever uttered. Without any doubt Jesus had directed that wave and every so gently deposited him on this rock. "Wasn't there a scripture about Jesus "this rock," he pondered? Maxwell knew what his future was now; he had been given a reprieve and had committed to serve the Lord the rest of his life. He had no regrets, and because of what Jesus had just done, he would without doubt carry out his divine service with vigour.

After regaining his breath Maxwell's thoughts turned to conjuring up the courage to climb off his rock and get to the beach. He could see his father and Niles walking excitedly down towards him but that was at least a kilometre away. Jumping off his rock he was very surprised to find the water barely up to his knees and he quickly clambered from rock pool to rock and made it to the beach. "I thought you were gone," was all his father could say. Niles filled in the details of his swim for safety as the trio walked up the beach in the fading light toward the car. Maxwell never mentioned his miracle or his extracted commitment. But he sure was very thankful to be safe and knew things had changed in his relationship with his Lord.

A few weeks later Maxwell was hard at work attacking a car door frame that had been rearranged in a recent crash. He had repaired the damage but the overall shape still prevented the door from aligning correctly. With a chain tied beneath the car and a large block of wood wedged at the top of the door Maxwell sat on the ground and pushed hard with both feet against the protruding door while pulling on the chain for balance. He tried the door and yes, it had improved. "One more good push and it should be right," he told himself. Again with his knees suspended high he pushed with all his considerable strength. Just as he thought he'd achieved the right bend he felt a slight burning in his right knee but thought nothing of it. He jumped to his feet and tried the door and much to the surprise of his passing workmate the door clicked shut aligning perfectly. "Job done," Maxwell declared little knowing exactly how prophetic those words would prove.

Chapter 2
The Law

Maxwell gathered up his tools and began to walk towards his tool box when suddenly he felt a sharp piercing pain stab through his right knee and he crumbled in a heap on the ground. His colleague rushed to help him up but Maxwell couldn't walk or put any weight on his right leg. He could however hop and too proud to admit defeat he hopped to his toolbox carefully placing all his prized tools. Hearing the yelps of pain Maxwell's boss came by to see what the prank was this time. After hearing his predicament he order Maxwell to go home and rest his leg and see how it was in the morning. Maxwell reluctantly obeyed, hopped to his car and made a one-legged drive to his home.

Next morning the knee was swollen like a pumpkin and Maxwell's mother ordered him off work and to the doctors. X-rays and visits to the specialists followed and finally it was determined the knee had temporally dislocated and while now functioning as it should there was considerable cartilage and ligament damage which necessitated an operation. Since it was a work accident and covered by medical insurance the operation could be done immediately and before he knew it Maxwell found himself lying on an operating table in a modern private hospital an hours' drive from home in a town that had no Assembly in it! The thought unnerved Maxwell somewhat but he knew his family would visit when time permitted and he had his Bible and prayer was always available.

The first operation was a moderate success which allowed Maxwell to walk again but with some pain. After several months and little improvement further surgery was scheduled and Maxwell found himself back in the ungodly city and under the surgeon's knife. This time, however, a strict recovery program, involving weeks in a rehabilitation hospital, was ordered and, thankfully, the final outcome was considerably more successful. The damage unfortunately had been done and the knee could not tolerate a lifetime of heavy lifting so lighter employment was required. Maxwell was disappointed as he really enjoyed fixing smashed cars and was very good at it. He'd always been top of his class in his annual exams and was even named top automotive apprentice of the country one year. Unfortunately, because receiving the award required attendance at a social event Maxwell was never able to receive it. "Who needs worldly awards," Maxwell thought, "I am part of God's Assembly and we have the Elect Vessel, what can the world add to that."

Fully recovered Maxwell began work at the engineering office of the Telecom Department as a trainee draughtsman. The department was government owned and the pay was good and Maxwell excelled. What's more, further studies were encouraged and paid for by the Department and Maxwell soon found himself in correspondence study working towards a qualification in professional engineering.

Chapter 2
The Law

His new office unfortunately was based in a neighbouring town about an hour's drive north of his home but because that city had an Assembly his elders had given him permission to work there. Maxwell boarded with an Assembly family during the week in the city but always made it home for the weekends. He missed his family and with so many brothers and sisters something crazy was always just around the corner. Weekends at home became cherished.

All this while Maxwell strongly sensed the Lord speaking to him, telling him his life was going to be similar to the life of Joseph, the son of Biblical Jacob. He had no idea what that could possibly mean or if it was even really the Lord speaking to him. As far as Maxwell knew the Lord only spoke through the Elect Vessel. "Perhaps it's just my mind playing tricks on me," Maxwell told himself. The Vietnam War was on and he was subject to call-up for military service if his birthday was selected in a national ballot. "Perhaps I'm going to get called up and taken prisoner and held in prison for years," Maxwell mused with a cold shudder. Despite the dates each side of Maxwell's birthday being balloted he wasn't drafted into the military and he thanked the Lord his nightmare scenario never became a reality.

Thus were Maxwell's teenage years. He fully embraced the copious teachings of the Elect Vessel and strongly believed in his heart that because of his privileged position in the Assembly he lived a fully righteous life. He piously read his Bible night and morning and never missed a single Assembly meeting. After all he had made a promise to the Lord when He saved him from the raging seas and how better to honour that promise than to live the way he now was. In his mind he was at the pinnacle of living a fully righteous – white linen bright – life. What more could he do? Little did he know but God was about to answer that very question in a most unorthodox way.

*"The Ten Commandments
Are Not Multiple Choice"*

Chapter 3

The Veil Is Lifted

Maxwell sat across from the lawyer as they reviewed a document for his land purchase. He disliked lawyers but there were none in the Assembly so he was forced to take advice from a heathen. He had received a $1,100 settlement for the injury to his knee and with the help of a $200 loan from his Grandfather he had purchased a small section of land. "Someday," he declared "I'll start married life on this spot." He was certainly old enough at 23 and Maxwell, while having plenty of friends who were girls, never actually managed to make one of them his 'girlfriend.' Perhaps if he prepared the nest then that may attract 'the one,' he mused.

Unexpectedly the door to lawyer's office burst open with the secretary making her excuses. "Excuse me sir but are you Mr White?" she asked. Without waiting for Maxwell's reply she continued, "There's a phone call for you, they say it's very urgent." Maxwell picked up the phone and was surprised to hear his father's voice. "We've got some bad news," his father blurted out, obviously a bit upset. "Your grandfather dropped dead this morning," he quickly continued, desperate to keep his emotions in check. Now it was Maxwell's turn, "What, how, when - what?" he stumbled. Maxwell had seen his grandfather at the meeting just last night and he seemed in fine spirits, now he was dead? He hardly heard his father's answer but he had suffered a massive heart attack while out digging in his garden – "dead before he hit the ground," Maxwell's father recounted as he finished up. "Thanks for letting me know, I'll see you when I get home tonight," Maxwell answered and ended the call.

The call finished, Maxwell explained to the lawyer what had just happened then continued with his business. He was close to his grandfather but strangely instead of grief he felt content. He knew he had gone to be with Jesus so why the need to grieve, he debated. He'd been to plenty of funerals before and he'd known most of the departed personally so why was this any different, just because he was a blood relative? Besides, he'd seen so many of his friends and relatives withdrawn from and that was effectively the same thing as them dying since he never saw most of them again. "Yep," Maxwell told himself, "another door closed in life." And with that he accepted his grandfather's passing and went on with his day.

Maxwell had completed his training and received his qualifications but, tiring of working for the government, he had started his own consultancy firm specialising in house and engineering design. It was the 1970's and the country was thriving with opportunities abounding. He still worked in the city but because he now owned a nice set of wheels he lived at home and commuted the 50 kilometres to work each day. Petrol was cheap and business was good. Maxwell enjoyed living in the moment and the moment was sweet.

Funeral meetings at the Assembly were little unchanged from any other meeting except an open casket sat in the middle of the seating oval. The Elect Vessel had decreed that the lid not be placed on a casket until the body was to be taken to the grave. No particular explanation was given expect that why would you not want to gaze on the face of a loved one instead of a polished box? Maxwell felt it a little creepy but the Elect Vessel had decreed it, so there was no question. His grandfather lay as asleep with his casket open to the heavens while a hymn was sung, followed by a prayer. Three brothers followed each other in giving a stirring account of how Gersh had lived his life serving the Lord and honouring the Elect Vessel. That was quickly followed by a further hymn then a prayer and the service was concluded. The lid was screwed on the casket and everyone shadowed the hearse to the cemetery where a final gathering was assumed to commit the body to the Lord. That complete, the casket was lowered into the grave and all the Assembly men got busy filling in the hole. That was another edict from the Elect Vessel – "why would we leave our loved ones to be buried by a 'worldly' person?" With the grave filled, Gersh was gone and everyone resumed their busy lives.

Assembly life continued unabated for Maxwell. Righteousness was an anchor point for life in the Assembly and living a life completely separate from every possible contact with the world was the only solution. The only allowable contact with worldly people was through earning a living - money was not an evil thing, just the love of it, the Elect Vessel pointed out. Earning as much of the stuff as possible only served to allow a greater separation from worldly contacts. Amassing useful worldly items was encouraged as then they can be turned to necessary use in the service of the Assembly.

Strong encouragement was given for different assemblies to mix with others, as frequent as possible and gone were the days of letters of introduction. Fellowship meetings, with an invited spiritual leader, were held in various areas most Saturdays and Assembly members were urged to drive, sometimes for several hours, to attend these day meetings. Maxwell enjoyed them and attended as many as possible. Not only did it widen his circle of friends, some of the young ladies in various towns or cities were definitely a sight well worth a four hour, each way, drive! Oh, and besides it was always good to hear a stirring word from a spiritual brother! There was always plenty of whiskey to drink during the break and a bring-your-own-lunch was a bonus.

In addition to the one day fellowship meetings were the three-day-meetings. Each Assembly was 'encouraged' to hold a once a year event called a three day meeting. These were invite-only events and all attendees were accommodated and fed in member homes. Every available sleeping space was taken with some homes managing to billet 10 - 15 guests. To say there was a competition would be unthinkable but the number of guests your home took in was a widely announced secret.

Guests arrived on Thursday evening and the first meetings started 9am Friday with another at 12 noon and a closing one at 3pm. In between was a time to fellowship. Eating or drinking in the Assembly meeting hall was forbidden, as that was the house of God. The best place to accommodate the food and booze locker was from the car boot (or trunk depending on your location). Small groups would huddle around the various cars with the fathers lashing our liberal portions of the golden nectar and the mothers offering various finger foods to soak up the consequences. The 3pm services were often the most liberated (or was that lubricated) gatherings of the day. The same order was repeated the next day but Sunday of course started at 6am, then 9am with the final round up at noon after which everybody said their goodbyes and set out for home, wherever that might be.

A liberal number of young adults were invited to three day meetings and for Maxwell this was the most enjoyable part. The free evening time started at 4pm which left plenty of time to mix and mingle. Depending on the weather large groups of young folk would gather for a barbeque at a river or beach.

Singing around a campfire, fuelled by whiskey competing for the eyes of the lovely brunette from a distant town was close to Maxwell's heart.

Not all the Assembly youth were as devoted to the Elect Vessel at these gatherings as they were during the daytime meetings. There was the occasional pairing off but peer pressure generally held that in check. Other less serious but extremely worldly things however often made an appearance. Record players (turntables) or, later, cassette players were commonly used to complement the camp fire singing or just to listen to the latest pop single that someone had managed to secretly acquire. Very rarely was the Elect Vessel mentioned, at least in a positive context. Frequently much discussion was centred on the latest edict, involving yet further containment of natural enjoyment, followed by creative discoveries on ways to circumvent it.

On the negative side there were always those one had to watch out for – known snitches. The occasional too-goodie attended such occasions solely for the purpose of observing events that would later be recounted with embellishments in a letter to the Elders of a poor unfortunate's local Assembly. Not infrequently, the subject of such an account quickly found themselves being visited by the priest, shut-up or worse summarily withdrawn from. Maxwell frowned on such despicable individuals and trod the fine line between being worldly and saintly. When travelling he remained a willing participant, once a year however, on home turf, under the guidance, or shield, of his five sisters, he was often the instigator of marginal worldliness. Just so long as none of the Elders find out, was his motto.

Maxwell's status within the Assembly had also matured and he had become somewhat of an able speaker and was often used at fellowship meetings and occasionally at three-day-meetings to bring a short word or gospel message. Although always a little nervous at public speaking, Maxwell found he enjoyed it and very quickly became adept at it. He had become well known throughout the country and even into Australia and was always in demand to speak. Finding a topic was easy as the Elect Vessel's edicts were copious and, if all else failed, he could always revert to good old guilt. Guilt was strongly used as a weapon within the Assembly and even if one had not actually entangled in any form of worldliness there was always room for repentance anyway. For Maxwell, he knew that he knew that Jesus had died for his sins so repenting to Jesus for anything and everything became second nature. How else was he going to maintain righteousness in the Assembly?

At times the Elect Vessel himself would travel in person from his overseas sanctuary and a series of three-day-meetings were convened in various cities during a month. These gatherings were particularly large and dedicated followers travelled from far and wide to hang upon the enlightenment words which flowed effortlessly from the fearless leaders whiskey laden lips. Maxwell had attended several presided over by the Elect Vessel, and had even been invited to speak at one or two of them. It was the pinnacle of Assembly life to be invited to attend a meeting where the Elect Vessel held sway. Maxwell cherished the words of this man of God and firmly believed they were equal to Scripture itself. He really had matured to manly status in the ways of the Lord and clearly his righteousness was pretty well matured – in his opinion.

The meetings with the Elect Vessel in Sydney had concluded but Maxwell had stayed on for a couple of days with his host and ventured off to downtown for a spot of shopping, searching for items unobtainable in his small country town. Later in the afternoon Maxwell found himself in the tourist sector, souvenirs always made good mementoes he felt. "Hello, do you want some?" a female voice asked. Maxwell quickly turned towards the voice only to melt into a pair of the prettiest young eyes he had ever seen on this earth. "Want some what?" Maxwell asked innocently. "You have cash?" she asked professionally. Maxwell quickly felt his wallet in his pocket then replied, "Yes, plenty." "Then follow me," she replied and quickly turned towards an open door and stairway.

Maxwell watched her walk and something within him said, "Watch out, she's trouble." She reached the door and seductively turned towards Maxwell and slowly beckoned with her hand. Maxwell went weak at the knees; he had never seen such a beautiful woman close up and really wanted to learn

Chapter 3
The Veil Is Lifted

more. Every thought of Jesus, the Elect Vessel or anything to do with righteousness completely vanished from his mind as he stepped forward to follow her up the stairs, youthful hormones surging through every vein in his body.

Fifteen minutes later Maxwell was back on the street twenty dollars lighter and no longer a saint. "Wow," he thought, "the half was never told me!" He floated down the street as if walking on air. The next hour passed quickly and shopping seemed a distant memory. Suddenly he caught sight of a sign for his train station. His heart stopped; "What have I done," he said to himself. "The Assembly - the family I'm staying with – the prayer meeting tonight." An immense flood of guilt gushed through his body rapidly followed by recurring memories of his recent pleasures. "I can't just stand, here," he told himself and with a step of purpose he marched himself toward the train. "What's the problem, anyway," he reasoned, "nobody saw me? Yes, exactly," he exclaimed hopefully to himself, "the Assembly need never know." With that he boarded the train and continued his travels. Standing to pray that night wasn't as easy as usual so he left his run to last and later, upon self-evaluation, considered his cant was impressive enough to convince the locals he was a budding man of God.

A few weeks passed and back home Maxwell grew more and more uncomfortable. It seems that at every meeting he attended the only talk was of sexual immorality and the need to keep oneself unspotted from the world. Racked with shame and remorse Maxwell was beside himself. "Oh Lord, what do I do?" he cried aloud while driving in his car. It was distant but from deep within him heard a soft still voice say, "You've always known Jesus died for your sins, confess your sin to Him." "Of course," he exclaimed aloud. Right there in his car Maxwell recounted a very sincere and deep confession of his immoral sin asking Jesus to forgive him for turning his back on Him like that. From the depth of his heart the confession sprang and at that moment he truly felt the love of Jesus like he'd never known before. He knew that he knew that Jesus had truly forgiven him of this devastating sin. Finally he was cleansed. With a spring in his step he completed his day and, for probably the first time in his life, he more fully appreciated what Jesus had done for him when He bore his punishment for sin by suffering so terribly on that cross.

Unfortunately the message from the Assembly meetings never changed. Every day he came home recharged with guilt; what was he to do? Jesus had forgiven him, how did he overcome this guilt. Finally he decided, enough, he must tell the priests. But how on earth does a budding man of God just bowl up to a saintly Assembly priest and tell him you've committed such a grave sin? This troubled Maxwell as much as the guilt that swamped him. "I'll write it out and drop it in his mailbox," Maxwell thought with sudden cunning inspiration.

Maxwell attended the meeting that night and though the local priest was there too, he never even looked Maxwell's way.

"Strange," he thought, "he must have my letter by now?" A couple of nights later he got his reply. Mr Davies approached him after the meeting and asked if Maxwell could come round to his place at about 9pm that night. "Gulp," thought Maxwell and replied in the affirmative.

Mr Davies and Mr Trevor sat across the room. These were the two most senior priests known to man. Mr Davies began, "Got your letter," he said abruptly and paused for what seemed an eternity. "Tell us what happened, Maxwell," he continued. "The dirty old man wants all the gritty details," Maxwell thought, and then thinking better of it he gave a matter of fact account of the events of that afternoon in Sydney. "I see," Mr Davies replied and following one of two clarifying questions he said, "We'll have to talk to the Elect Vessel about this and it will come up at the Assembly meeting this Saturday." Not sure of what to do next Maxwell told the priests of the very moving account of his confession to, and forgiveness from, the Lord Jesus. "That's very good," Mr Davies said in reply, "but this isn't about Jesus, this is about the Assembly. She has to clear her name."

Confused Maxwell made his way home and just in case Jesus hadn't understood his initial confession fully, he made another lengthier one that he felt covered all possible variations. Strangely he didn't feel any difference, unlike after his previous one.

Saturday meeting came and most had already heard the basics of Maxwell's case and what wasn't known precisely was simply manufactured by the teller. To some Maxwell became a folk hero but to others he was the devil incarnate. Finally Mr Davies said, "There is a serious matter involving Maxwell White that we've been looking into and have spoken to the Elect Vessel and we feel he must be shut up for a week. We'll meet with him and report back next Thursday night." With that statement he turned to Maxwell and said, "Will you now leave the meeting." Maxwell had sat on the front row as usual and hadn't been expecting to be shut up as he had definitely repented of what he'd done. He got up and avoiding eye contact with all of his friends and relatives present walked the walk of shame out the door to his car. Little did Maxwell know that this would be the very last time he would experience the Assembly.

The same two priests visited briefly again on Tuesday evening but very little was discussed except the Elect Vessel had been spoken to again and he reiterated that the Assembly had to clear its' name and the matter would be brought up Thursday evening. Maxwell understood and felt sure the process of being shut up was achieving that means and his repentance would be recognised and on Thursday he would be allowed back again.

The Thursday meeting went on for some time and Maxwell waited at his home for his family to return and tell him the result. It was 11pm when just his father and mother arrived home – by themselves. His mother disappeared straight into her room without saying a word and slowly Maxwell's father walked over and sat on a kitchen chair. "You got withdrawn from," he said, his voice breaking as he spoke. "Your repentance to Jesus was considered but the Elect Vessel stated that given the nature of the sin, then the Assembly had to clear its' name and there was no other option but that you are withdrawn from immediately." Maxwell wanted to vomit. He knew exactly all that that entailed. He'd seen quite a number of his friends withdrawn from over the years and not a one of them had ever come back. Just then Maxwell had a puzzling thought, "Where's the rest of the family, Dad" Maxwell asked? His father answered, again matter of factually "Your Mother and I spoke up against the Assembly judgement and we have both been shut-up too. Your sisters and brothers have gone to their uncles tonight while we sort things out. Your two brothers will be home tomorrow as they are young and need their mother."

Maxwell quietly cursed travelling to Sydney and felt overwhelmed with hopelessness about the situation he had caused. "Dad, you and Mum have to get back to the Assembly. You can't break up the family over me. I'll be ok," Maxwell assured him, "I'll find somewhere to live and I'll be gone by the weekend." Maxwell didn't sleep well that night. What a mess he'd caused but most of all he was totally confused. How come Jesus could forgive him so clearly for what he'd done but his fellow Assembly members just could not? How could that be, did they not even talk with Jesus?

Back at the office next day not much work got done as Maxwell busied himself with finding somewhere to live. Fortunately an acquaintance he'd done previous work for was renting a small partly furnished apartment. He took it. The apartment was small and had one bedroom, the wall to the adjoining unit was paper thin but it was somewhere to lay his head. The possession date was in four days.

The days that followed back at his home were just plain weird. Maxwell was barred from the family table even though his parents were also shut up. Every time he crossed paths with his parents around the home neither of them spoke or made eye contact – he'd become invisible. His father eventually broke rank and offered an apology saying the treatment was necessary if they were to find their way back and have the family restored to them. That part fortunately for them didn't take long and on the Saturday they were advised by the priests that they could break bread the following day and receive the family back home. The condition – Maxwell must be gone immediately. Distraught but understanding, Maxwell left the house that day and booked into a city motel. He would come back Monday evening while they were at the prayer meeting for his possessions, when his apartment was ready.

Monday night, with the whole family at the prayer meeting Maxwell packed his belongings and loaded the car ready to leave his family home, perhaps for the very last time. He walked around the empty house in unbelief, numbness invading his body and disbelief his brain. From every room he entered family memories screamed out to him. He collected small mementoes here and there and the occasional photo to remind him he once did have a family. While soaking in a final imprint of the family living room Maxwell heard a crash outside as the door burst open, the family was back. His mother was first inside and without a glance and with distinct anger in her voice said, "You still here, you better get on your way." Snatching the last of his stuff Maxwell called out the all clear, he was going now. None of his seven siblings said anything except one sister who in solemn formal tones just said "Goodbye Maxwell." Those words burned into his soul, that goodbye sounded very final.

Out in his car Maxwell collected his thoughts and began to reverse down the drive. Something moved near the house, he stopped the car to see his nine year old brother whom he loved so dearly standing forlornly outside near the front door. Maxwell had waited 14 years for a brother and the two of them had become inseparable. His young brother's face said it all, his little world had completely disintegrated; his beloved Maxwell was leaving forever – without him! Maxwell wanted to rush over and give him a huge hug and tell him to look after mum for him, but he just couldn't. The very best he could muster was a passionate wave and with tear-filled eyes and a huge lump in his throat he reversed out on the street and drove off into the night. The vivid picture of that sad, young, deeply loved brother quietly waving broken hearted from the side of his family home forever engrained in his memory.

It would be more than 20 years before Maxwell saw his brother again. He never saw his mother, ever, and was not allowed to attend her funeral even though many years had passed. He wondered if she ever regretted her last words to him.

Maxwell didn't recall much of the 50 km drive back to the city and it was a very sober young man that quietly unloaded his car and arranged his meagre belongings around his sparsely furnished abode. Mission accomplished Maxwell went inside and locked the door. Suddenly the enormity of the moment overwhelmed him – he was utterly alone. Every single person he'd ever known - friend, relative or acquaintance - had banished him from their lives. For his entire 23 years he'd been instructed that every unknown worldly person outside his locked door was an agent of the devil himself and never to be befriended. A massive black cloud of utter abandonment and hopelessness overwhelmed him and he burst into inconsolable tears. Hours of tears followed until eventually he was consumed by exhausted sleep.

Next day Maxwell couldn't face going to the office and stayed in bed. The grief had passed but was now replaced by confusion mingled with sheer terror. All his entire life he'd been taught that Jesus had died for his sins but yet the beloved

Elect Vessel had decreed he had committed a sin the Assembly could not forgive. Why was that, the Assembly or the Elect Vessel hadn't died for his sins, that was Jesus. But the Elect Vessel spoke the words of Jesus, didn't he – how could this be? This circular puzzlement ran rampant through Maxwell's brain. He tried to read his Bible but that only served to muddy the waters further and as for prayer, why would Jesus ever listen to him now – he'd been withdrawn from. Was he even still saved?

The days passed and the turmoil in his brain raged. Maxwell threw himself into his work hoping to reengineer his focus. He longed to be back in the Assembly, he longed for his family and especially his young brother. Unfortunately the only way back was via the priests and Maxwell knew it wasn't permitted for him to approach them - he had to wait and they would come to him when it was time to gauge repentance. They will come, he told himself. In the meantime he maintained complete separation from every worldly person and the only contact he had with any humans were his work acquaintances and customers. Strictly business he told himself.

The weeks passed and no priest materialised. His father had called one evening, just to check he was still alive and doing ok. Maxwell could detect the pain in his voice which only served to regurgitate the self-suppressed emotions and yet again a few tears were shed.

The apartment adjoining Maxwell's was occupied by a young guy, perhaps a few years older than him, but he could never talk to him —he was worldly. He did however have good taste in music Maxwell thought, so he can't be all bad. Through the paper thin walls he could hear his radio clearly. The latest John Denver pop song, Country Roads had just been released and seemingly was playing every fifteen minutes. The vision of a country road taking him home resonated with Maxwell, it numbed the hurt. That was a good thing he reckoned.

A few days later, Maxwell passed a music shop displaying a large poster of the country singer, guitar over his shoulder swaggering down his country road. "I've got a cassette player in my car, Maxwell told himself. "It's not really a worldly song, is it?" he confirmed internally. And with that a purchase was made and Maxwell had bent the invisible blurry line defining worldliness and his version of righteousness.

A few weeks later one of Maxwell's customers offered him a contract to work with his firm on a major engineering project they'd just been awarded. Oil and gas had recently been discovered off the coast and his adopted city had overnight become invaded with sub-sea petroleum specialist from all corners of the globe as the construction phase of the country's first offshore oil rig began. His American client required him to be available seven days a week as they had vessels at sea which only operated within specifically defined weather windows. When the ships were working engineering information had to be interpreted and relayed back to them. Maxwell had nothing else to fill his time while he waited for the priest, so why not?

Chapter 3
The Veil Is Lifted

Working on a Sunday, in these circumstances, was ok, he consoled himself. Also the money was excellent.

A few weeks passed when late one evening one of his superiors dumped a large bottle of whiskey on Maxwell's desk. His eyes lit up immediately – the nectar of the Elect Vessel he thought. He'd be in for that. "We just won a large extension to our contract," Tom explained, "we're expanding". With that Tom thrust a large glass of whiskey into Maxwell's hand, "Cheers," he said, raising his own glass and throwing back a large swig. The situation compelled Maxwell and instinctively he did the same. It was the first whiskey Maxwell had enjoyed in weeks, such a fine malt it was too. The fact he was consuming it with a worldly person totally eluded him. The moment felt right.

Several more glasses followed during which Maxwell discovered a lot about Tom. Even though they had worked together for a few weeks, Maxwell had kept completely to himself. He knew nothing of the lives of any of his workmates except he deduced from their accent they were mostly from the US or perhaps Canada. Tom opened up first; he was from Vancouver, married with a four year old daughter. "Take a look at this one," Tom exclaimed, handing Maxwell a photo. "Isn't she adorable? That little girl changed my life!" "Ah, this is the wife," Tom proudly announced, thrusting yet another wallet photo in Maxwell's direction. "She sure is," Maxwell agreed with little persuasion.

The two drank and talked for at least two hours. It was the first real conversation Maxwell had had with anyone in weeks. What surprised him most was that Tom seemed completely normal. He loved his wife and daughter and everything he said about his life displayed normal family life, to Maxwell. But wasn't he worldly and a son of the devil? Perhaps it was just the whiskey clouding his judgement, but he came across just like so many of his old friends from the Assembly? The only difference was that Tom made no reference to the Elect Vessel or Assembly rules. Then it dawned on Maxwell, the conversation never once made him feel guilty. Maxwell went to bed that night somewhat more relaxed. Maybe, just maybe, he thought, he could find some friends among these worldlys? "He would have to be selective," he told himself, "Tom was obviously the exception, not the norm."

The weeks passed and the office grew as Tom's team was joined by experts from all corners of the globe. All were under 40 and mostly single, here to earn big bucks and play hard. At Tom's encouragement Maxwell was quickly adopted into the international gang. He was the local and who better to serve as guide to all the intricacies of their newly adopted home town. Although he suffered from the occasional pang of conscience Maxwell felt good. He was part of something, he had friends and what's more they weren't warped or depraved as he's always been told. They seemed perfectly normal and all had mothers, fathers, brothers and sisters just like him and there wasn't a devil worshiper among them. A stark realisation hit him like a sledgehammer – he'd been lied to, big time!

Alone that night contemplating his new enlightenment his imagination clicked to warp speed. He certainly had been lied to about those that didn't belong to the Assembly. "Name them worldly if you must," he mused, "but they're definitely not evil, deprived or agents of the devil. Some of them even said they went to church – occasionally!" So if he'd been lied to about that, exactly what else had he been lied to about? Millions of questions sprinted across Maxwell's brain. The Bible was very clear on what God thought of liars. Yet these were the direct words of the Elect Vessel! Did this mean the Elect Vessel was a liar? "No, surely not" Maxwell told himself in disbelief. "That couldn't be possible, could it? On the other hand the evidence of my new friends definitely says the opposite." Now Maxwell's dilemma really took hold. If he lied about people not of the Assembly, what else had the Elect Vessel lied about? What about the Bible, what was right, what was wrong? Wallowing in a fog of bewilderment, Maxwell finally fell asleep. He hadn't read his Bible that night. It was the first time he'd not done so since he began to break bread more than 15 years ago.

It took a few weeks but eventually a firm conclusion matured in his mind; the Elect Vessel was anything but chosen of God. He was nothing more than a leader of a cult and he held his little flock together with absolute fear of eternal damnation. The reality was that whoever disagreed with him was banished in punishment until they 'repented,' and all this was done under a guise of maintaining righteousness before God. What a fool he'd been. Armed with the stark revelation of what he'd so recently been such a willing participant in, Maxwell's previous sorrows quickly morphed into heart-filled thankfulness. No longer did he pang to go back to his past, but what was the future?

Maxwell felt like a caged bird that had unexpectantly been released into the vast mountain skies. What were the boundaries? What were the limits? Height, depth, length and breadth! What exactly was right or wrong? Who said so and who made up the rules. What about God, Maxwell ventured? Deep down, he certainly wanted an immediate answer to that question. He knew that Jesus was real, he'd experienced His forgiveness and after all He did save him from the ocean that day! "Ok," Maxwell declared. "Jesus is real, that I know and I know He died for my sins. What else is, I have no idea." With that Maxwell took it on himself to determine exactly what and where the boundaries were. His former understanding of righteousness was completely in tatters.

"Time is short, hell is hot
the King is coming ready or not"

Chapter 4
The White Standard

"What sort of name is Maxwell," Mike shouted above the noise of the little bar. "From now on you are Max," he declared. The small group roared their wholehearted agreement and thus Max was born. Max had been ex Assembly for nearly a year now and had more-or-less come to terms with the situation. Not a squeak from any priest though and Max declared, "Good riddance." One thing he was sure of was that the Elect Vessel was certainly no messenger of God. His self-determined rules and edicts had very little to do with righteousness, that much was clear. But what was true righteousness then? Max didn't know and right now didn't really care. Life was good and he was free.

Max had developed a strong friendship with Tony; both were about the same age. Tony had recently returned to New Zealand after a savage marriage break up and, while never discussed, the mutual affinity of abandonment and hurt formed a common bond between them. Together they shared a house as flatmates with two other expatriate workers. Although unplanned the residence had become an unofficial clubhouse for these highly skilled international workers seeking respite from their demanding round-the-clock work schedules. Max and Tony both with much to forget took up the roll of club patrons with gusto. Sex, drugs and rock and roll prevailed! Max's Bible lay unread in his top draw with his prayer-life, negligible.

Thursday, Friday and Saturday nights' routine would usually kick off at a little wine bar in the city centre and end up at a popular tavern/nightclub. Regulations of the 70's forced these establishments to close at 10pm so everyone was invited back to the clubhouse where festivities would continue into the wee hours. Sunday afternoon/evening was gambling time. Surprisingly despite very little experience Max became an adept gambler and an afternoon stake could easily reap a few hundred dollars. The remaining weeknights were just hangout evenings, time to catch up and share a drink with those new to town or back from a three week offshore stint. Life was busy but somehow Max managed to keep up an active work schedule and was quickly becoming an expert in his new-found discipline – offshore oil and gas engineering.

Max had few boundaries, to him if someone else was doing it, why not. Everyone seemed to smoke cigarettes so why not. Just one or two offered by friends initially but that quickly matured to continuous smoking during a night out. The habit only kicked in when he was drinking and since he didn't drink at work, neither did he smoke.

One particular Sunday he'd been called into the office early, a serious problem was developing and his urgent attention was mandatory. Max's work ethics sprang into gear but his body screamed a completely different melody. The past evening had been a particularly celebratory one which had finished up close to 3am. Not only was Max's head performing the continuous drumbeat of a mature hangover his lungs felt like the bladder of a bagpipe after a kindergarten lesson. Later that day, crisis alleviated, Max sat alone in his car. He'd driven to the beach to walk and clear his head. A sudden thought leaped into his mind – he didn't like smoking. He didn't have to do it, just because others did. Right at that moment Max resolved to never smoke another cigarette – and he never did! Strolling down the beach Max reflected on his decision. He didn't need to be told what to do, some things were right, some were wrong and others just plain stupid. Could this be criteria to establish boundaries for his life? The fresh sea breeze invigorated him and he felt his head and lungs finally clearing after his lacklustre day.

Over the next few months Max learned to apply his smoking principle on other areas of his life. Drugs, while rarely on public display at the clubhouse, where certainly present. Red, one of Max's close international friends was an ex heroin user and he'd recounted some horrific accounts to the gang on his unpleasant experiences. Not that Max had any particular view on the subject but he went along with Red's opinion and the use of hard drugs was unofficially excluded from the club. Marijuana, on the other hand, freely abounded. Max participated readily as the effects were similar to alcohol he reckoned, so what was the harm. Deep down however something didn't sit right with him about the drug but no matter what, he couldn't figure the problem. So like everything else he embraced it with a passion.

Back from the tavern one Saturday night one of Max's friends produced a stash of rolled cannabis joints. The small group enthusiastically lit up and sucked in the toxic smoke like fresh mountain air. It was a barmy summer's night so Max retreated outside to the steps waiting for the effects to take hold. The results of a night of heavy drinking presented itself and Max went off to give relief. The bathroom was occupied and reeked of vomit so Max wandered back outside and down to the back of the garden where, after checking there were no observers, emptied the content of his bladder into the small garden stream. Making his way up the path to the steps he felt the effects of the drug beginning to take effect, so he lay back on the grass to gaze at the moonlit sky and enjoy the ride.

The ride however was anything but normal. Max sensed himself being gripped with paranoia - this was not usual, he reflected. He got up eager to get inside as suddenly the darkness posed countless unseen dangerous threats. Inside nothing changed, perhaps if he went to bed, he figured. As he entered his room a particular panic flooded in. What if someone had seen him relieve himself in the garden? You can be arrested for public indecency he told himself. He didn't want to go to jail – oh dear Lord what was he to do. At that very instant he thought he heard someone at the front door. The voices were loud and didn't sound hospitable. He couldn't make out what they were saying but in his self-induced haze he was convinced, it was unquestionably the police. No doubt they must be here in search of the pervert who'd been exposing himself late tonight down the bottom of his obscured dark garden! Paranoia became reality, what to do? With a flash of brilliant ingenuity Max dived into the cloths cupboard and slid the door firmly shut behind him. "They'll never find me here," he told himself, very pleased with his cunning plan. How long he was there Max never knew but it was hours before the loud voices abated. It sure takes a while to search a house Max decided. Strangely the members of the local constabulary seemed totally unaware of the master bedroom attached to the end of the house or the large wardrobe it contained. In the ensuing quietness Max crept from his safe-place and into his bed and fell asleep almost immediately.

Next morning he tried to piece together the night's events. "No, didn't see any cops here," Tony assured him. "You were here all night?" Max questioned him, doubtfully. Others confirmed the facts but that wasn't the reality Max believed. However, he was not quite ready to endure the raucous friendly ridicule he was certain would ensue for spending most of last night in a clothes closet, so he let the matter rest. Later that day Red bought up the cannabis they'd smoked. "That stuff was laced with something," Red announced knowledgeably. "I've done some stuff in my time and that one was up there," he continued. Max didn't say anything but perhaps Red was on to something. "This is not good," Max thought. Last night had shaken him immensely. He skipped gambling that afternoon and took a walk along the beach.

Kicking up the hot sand with his bare feet Max tried to put things into perspective. What was right and what was wrong? He wished he really knew but there was no one to tell him anymore. But then there was the law of the land, he stated as he recounted the events of the previous night. There were clear laws about public decency, laws about drugs. While he felt he wasn't really in serious breach of those, he did actually break the law. "Oh, my goodness," he said aloud as the stark realisation as his thoughts soaked in. Breaking the law on any level isn't living right. What if he continued breaking it, what was next? Things had to change, but what and how? He'd lived as club manager for almost two years now, but the club had evolved. He didn't like some stuff anymore. And yes, no more drugs, at any level! Hallucinations were scary – so, "No Thanks."

Max couldn't face going back to the house that evening so dropped by his friend Lear's place. They weren't lovers, just very good friends as were most girls he knew. She reminded him of his sisters; he felt he could talk to her about anything. Lear, about the same age as Max, had also been through tough times in her young life, although she knew little of Max's shielded background. She'd had a son out of wedlock, much to her father's disgust but she'd worked through her issues and in Max's opinion, seemed to have her stuff together. "Some people had no boundaries," Lear explained, "Absolutely anything goes with them. Unfortunately all actions have consequences," she concluded, nodding towards her son. Max was impressed; this was deep stuff from his world savvy friend. "So how do you tell the good guys from the bad?" Max questioned. "Hell I don't know," Lear laughed in reply. "For me I just push the door open a little and if I like what I see, I let them get a little closer – in stages mind, not all at once. Some people just feel creepy so I move on quickly. It's up to you to choose and you have to develop your personal criteria of the people you need around you, ones that will add enjoyment to the way you want to live your life and makes you feel comfortable," Lear expounded, keen to help close the gaps in Max's life skills.

After an enjoyable dinner and most of a bottle of wine a plan had been hatched. It was time to do something different. Max needed to select his friends, and establish his criteria for doing so – and fast. It wasn't necessary to do everything everyone else did; it's okay to be independent. Lear mentioned her friend Robin was looking for a place, "Why not rent a four bedroom house and share it with her and get a couple of other flatmates. She would select one and you the other." Lear suggested with sudden inspiration and excitement. Max knew Robin well and quickly agreed she would make an excellent housemate in his newly creating world. With that Lear called Robin and the deal was done.

Next evening Max explained his new plans to Tony. "Oh, thank God," Tony answered. "I've been wondering how to break it to you. My father's been in touch and he wants me to move back home to help him manage the family farm." A few weeks later Tony and Max moved out of the old expat clubhouse and said their goodbyes. The past years together had been action packed and there was very little they hadn't experienced together. That phase in Max's life, however, had ended with few regrets.

Robin, her friend Christine and Max set up home together in a modern three bedroom house in a new subdivision on the city outskirts. Gone were the late night, after pub, parties and in were dinner parties and evenings at home watching the telly. Max still crossed paths with his expat friends but many of them had moved on too. Phase one of the offshore project was nearing completion and so was the requirement for the multitude of international experts.

Sitting on his deck, overlooking the city and the ocean beyond, Max reflected on his recent life changes. Did he have regrets – no, not really. The last two years had taught him so much. There were things that were right and there were things that were wrong. But strangely there wasn't anybody hovering over him telling which was which. Something deep down inside Max was guiding him. He didn't know who, what or how but very slowly he was beginning to discern it. But, was that righteousness or was it something else, he debated. Was righteousness about doing what was right? Perhaps not, he concluded. If that were the case then his new friends would be righteous, they did right things. Only problem was as far as he knew they weren't Christians, didn't know about the work of Jesus. Satisfied with his progressive life changes Max packed away his debate for another time. One day I'll understand, he thought. Focusing on God was not part of his life right now; he was content to simply believe. Max knew that he knew that Jesus had died for his sins, the penalty was paid. That gave him peace enough for now.

A couple of years passed and all the expats were gone. The bars seemed empty and strangely unappealing to Max. He still drank but seldom got drunk. He didn't feel convicted of it; he simply didn't like waking up with a hangover any more. One of the incredible benefits for having female flatmates, Max discovered – they had female friends! Some very beautiful friends in fact and receiving introductions, kids play. Several romances blossomed but somehow Max couldn't allow anyone to get too close to him. Deep down the raw scar of abandonment by everyone he'd ever loved, had not healed yet. He'd never told a single sole about his Assembly past, only advising his friends he'd fallen out with his family and didn't see them anymore. His secret burned in him and he came close to confessing all to one close girlfriend but just couldn't so, as usual, he moved on.

Although he had no desire to set foot into an Assembly meeting ever again he yearned to see his family. Christmas time was particularly hard. Although the Elect Vessel had forbidden celebrating the day, even with family, Max's friends always went off to be with family, it was then the loneliness hurt. They'd invite Max to join them and he did once but experiencing normal joyful family life only served to make him miserable.

Further complicating things was his knowledge that if he married then the link back to his family on any level would be severed completely. Access to his family was only possible through the Assembly but having an unbelieving (non-Assembly) wife would make that access impossible. The choice was either a wife or his family, he could not have both.

This paradox bothered him as now he was trying hard to do the right thing and perhaps he had even establish his own family of sorts. Doing right however paralleled so many things from his previous life. He had no desire to go back to his expat club days as much of that life was intolerable now. Yet his current life of contentment and normality brought with it so many memories of family fun days at his own home which distressed him too. Doing what was right wasn't easy, he decided.

A few weeks later Max was presented with a new alternative. Pete, his expat friend, phoned from Sydney, Australia telling of a new project starting over there, "Why didn't he come over?" "They're screaming out for people with your experience," Pete explained. "Besides," he continued, "you can stay with me until you get established." Max had never seriously thought about joining the expatriates' job-followers pack, but why not. Who says he can or can't and besides the money is good and I don't need to live their lifestyle, he reasoned. "Nobody will care about my past Assembly life over there" Max reckoned. He was well qualified so yes, he would go.

It took a week or two to finish up his current contract and sell off all his possessions. The farewell dinner parties seemed endless but finally he was to travel next day. At the urging of Lear, Max called his father to advise him of his international relocation. He hadn't spoken to him in four years but elected to do it by phone rather than in person. The call was short and matter of fact. His father thanked him for letting him know and asked if he was well. Max asked how the family was. "Everybody's fine and doing well, Maxwell," his father answered. "Maxwell!" Max thought, "I haven't heard that name in years, definitely no one he knew anymore." With messages conveyed the conversation ended. The following day Max set off to meet the world, all his life's possessions neatly packed in one standard suitcase. Little did he know that would be his life for the next twenty years, and it would take him to more than one hundred independent countries.

Max lodged with his friend Pete for a few days. Pete's friend Bruce (yes Bruce really was a common Australian name in the 1970's) told him his mother was looking for a boarder, if he was interested. Max was and he liked the concept of full board, it would cost him more but he'd have his meals cooked – the most appealing part.

Bruce's mum Pam had become pregnant with him when she was just 16 and as was the custom at that time had married the father to reduce the shame. Since love had little to do with the marriage it ended in a nasty divorce four years later. Pam lumbered on alone and raised Bruce, now in his mid-twenties. Max quickly settled in and, as usual, engrossed himself in his work. With little time available for socialising, after several months Max had not made many new friends.

One evening Bruce asked Max if he'd like to go to a solo parent's party that coming Saturday. His mother would be going so there'd be someone there he knew. Max wasn't sure but Bruce assured him he'd often attended and thoroughly enjoyed it. Unfortunately he couldn't go this time as he had a hot date. The night finally arrived and much to his surprise Max found the place wasn't full of men haters as he presupposed but fun loving women and men, many his age. The evening unfortunately was cut short when Pam announced she was leaving and since she provided the only transport option Max left too. Driving home Pam talked on, inquiring about Max and how he liked Sydney and living with her. Max replied politely but deep down was disappointed at his party time being cut short. Pam turned the car into a beach car park and stopped the engine. Beautiful night isn't it she exclaimed and in a seemingly well practiced move slid across the bench seat of the old car. Next thing Max knew he was locked in the embrace of his friend's 41 year old mother, desperately trying to avoid reciprocating her deep tongued kissing. Not sure of what had just occurred Max made a leap for the door handle and escape to freedom. While on one level he did find Pam attractive, but;

a) She was the mother of his friend and therefore old enough to be his mother and,

b) She was forty-one!

"I'm sorry Mrs Browning," Max said from the freedom of the outside, "I just can't do that." Max left the door open and walked away towards the beach. The cool summer evening air felt good but on the inside he felt yuck! The thought someone of his mother's ilk had tried to seduce him sent shudders down his spine. Max heard the car door slam shut and it drove off. Max didn't care, he never intended getting back in there anyway.

Fortunately Max knew the beach he'd been abandon at so decided to walk back to his lodgings – he was in no hurry! As he walked he pondered on his revulsion. He'd never been one to shy from the offer of gratuitous sex previously, so what was different? Yes she was 41 but he was only 13 years her difference. Her body wasn't unattractive; but the more he thought the more revolted he became. It's because it just isn't right, Max told himself.

This concept was completely new to Max. "You don't do things because they're just not right?" Max puzzled. His analytical mind raced away

– Things you don't do because you don't like it; hard drugs etc.

– Things you don't do because it's against the law; again drugs, oh and weeing in the garden!

– Now this, things those, that just aren't right.

"Moral law," he exclaimed a little stunned at his eureka moment. A general rule of right living, he recalled. "Bit different to the Elect Vessel's moral laws," Max thought. Conclusion reached, Max tucked it away as usual. Back at lodgings the place was in darkness, Max crept inside and shut his bedroom door firmly. He never saw Mrs Browning again and later the next day he went looking for new lodgings.

Max's project had moved to the commissioning phase therefore he was relocated to live at the project site. It was a large copper and zinc open cast mine and processing centre about 150km west of the federal capital Canberra, right in the middle of nowhere. The site operated 24/7 and although Max only had to work five days a week to relieve the boredom he worked every day. Pete announced he planned to backpack through South East Asia when the project was done and Max was invited. Money was therefore the sole focus for Max during his five months on site.

Asia beckoned and the next several months were spent exploring all the non-tourist regions of Southern Asia. Max was stunned at the huge variance from his culture; the foods, the clothes and living conditions, all so different from anything he'd ever imagined. He loved it; the people were incredibly friendly and never once did he feel afraid or threatened. Nobody has ever been able to figure out what made India work. A symphony of one billion ungracefully choreographed inhabitants scampering about their day focused on one single ambition – survival. Somehow India happened. As the sun abated the people became quiet, at sun up the same ungainly dance was repeated.

To Max's surprise it was their gods that perturbed him most. Little carvings of wood and stone each represented their favourite so-called god. Shrines on street corners faithfully maintained with devoted allegiance. Max marvelled at their belief, there were gods for travel, gods for fertility, gods for rain, for food, for animals, plus a thousand others. Not a one spoke or had any powers but none of that mattered to any of their followers. Max reflected on how real his God was. The feeling of forgiveness when he'd confessed his sin which the Assembly could not. The God that had answered him when he'd cried out to Him to save him from the waters all those years ago. Max prayed to his God a little more in Asia.

Pete had gone back home but Max's travels continued between spells in civilization to earn the cash required to feed the next sector. The UK proved an ideal base and once again Max found himself engineering offshore installations, this time for the North Sea oil boom. Next adventure was an extended tour through Scandinavia, Soviet Union and Europe. Max loved the diversity, the cultures and peoples. Switzerland bordered on a love affair - such a beautiful country, it reminded him of home. Back at work again Max budgeted carefully, he always worked long enough to save just enough money to get him established in his next job location. This time it was Rio de Janeiro. Two days before he was to leave he received a telegram – "Project cancelled, no longer any job, don't travel." Unphased Max dug out his favourite map of the world and leaned it against the wall, stood back and threw a dart towards it. Whatever country it lands in I'll go there next he determined. That afternoon he went off and booked his passage to Canada. Deep down though he was moderately thankful the dart hadn't landed in Mongolia.

Chapter 4
The White Standard

Max counted his money. He had money for his fare and living for about 30 days travel in 1st world Canada plus an airfare back to New Zealand. He wasn't sure what the work requirements were in Canada so uncharacteristically, as a backup, he kept aside his airfare to NZ. Didn't want to be trapped in a foreign land he told himself. Not a sole back home had any idea where he was and the thought occasionally crossed his mind, quickly followed by a dismissal. "Na, they don't care a brass-razoo about me," he reiterated to himself.

The day, in Canada, when he crossed the point of no return remained firmly imprinted in Max's mind. He loved the country and found it a little bigger than anticipated. His vague ambition was to get to Calgary, he'd heard they'd discovered oil-sand near there, whatever that was but felt sure they needed his skills to help extract it. He had a choice; he could catch a flight from Winnipeg back home or have a steak dinner and venture on. Coin flipped he went to dinner. Eventually in Calgary he scrolled through the newspaper but surprisingly not a lot of prospects when he noticed an engineering agency advert. He called the number, "You have experience in what?" the voice questioned. "And you're in Calgary right now?" the agent continued. "Stay right where you are, I'm coming by to collect you." Max started work the next day and that city was to be his home for the next four years. As events unfolded he realised that perhaps the dart landing on the map of Canada, or the coin flip, may not have been entirely by chance.

Max assured himself; undoubtedly it must be his strong rugged physic ensconced in his near six foot frame, or perhaps the magnificent moustache he supported, that made him irresistible to the Calgary ladies. Sadly the truth was more closely related to the local's obsessions with unfamiliar English accents that caused them to swoon at the knees. Whatever the real reason Max didn't care, he revelled in his new found notoriety. The work was great, the money was excellent and Max enjoyed the good life.

Thirty is a huge milestone his workmate Wendy assured him, your life is almost over now. Of course Max knew her words were rubbish but he couldn't shake them from his thoughts. His friends had arranged a lovely surprise party for this addition to his age - almost everyone he knew in his adopted country was there. However Wendy's words still rung in his ears, he couldn't help wondering what if it was? What had he achieved, what was his legacy? He'd done a lot of stuff, visited copious countries and had celebrated at every possible opportunity but what had he built? If he died today who would care, who would mourn once the initial loss was passed? He had no family, his friends were great and kind but he was certain that if he moved on he'd soon be forgotten. "There's got to be more to life than this," Max complained to himself.

After several days of self-debating Max made a decision – he would find a wife. The decision carried with it the finality his natural family was gone forever but he'd come to terms with that now. It had been seven years since he'd last seen them or had anything to do with them; enough was enough, time to rebuild. The thought of his own mortality had also focused his thinking more clearly on things of Jesus. He elected to keep short accounts with the Lord from now on and began semi regular prayer and confession of his numerous shortcomings. He knew he believed in the power of the blood of Jesus; that remained an anchor to his soul.

Max had never viewed women as sexual conquests even though there had been plenty. They were far more than that he'd learned and they came in all kinds of packages. Some were sweet and elegant, others strong and sporty and of course the strong and domineering. But what kind would make the best wife and, hopefully, mother of his future children. Max had no idea so true to form he abandoned the analytical approach and simply assumed he'd know her when he saw her.

It was during this non-analytical period when Max found himself dating Sally, a registered nurse. The topic of abortion was hot in the news with views for and against strongly voiced. Max didn't have a strong opinion either way but considered destroying the foetus was certainly a very efficient method of terminating an unwanted pregnancy. At various dinner parties Max would regularly take an opposing view, not that he maintained any strong opinion, it amused him and always made the debate interesting, in his opinion. Max called round to pick up Sally on their prearranged date to find her extremely upset and still in her work clothes. "I'm sorry," Sally explained, "I've had the most terrible day." The date is obviously not going to be happening and since my evening is now free I might as well stay and listen, Max debated to himself.

Sally explained she'd been rostered onto the surgical ward and just after lunch she'd gone into one of the surgeons rooms to find him anguishing over a dish on the bench. Sensing his distress she'd asked the problem. "Take a look," the surgeon suggested. Sally tearfully described the tiny squirming body, lying helplessly on that cold stainless steel tray, gasping for air through lungs not yet fully fit for purpose. "I quickly pushed the stunned doctor aside and immediately set to work," Sally continued. "Get me some suction," she'd ordered. The two of them worked desperately for more than an hour to revive the little boy but to no avail. "He was just too young to live – he was only at 26 weeks," Sally cried, "Yet he was so perfect." "He'd been aborted by the surgeon," Sally continued. "He told me he was ethically confused, he was under strict instructions from the mother to terminate the pregnancy, which he did. Yet here was this little child, snatched from his safe haven before his time, desperately clinging to life. As a doctor what did he do, obey the mother or help this struggling infant live?"

Now it was Max's turn to be upset. He was stunned. He'd always thought of abortion as destroying a foetus not killing an otherwise healthy child. Finally he asked, "So under the right circumstances the child might have lived." "It would be touch and go," Sally explained, "but yes, it is possible for a child born that early to make it." At that very moment Max resolved to never support abortion rights, ever, and certainly he would never use the debate as entertainment. His life skills were yet further reinforced – there were things that just are not right!

It was a year later and Max was now sharing his house with two other young women, one a local but the other, Jenny, was from New Zealand. Jenny reminded him of his roots and he liked that idea. During dinner one evening Jenny announced that her cousin from her hometown Timaru was coming over on holiday and would it be alright with the others if she stayed at the house? Quick agreement was forthcoming and Hazel was accepted to arrive in three weeks.

Max arrived home from work at his usual time just as newly landed Hazel was being introduced to Carol the other housemate. "And," Jenny continued as Max entered, "this is our other housemate, Max. Max, meet Cousin Hazel from New Zealand," Jenny concluded. Jenny while attractive, could not be described a natural beauty, but her blood relative was a knockout. What a stunner Max thought, then, unusually lost for words, stammered out "Pleased to meet you, Cousin Hazel, from New Zealand." What a stupid thing to say Max thought and to cover his momentary stupidity he burst out laughing. Quickly the small group joined in – embarrassment averted, Max thought with relief.

The days passed and Max found himself less interested in work and very keen to get home of an evening. After a few nights Max plucked up the courage to ask Hazel out for dinner – just her, not Jenny, he clarified. "Oh, so it's a date then," Hazel teased. The two sat and talked for hours. Max really liked what he saw, what exactly he saw he couldn't figure out but she was different. Not only was she a stunning beauty she had a brain to match with a wide knowledge on most subjects, unashamed to voice them. What's more she liked the same things he did, the foods he did, she even loved to travel. This was too good to be true, Max thought, there has to be a catch.

The next weeks flew by, Hazel and Max became inseparable. Max had done all he could to show her the very best of his adopted city and its' surrounds but as with all good things, it was time to say goodbye. Hazel was to fly out to Toronto, staying with family for a week, then return home via Vancouver. She had a six hour window in Vancouver so Max agreed to fly over to see her on her way. They'd toured around the city to see the sights of the coastal metropolis. Neither of them enjoyed it however, the fact her all-night flight left in a few hours weighed heavily. On the bus to the airport Max suddenly blurted, "You don't have to leave." Calmly Hazel replied, "Are you asking me not to?" Max thought for a moment and yes he'd never been more certain. He didn't want her disappearing from his life, not just yet anyway. Despite their promises he knew if she returned to New Zealand their romance would quickly fade. "Yes, I am asking," Max replied. "Okay, I will," Hazel answered quickly, disregarding completely, her usual cautious nature. That night Max and Hazel few back to Calgary and set up house together.

Max for the first time in nearly nine years felt a true glimmer of normality return to his life.

*"The mighty oak
was a little nut that stood its ground"*

Chapter 5
New Beginnings

Max wandered along the path around the shoreline of Lake Lugarno. He'd jumped at the chance to travel to Switzerland, his favourite oasis, for a few days of business meetings. Hazel and Max had been together for a few months and life was good! This was the first time they'd been separated since Vancouver and Max wasn't sure he liked that.

Several weeks back Hazel casually mentioned that she'd gone to school with several Assembly children. Max appreciated her small town was a strong breeding ground, literally, for the Assembly and it wasn't at all surprising Hazel had run across them. She mentioned one or two and of course Max knew then too, at least by name. She continued, volunteering the fact that these poor unfortunates had to live lives isolated from every worldly person, attend meetings every day, obey the Elect Vessel and compete with each other in consuming whiskey. What didn't this women know, Max marvelled.

Chapter 5
New Beginnings

Max had never told a soul about his Assembly past, he firmly believed the only way to eliminate the memory was to keep it well buried. But here sat a beautiful young lady who completely understood the people of his past. An unfamiliar feeling of extreme openness overwhelmed Max as he gazed upon her, urging him to reveal his deepest secrets. Max cautiously opened a small door in his self-applied impenetrable armour, here goes nothing, he thought. "I used to be one of them," Max stated as calmly as he could muster. "Got kicked out about nine years ago," he quickly added. Hazel laughed, you mean I've come all this way round the world to connect up with an Assembly guy?" she teased. "What did you get kicked out for," she asked. "Sex," Max replied, not keen to add any more detail. "Yep that would do it," Hazel laughed, knowledgeably. And with that the subject was accepted. Max felt a huge unseen weight lift off his shoulders. No longer did he have to hide a shameful secret, it was in the open now. What an amazing women he thought. She was the first person in a decade he'd ever been able to share that with. A bond had been established.

With that unseen barrier gone in Max's mind, he felt he had to go deeper and uncover Hazel's true thoughts on God. While he'd turned his back on the Elect Vessel he hadn't with his God. Deep down Max loved Jesus very much as he knew what he'd saved Max from. If Hazel was to be a part of his life he must know what she really believed.

Following a news article on prayer in schools a few weeks later, Max saw his chance, "Why ban God from everything," Max stated emphatically. The statement left little doubt on which way he inclined. "I thought you didn't believe in God anymore," Hazel inquired. "Oh, yes I definitely still believe in Jesus," Max replied. "Never any doubt on that, it's just the Assembly and all its rules I couldn't stand." The answer seemed to satisfy Hazel who sat in contemplative thought. "I'm not really sure what I believe," she volunteered. "I do believe in a "superior supernatural being" though," she added almost as an afterthought. "Isn't a "superior supernatural being" just another term for God?" "What makes you believe that?" Max inquired. "It's the only way I can make sense of everything," Hazel answered. "We have to be here for a reason and if so then someone or something must have put us here for that reason." That's deep thinking Max thought, and also very true. "Have you ever been to church?" Max asked, inquisitive to understand where that thinking had originated from. "No, but Dad insisted we all attended Sunday School when we were little. I went for about three years" Hazel responded. "I guess that's what instilled my belief about God." She believes, Max confirmed to himself. He could live with that even if she didn't know Jesus the way he did, at least she did believe in God. With another tick confirmed Max changed the subject.

Max was snapped from his deep thoughts by an angry cyclist screaming something in Italian as he swerved past him. He'd been away from home for a few days now and suddenly it dawned on him, he really truly missed her. Max felt a surge of emotion well up within him; "wow I actually do love her." He thought, the reality of the moment consuming him. Yes, okay, as soon as I get home I'll make things permanent – Marriage it is then, he confirmed.

Hazel had made her intentions clear on her desire to marry on several previous occasions so it was with some confidence that Max popped the question soon after his return. However to his surprise her answer wasn't yes or no but "what changed your mind?" Max briefly toyed with the idea of teasing that he'd just discovered she was due a large inheritance but wisely took another tack. "I had lots of time to think in Switzerland and realised I needed you in my life – permanently," Max answered honestly. Hazel stood back contemplating Max, unknown suspicions flooding her mind. "Are you sure?" she asked, "I can have a bit of a temper sometimes you know." True enough, Max acknowledged, he had experienced that once or twice. Her strong character was one of her attractions. He needed that, she was naturally pessimistic he was naturally optimistic. "Well, what is it?" Max questioned keen to conclude the deal. "Yes, I'd be delighted to be known as Mrs Hazel White," Hazel finally confirmed. "Wonderful," Max replied, truly delighted, "we'll go ring shopping at the weekend. With that Max produced the chilled champagne and proposed a toast.

The ring was bought, the announcements made and her family back home shared Hazel's excitement. No date was set for the wedding, "We'll have it when we get back to New Zealand," Hazel informed, and Max agreed.

Hazel had travelled to Canada on a visitor's visa and was therefore unable to work. Not only was she bored with the confines of the home but immigration advised her that on the next expiry date of her tourist visa she would either have to get a permanent resident visa or leave the Country. She had three weeks to decide.

Max's job was great and the pay excellent, for him, moving on was not an option. Seeing the love of his life move on wasn't an option either. For Hazel to become a permanent resident she had to have a job offer, leave the country, make application and wait there while the visa was processed. However there were no guarantees it would be granted as unlike Max her skills were not in the shortage category. Finally a friend suggested they just get married as then she'd be covered under Max's visa. "We can keep it secret and do it all properly when we finally get back home?" Max suggested. Hazel agreed and she made the arrangements.

Judge Parker's office was on the fifteenth floor of the courts building and before him stood Maxwell White and Hazel Williamson. Max had taken his best clothes into the office that morning and had changed in the bathrooms on the ground floor. Hazel, dressed in a stunning new dress purchased especially for the occasion, had taken the bus into the city a little earlier, and met Max in the foyer. The Judge picked up his phone, "The witnesses can come in now," he grunted. And with that the door opened and the receptionist and one other court worker entered and sat at the side, by the Judge. "Shall we start," Judge Parker stated, seemingly bored with the process already. "Maxwell, do you take this woman to be your lawful wedded wife?" "I do," Max stated enthusiastically, admiring his catch. "And Hazel," Judge Parker continued, "do you take this man to be your lawful wedded husband?" "I do." Hazel answered confidently. There was a short pause while Max clumsily pushed the matching wedding ring onto Hazel's outstretched figure. "On the basis of the power vested in me by the State of Alberta I therefore declare you man and wife." Without pausing for breath Judge Parker continued, "Please show me your passports?" The Judge recorded all the details from the passports and asked Max and Hazel to sign their agreement. The two witnesses duly acknowledged their presence; the judge signed the bottom, and handed the form to Hazel in return for the $50 fee. Mr and Mrs White, papers in hand, conveyed their thanks and headed for the elevator. "If I'm quick I'll just get back to work for 1pm and nobody will be any the wiser," Max told his new wife. "Yes and I better get this paper down to the immigration office," Hazel replied. "Let's have steak for dinner tonight as a little celebration," Hazel added. And so it was in his thirty second year that Max and Hazel began married life together.

The weeks turned to months and then to years and finally Max's job came to a close, it was time to move on. Try as they might, their secret marriage became impossible to conceal. It was Hazel's Canadian cousin Jenny; she demanded to see Hazel's immigration papers, convinced she was working illegally. "Mrs" Jenny exclaimed! Hazel quickly explained the reasons and begged her cousin's silence, ensuring her she definitely would be invited to the main event back in Timaru, eventually. The news however was just too much for poor Jenney to contain so tele-Jenney quickly became telephone, telegraph. The reasons for a big family celebration back home evaporated quickly. Judge Parker's marriage ceremony was however completely legal so despite the lack of festivities that remained the sole event that entwined their two lives together. "It will be very nice to finally meet your family though," Max told his loving wife of two years.

Max was enjoying married life and also being back in New Zealand after six years of carefree roaming of the world. He enjoyed having family again; Hazel's family had accepted him as one of their own. Finally he felt his life rebuilding had really begun. This inward contentment led to thankfulness as he reflected on the unplanned path he'd taken yet, somehow, the result had turned out perfectly. Obviously it was the Lord's hand controlling everything. A Bible verse from his youth came to mind *"God maketh the solitary into families; those that were bound he bringeth out into prosperity:"* Psalm 68:6 (DBT). God had indeed placed him back into a family. Max began to pray

Chapter 5
New Beginnings

words of thanks to Jesus and quite frequently too. He maintained short accounts with Jesus about his sins, regularly confessing anything he'd done to displease Him. Because of his willingness to please Jesus Max made a conscious effort to avoid certain situations that he knew could lead to sin. He knew he was maintaining a form of righteousness but something was missing and he had no idea what. Regardless Max continued on doing his best and maintaining close contact with Jesus. This relationship however was maintained in total privacy, he believed it best that way. His connection with Jesus was solely his business.

The only work available to Max in his native country was high-rise construction which necessitated them living in Auckland. It was a pleasant city and their home, in one of the sea-side suburbs, enjoyable, however Max soon became bored with the routine of staying put and itched for a new international project. His opportunity came soon enough when Hazel noticed an advertisement in the paper for a position in Papua New Guinea. A few months later Max and Hazel found themselves setting up house in a company provided cottage in Lae, Papua New Guinea. Living and working in a third world country offered a new experience for them both. Things that Max deemed important such as money and material comforts were of little esteem in that wider community. The importance was family, or "one-talk" in the local speak; sharing was the norm with the concept of personal possessions, foreign.

Max and Hazel jumped at the chance to join a small group visiting a nearby village for the weekend. The settlement was set by the sea some two hours walk from the nearest road with electricity, running water or sanitary options non-existent. Upon arrival they were welcomed by some of the friendliest people Max had ever known. Sleeping arrangements consisted of small wooden huts with palm branch roofs and a dirt floor but it was comfortable and the sound of the lapping beach, soothing. The combined income of the entire village was only a few hundred dollars per year and in every international statistic they would be termed as living in extreme poverty. Yet here were a people, clean, well fed and very happy. They lived off the land, slept when it was dark and cared for each other. Max and Hazel very quickly felt ashamed of their stressing for material possessions after a night of festivities with such a happy caring group.

Max couldn't help thinking that they could improve some aspects of their lives with a little education to upgrade their skills. But apart from the children being taught to read, write and do arithmetic via the national government all other life skills were acquired in-house. This fact was demonstrated in dramatic fashion to the visitors the next day.

The options for returning to Lae were either a long hot walk through the bush or a pleasant one hour boat ride across the bay; the small group quickly opted for the latter. The transport was a twenty person lifeboat which the village had found washed up on its shores several years back. It had the luxury of an outboard motor which exhibited many signs of a brutal existence but after considerable tinkering it burst in to life. Amid much excitement twenty souls quickly scrambled aboard accompanied by luggage, sacks of coconuts, flax matting rolls together with numerous other bags of locally made items, some chickens and a pig for selling in the Lae market. Max being larger was directed to the back of the boat and Hazel to the front. Max checked the freeboard, it was a few centimetres from the top but at least the bay was very calm, he consoled himself.

At that moment the engine roared into life and the little Noah's Ark headed out across the bay. It was then that Max noticed the person at the throttle. A very tiny man well into his sixties, chewing on beetle leaves with vacant eyes fixed on some distant horizon. Max said a little prayer; surely they had someone in the village with more skills than this old man! No one else in the boat seemed concerned so Max sat back to enjoy the ride, the day was sunny, the sea was calm.

The Markham River runs from the nearby mountains and feeds into the bay between the village and the city of Lae. As the boat neared the river mouth the effects of the large river rushing down the steep incline and hitting the calm ocean were painfully obvious. The massive flow of fast moving water pushed up large waves in a swirling mass. Waves, some as high as two metres, broke in every direction towering high above the little craft. Calling it a lifeboat was a cruel trick, Max surmised. He looked at the waves then to the driver of their floating ark who had slowed the boat, manoeuvring it up and down beside the foaming waters. The expression on his face unchanged, the vacant stare still transfixed on unknown objects. Taking the boat any closer to the raging sea seemed certain death. Max tried to keep calm but panic was rampant, he looked across to Hazel sitting at the front and she too clearly envisaged her imminent death. "I love you," he mouthed. Next thing the little driver wound the throttle to full speed and turned it directly toward the raging waves. Much to Max's utter astonishment, as the boat approached, the waves ahead suddenly cleared as if some giant hand had created a path and almost instantly the laden craft was on the other side. Max looked back in stunned amazement as the waves quickly returned to their previous agitated churning. Perhaps the Captain had done this before!

Max felt a massive invasion of shame condemn his soul. The driver was obviously uneducated, and of unfamiliar character, but Max had automatically classified him as stupid. Yet if Max, with all his years of education, had attempted to do what he's just witnessed the loss of twenty souls would have been assured. Life skills were equal with educated skills and there were no class barriers. For the first time in his life Max completely appreciated that all men on the earth were equal. Some were good at some things, others something else. There were no classes, no rankings. *"God so loved the world,"* Max recounted, and he loved that little old lifeboat driver just as much as he loved Hazel and himself. Jesus gave his life to save all mankind.

Armed with this new found understanding Max finally put aside a major root of Assembly teaching. He long since knew that those outside the Assembly were not all sinners and heathens, there were many genuine folks. But this experience cleaned the path completely; all outside the Assembly were precious in God's eyes. Not that they were all saved of course, it was that God loved them and yearned to have them know Him too. Salvation was open to every person on this earth.

All too soon the PNG project ended and Melbourne beckoned, and again Max and Hazel set up camp in a new land. A few months later, after celebrating five years of happy marriage, Hazel announced she wanted to start a family. "I'm thirty one," she declared, "and that's prime child bearing age." Max didn't have a strong view on the subject and with a somewhat flippant attitude said, "Yea, why not."

Hazel insisted her children must have the same nationality as her so back to New Zealand the couple moved but this time to a lifestyle block and work near the city of Whangarei. Hazel felt Max's income was ample to support a wife and a family so for the first time in her married life she became a kept woman and almost immediately fell pregnant.

At first Max was nonplussed at the idea of starting a family but that all changed when Hazel attended her first scan. "It's a boy!" Hazel cried in joy and thrust a grainy image towards Max. Max considered the photo for a while; he honestly couldn't make head-nor-tail of it; however he knew better than to question his pregnant wife's knowledge. She was happy and that was a wonderful respite from her recent mood swings, "Wonderful news" he exclaimed, scooping her up in his arms. "Due date is about your birthday," Hazel added. About then something clicked in Max's brain, he was going to be a father! His first child was to be a son. He was gaining a family of his own. For the next few months Max walked with a spring in his step and a whistle in his heart.

Finally the day arrived and Hazel was to be induced, it seemed the little fellow was reluctant to make his appearance. They drove into the city hospital and with Hazel formally admitted and the process started Max went off to stay the night with Hazel's aunt, who lived nearby. About 1am the hospital called, "Hazel has gone into labour." Certain the birth would be well over before his arrival Max raced through the empty streets of the sleeping city, avoided the slow lift and bounded up the steps to the fifth floor to find his still very pregnant wife sleeping soundly and alone in her room. Max sat to catch his breath and wait.

Eventually, about 7pm next evening the doctor was summoned. "It's baby time," the nurse confirmed enthusiastically. Max oscillated between holding his wife's hand while uttering encouraging words, to quickly observing progress at the other end. "Just one more big push," the doctor urged. My son must be close now, Max thought as he hurried back to check progress. To his shock and horror, protruding from the birth cannel was not a sweet little baby boy, but a large unrecognisable black mass. "What the hell is that?" Max exclaimed loudly. As if unhearing the doctor continued his work, "His head is almost out, just one more push. He sure has a lovely crop of black hair," the doctor reported. "Oh – a head of hair…." Max sheepishly acknowledged to himself as his brain finally translated what he'd just witnessed. He scurried back to hold his wife's hand, he'd leave the other end to the experts, he determined. At 7.35pm the doctor handed Hazel the loveliest little bundle of joy Max had ever seen. This was HIS son, he was now a Father! "What's his name?" the nurse asked. "Austin Frank White," Hazel proudly announced.

Max revelled in the delight of being a dad, announcing the news to everyone he met. He couldn't wait until Austin grew and he could take him places and do things with him. It had been a few weeks and with Hazel keen to get out and enjoy the summer they set off to attend a demonstration of life-style block management. They'd taken a picnic lunch; it was their first family outing. Hazel was keen to explore and catch up with friends so Max found himself alone with Austin as he sat under the shade of a large oak tree. Austin, recently fed, slept soundly oblivious to the stunning surroundings and the love welling from his father's heart. Max admired his tiny son sleeping so confidently in his father's arms. I wonder if my father ever did this, Max considered? His thoughts quickly drifted off to all the events of the past fifteen years since he last saw his family, the hurt, shame, betrayal and suffering he'd experienced all popped up. But so did all the things he'd learned from those experiences, things that were right and things that were just wrong. He had met people that were kind and nice, others who were just plain mean but most importantly he now knew how to tell the difference and who to associate with. Finally there was Jesus; the forgiveness he'd experienced, the miraculous plucking from the raging sea, the guiding hand that had brought him through all his troubles, had given him a lovely wife and now a son. "If only dear Lord Jesus," Max prayed, "I could pass my life knowledge and experiences on to my son so that he can be spared from the same path." Max gazed upon his sleeping son so full of innocence and dependency. If only there was a way? The thought of his precious son being hurt by others saddened Max, but just as if someone had whispered in his ear, Jesus answered, "Give him to me, I'll take good care of him? He'll learn from experience just as you did but just like you, we'll do it together." At that very moment sitting under that shady oak tree, Max dedicated his little son to Jesus.

Max felt closer to Jesus than he'd been in a long time and he prayed more frequently. Other than that there was little more that he wanted to do. He liked his life and in his eyes he was living right. He wasn't walking in sin, that he knew of, but still kept short account with Jesus, confessing any regularly. Max had been working hard and one night as he slept, he suddenly found himself in the presence of a friend chatting with him face to face. Max stood there embedded in the vision, he could make out a face but no particular facial features, but without a doubt he instinctively knew it was the face of Jesus. The hair was white but opaque, the face however absolutely radiant, shining like the sun; such an incredibly vivid and bright white but not burning to his eyes. It was as if he could see deep inside the man who had not a single shadow or obscurity present – *in Him was no darkness at all.* The radiant whiteness extended as glory from His presence. An incredible feeling of the presence of Jesus in person flooded Max's heart. The sensation was of a simultaneous overflowing of peace, joy and love – not separately but all three together at absolute maximum flow.

To this day Max cannot recall exactly what they were talking about as the conversation was similar to a verbal download directly into his spirit. Something his natural body was completely unable to comprehend. Max soaked up the unexplainable feeling of the moment as the download continued. Finally Jesus spoke in Max's native tongue, "It's time for you to go back now," Jesus said. That was the last thing Max wanted, he was hooked and determined he'd never leave. "Please let me stay," Max begged. "No," Jesus answered kindly,

"I've got a couple of things for you to do yet." The next thing Max knew he was sitting bolt upright in his bed, his wife sleeping obliviously beside him. "What was that all about?" Max questioned. But then the feeling of His presence returned, much weaker now but very real all the same. The words of Jesus kept repeating in his ears, "I've got a couple of things for you to do yet." What things? A couple – was that general or specifically two things? So many questions he just wanted five minutes more back there to get all his answers. No more answers came that night, but the sensations remained with Max for the rest of his natural life.

The days turned to weeks and no further answers came. For some time Max had felt the urge to call his father. He was heading down that way to visit Hazel's sister and perhaps they could meet briefly. Max plucked up the courage and after 15 years he heard his father say, "Certainly Maxwell, we'll be glad to have a chat."

The day arrived and Max, Hazel and Austin were ushered into the family home. Father shook Max's hand and directed him to the lounge where there were two priests whom he recognised. Also there were two other young men he assumed were his now grown brothers. Neither looked anything like the broken-hearted little boy he last saw waving sadly from the front door. His mother was nowhere to be seen. After some small chat one of Max's younger sisters entered the room and asked Hazel if she wanted to come out to the garden with her while the men talked. Max watched as his wife and son left the room, the serious stuff was about to begin.

With pleasantries deserted one of the priests began, "You need to get yourself right with the Lord and come back to the Assembly to break bread." The priest left it there, assuming his short sentence devastating enough to demolish the most hardened sinner. Max said nothing; his interest was in his father and his brothers. Just being in the family home again felt good, he had zero desire to debate the priests. The silence did its trick and his father changed tack, "The Elect Vessel died about two years ago," he proffered sadly. Before he could help himself Max blurted, "Well that's good news." In unison, the other five men in the room gasped for air and sat bolt upright. One of his brothers was first off the mark, "You shouldn't say that Maxwell. The Elect Vessel was a mighty man of God, in fact it's said he was the personification of the Holy Spirit." Max couldn't contain himself and burst out laughing. They sure had moved on, he thought, that was an extremely bold statement and certainly not one he shared. "I very much doubt that," Max replied. "I knew the man too, remember? Jesus in the parable about the unforgiving servant makes one thing clear. "*Thus also my heavenly Father shall do to you if ye forgive not from your hearts every one his brother.*" Matthew 18:35 [DBT] It was your Elect Vessel who told me he could not forgive me for what I'd done and that the Assembly had to clear its name." Max was mad now, how dare they?

The little group fell silent; this heathen had turned the conversation into a choice between the Elect Vessel and the words of the Bible. Without guidance no one dared answer. Max took the initiative; he stood up and marched over to the window, "That kowhai tree has sure grown," he exclaimed. I loved that thing when it was in full bloom." The priests gave up and left the room presumably to seek guidance. His father joined him at the window and agreed about the kowhai bloom. "Your mother spends a lot of time in that garden," he said. "How is Mum?" Max asked. And so the ice was broken and Max got what he'd came for, a bit of catch-up with his family. Who was married, what his brothers did for work, was everyone well.

After about ten minutes one of the priests re-entered the room and coughed loudly in his father's direction. Max got the hint, the respite was over; it was time to leave or get another lecture. "I'll go out the back way and get Hazel as I go," Max offered. Everyone shook hands politely and Max headed off to find his wife and son.

Back in the car Hazel inquired how it went. Max was choked with mixed emotions, he'd spoken to his family again after fifteen years but the pain was still very real. "Might have been a mistake," was all that Max could answer. "You know," Hazel said, "none of those men had any interest in Austin. Nor me either, I guess. I like your sister though. I wish we could see her

149

more often." It was however to be a further ten years before Hazel got her wish.

"Be ye fishers of men….

You catch them, He'll clean them"

Chapter 6
Obedience

The immigration officer scrutinised all the paperwork thoroughly, "How long are you intending to stay?" he asked. "Indefinitely," Max answered. "And you have only, how much cash?" the immigration officer questioned, "and you don't have a formal job offer?" Hazel's grandparents were English and under UK law Hazel and her family had a right of return to live and work there. The North Sea oil and gas work was booming and Max wanted a part of it. They'd completed all the necessary paperwork through the Embassy in Wellington, sold all their belongings and had just landed at Heathrow, London. Max didn't have a confirmed job but he'd spoken with a mate and was completely confident he could easily walk into a job to quickly have the necessaries to support his wife and growing family in this foreign land 12,000 kilometres from home.

Hazel was three months pregnant with their next child and the three day stopover in Singapore had been strongly marred by her violent bouts of morning sickness. Austin was now fifteen months old, walking and a cheerful bunch of joy. Max had enjoyed exploring Singapore with him while his mother rested and vomited, glad of the peace and quiet.

"No I don't have a confirmed job offer," Max answered, "but I have a contact at this company who assured me he'd employ me if I showed up at his office with the right to work in the UK," and Max handed him the paper showing his friends firm and contact details. The immigration officer seemed worried, he checked all the paperwork again, rubbed his chin thoughtfully then marched off to confer with a colleague. Ten minutes later he was back and without saying a word stamped the passports and with a smile and a strong Jamaican accent said, "Welcome to the UK, Mr and Mrs White, and you too young Austin."

A couple of days later following a brief meeting with his friend, the White family were on an overnight train to Aberdeen. If Max wanted to earn the big bucks then Aberdeen, North-East Scotland, was the place to be. It was the entry point to the North Sea oil fields. Two days later Max started work in Aberdeen and Hazel and Austin set to the task of finding a place to live. Within a few months they had bought their first home, complements of a generous bank mortgage, in a small village about 20 minutes' drive from Aberdeen. It was the first home they'd owned together. Hazel loved the village and presently joined a friendly group of young mothers as she set about furnishing their home before her new arrival.

Max worked long hours and the money was excellent. He, too, loved the village and quickly found a group of friends and thoroughly enjoyed his Thursday evening pass to the local pub. Life was good, the weather was terrible but Max didn't care; he had a happy wife and a vibrant son and another on the way.

Again Max found himself staring at a grainy photograph trying to fathom its meaning. "See the little heart about there," Hazel said pointing to a smudge on the black and white image. "And the other one over here," she continued, pausing to allow Max time to comprehend. Max puzzled on this for a moment, then the penny dropped. "What, two? You mean its twins?" he stammered. Another addition to the family was great but he'd never contemplated twins! Proudly Hazel confirmed, "Yes, a boy and a girl – fraternal obviously," she said. Max, sensing his wife's delight gave her a huge hug, "well done," he added. "Oh, that was easy," Hazel replied with a laugh. "So, apart from the double-up, everything else is completely healthy and on track," she concluded.

Max's petite wife's belly swelled to enormous proportions. The comfort of carrying the two infants to full term seemingly impossible but somehow her little body made it, almost. About 1am, one Friday morning, Max was awoken abruptly with Hazel exclaiming her waters had broken. Max's mind screamed "action plan" while his body demanded "more sleep please." Never-the-less the well-rehearsed plan sprang into action, the hospital given advanced warning, the neighbour awoken and escorted in to mind Austin. Within minutes Max was driving his labouring wife the 20 minutes to the hospital.

Aberdeen Infirmary, as the hospital was known, was also a training hospital attached the local university. Multiple births were a sort-after commodity and word had spread quickly, finally one was imminent. Much to their surprise, upon their hospital arrival the pending parents were met by the duty doctor, one medical professor, a specialist doctor, two nurses and seven student want-to-be doctors each smartly dressed in white jackets or uniforms. "Did you tell them Princess Di was arriving?" Hazel inquired dryly with a chuckle. Max laughed but the presence of so many medical professional did not instil peace. He couldn't help noticing the stark contrast of his arrival to the deserted room at the previous birth. Max's next thoughts raced to panic – was there something serious he didn't know about?

Hazel was ushered to a private room and eagerly inspected by a dozen peering eyes. "You're almost fully dilated," one of the doctors advised. "We'd like to take you through to the theatre now, if that's ok?" "If that's ok," Hazel exclaimed. "Just get those monsters out of me." "I have a question," Max interrupted, from the back of the crowd. "Why so many doctors?" Max asked, as calmly as he could muster. The duty doctor stepped forward and, in his broad Nigerian accent, explained that this was a training hospital and not to worry as the students were only there for observation. "And the others,"

Max said motioning towards the remaining horde. "Oh, yes, very sorry," he continued and introduced the specialist, the professor, the anaesthetist and the two nurses. Since they are three weeks premature we always like to have a specialist and anaesthetist present, you know, in case something goes wrong." He finished up as if trying to reassure himself. Max felt slightly more comfortable as his wife was wheeled off to the operating theatre followed by a crowd of professionals like seagulls around a discarded lunch.

Max was allowed into the theatre but only after donning a gown, wellington boots, a mask and hairnet. This is a sterile environment he was reminded. Hazel unmasked and barely in a gown, lay on the delivery table screaming in pain as the next contraction kicked in. Max stood quietly at her side, he would keep away from the business end this time. Besides, I doubt I could get near it with that multitude there, he reckoned.

Hazel had told the story of her sister who, during the birth of her second child, had looked over at her husband holding her hand seemingly oblivious to her utter agony. She had gently pulled his hand towards her mouth and chomped on it with all her might. While his screams didn't alleviate any of her pain it did provide great internal satisfaction at seeing him suffer too. Hazel loved the story and had recounted it several times in Max's hearing. It was then, as he stood, calmly holding Hazel's hand, desperately trying to be useful, that he noticed a sudden look of cunning flash across her face and he slowly felt his arm being drawn upwards. Instinct reaction kicked in as Max abruptly recollected her sister's story. I like all my fingers, Max mused as he rapidly snatched his hand from the widening jaws. Max looked at his wife in mock scorn, his wife, with a faint grin above the pain, said, "You remembered, I see."

"Here's the first one," the doctor announced, handing Max a tiny pink body wrapped in towelling. Max admired his new son and Hazel continued her work. Levi was his name, and he was strong and alert as he took in his surroundings for the first time. "Here's one for you too Mrs," the duty doctor said as he handed a very tiny bundle to Hazel. As the doctors finished stitching up at the other end and Max and Hazel admired their instant family, the specialist approached. "The little girl, does she have a name?" he inquired. "Maxine", Hazel replied happily, relieved that the pain had ended. "I'm sorry to do this," the specialist interrupted again, "but Maxine is exceptionally tiny so we'll have to get her to the Premature Infant ICU immediately." Hazel was hesitant to release her hard earned catch quite so quickly but, following repeated warning of the urgency, she finally relinquished her miniature daughter to be cared for intensively. "She'll just be down the corridor in the Intensive Care Unit and you can visit anytime," the doctor assured her as he hurriedly left the room carrying Maxine in his arms.

A few days later Max and Austin visited the rest of the family at the infirmary. Hazel was in the ICU with Levi and

Maxine had just been fed. Both were sleeping soundly. Austin was delighted to see his minute siblings but quickly bored, he had so much to tell his mother. Max, however, was allowed to hold Maxine for the first time. Because she was so minuscule her only attire was a napkin size diaper. "They don't have clothes to fit at that size, Hazel explained, "that's why it's so warm in here." Max's big hands looked absurd beside his miniature daughter's body. He looked at Austin now 21 months and he almost came up to his waist – what a monster, he thought, compared to this. He surveyed Maxine with his engineering mind as he laid her sleeping body across his hand. Her little head rested against his extended thumb and her perfect doll size legs swung off the side of his palm. The entire length of her torso was the same distance as the width of his palm, Max marvelled. "Will she ever grow?" Max asked. "She put on twenty grams yesterday," Hazel announced proudly. The doctor says we can all go home when she gets to four kilograms – only another 400 grams to go."

It seemed forever, but finally the expanded family was reunited in the family home. Max felt happy and, in genuine thankfulness, praised the Lord for His kindness in granting him a quiver full of arrows. *"Children are a gift from the LORD; they are a reward from him. Children born to a young man are like arrows in a warrior's hands. How joyful is the man whose quiver is full of them!"* Psalm 127:3-5 [NLT] He had his own family now, clinging to his past was no longer needed. Jesus was true to His word and had blessed him. While Max gave thanks in his heart his outward life reflected little acknowledgement for the blessings of the Lord. He loved the Lord and was living right – that was enough for now.

Max enjoyed his work; he worked long hours but relished getting home to be welcomed by his growing family. For Hazel, life was more like a continuous haze. Having three children under two years old was no game, up every few hours every night, feeding, washing, cooking and cleaning during the day. Max was quietly thankful his lot was earning the keep, out of the house each day – although he wisely never shared his thankfulness with Hazel. Austin attended a day care centre during the day, which he enjoyed as his thick Scottish accent quickly matured. Yet through it all Hazel coped and managed the house well. The unseen blessings of the Lord were ever present.

When a promotion was offered, Max jumped at it. No more being contracted by the hour but a set salary with health benefits and regular holidays. With the new job came considerable responsibilities. He now managed a design division of the sub-sea construction company, had a staff of thirty and a multi-million pound budget. Max savoured the challenge and excelled. It had only been eighteen months since they'd arrived in Scotland and already they were a family of five, owned their own home in a rural village, had a great job with a nice car and experienced summer holidays in the sunny regions of Europe. Life was great.

And so it was as Max lay in his bed one evening. Their five year home ownership anniversary had just passed. Austin was in his second year of school, Levi and Maxine attended kindergarten and the fog in Hazel's brain had cleared somewhat as she slowly got a little more time for Hazel. Max always prayed daily as he knew that Jesus was Lord. Outwardly however, Max showed little Christian exuberance, his relationship with Jesus was a private matter for him – or so he thought. It was on this evening while Max lay in his bed, listening to the frequent rain, that he thanked the Lord with a very grateful heart for His very abundant blessings. He worshiped Jesus in his heart, beholden to Him for all He'd done but most of all that Jesus had died for his sins and he was set free and blessed. As the euphoria abounded within, Max heard a soft, clear voice whisper in his ear, "You're okay because you know that Jesus has died for your sins and set you free. What about your three little children? What about Hazel? What do they know of this Saviours work and love?"

The soft voice hit Max like a sledgehammer. The thought of his three adorable children and his lovely wife spending eternity in the pit of hell because they never heard the gospel of Jesus shook him to the core. He felt physically sick. He hadn't read his Bible for a while but he knew the message was very clear. Eternal life was only for those who gave their lives to Jesus. What was he to do? Max begged for the voice to come again, he had so many questions. How was he to achieve this desperately essential and urgent task? No further voice was heard by Max that night and little sleep was gained.

Next morning Max's mind was still in turmoil. He didn't know anyone that was a strong Christian. He knew some that went to church but he was fairly certain they went more from obligation than any genuine desire to please the Lord. His village had three pubs so, as was the ancient law of Scotland, there were three churches or Kirks, as the locals called them. In order to combat the evils of the liquid amber copiously flowing from every glen throughout the highland and lowlands of Scotland, the staunch fathers of old had declared that before any public drinking house could be built in any city or village then first a Kirk must be built. This centuries old edict had led to a rapid explosion of churches throughout the nation, some of which were well attended. So it was that Max's little village of 1200 souls was blessed by the presence of three stately buildings dedicated for the worship of God.

Max drove around the village stopping at each of the three buildings. Two were locked but a notice was posted informing there was to be a service on Sunday at 11am. The final Kirk, a grand stone building in the village centre sporting the name "Free Presbyterian Church of Scotland" was open, and Max ventured inside. Throughout his years in the Assembly he'd been taught that every other church on earth solely taught lies inspired directly from the devil himself; so it was with much trepidation that Max entered a non-Assembly building for the very first time, in search for answers from God. Max walked up the centre aisle and took in the scene. The little wooden pews neatly arranged on each side along the nave. A massive stained glass window through which an image of Saint John threw a dim light across the sanctuary and a grand elevated pulpit stood to its right. Everything was clean, well-polished but completely deserted. A pile of hymn books sat on a small table. Max ventured over and thumbed through one. He recognised one or two but something didn't feel right – Hymngate flashed through his mind as he put the book down with a weary grin. The building was so cold that Max thought his bones might freeze. How could this be a happy place to enjoy God's presence he thought in disgust? Annoyed at the cold and the lack of any personnel, Max suspected most of what he'd been taught about non-Assembly churches could possibly be true. With no answers to be found in the deserted buildings Max returned home disappointed. He was on his own – what to do?

Packed away somewhere was his Bible. Where? Max racked his brain. Although he'd never read it in years, Max had kept his little pocket Bible. He'd been tempted to discard it once or twice but that felt improper as if he was tossing out the final vestige of his Godly past. "Where's my box of old travel mementoes," Max asked? "Somewhere in the attic, I guess," Hazel replied. "Why are you looking for that anyway?" "I'm looking for my Bible," Max confessed. Hazel didn't reply but the astonished look written across her face said it all.

Chapter 6
Obedience

Max rummaged through the boxes in the attic and, finally, he found it. It was small, pocket size, literally. The cover was leather and in perfect condition, still with his name 'Maxwell' inscribed in gold lettering across the bottom corner. Inside his grandfather had written to Maxwell, it'd been a present from him when Max turned sixteen. He thumbed through it and even though the print was tiny he could read it clearly without his glasses. That night Max announced to Hazel that he was going to begin reading his Bible again. Hazel enjoyed reading and saw the opportunity to extend reading time before lights out so raised no objections to Max's plan, although she later confessed she thought it would be a quick passing novelty. Opening at the book of Genesis Max began to read. His goal, one page or one chapter each evening and a few verses each morning. The habit that had been instilled in the much younger Max was again rekindled.

Exactly why Max began reading his Bible again, he couldn't say. He just knew it was what he had to do. Following on from his sledgehammer moment the question of the salvation of his family rang loud in his ears. Obedience to the voice he'd heard was the only response. As the father of the family the least he could do was lead by example and that example certainly had to be visual. Going to church had to be part of that example too. But what church? None of the ones in his village had any appeal and certainly were not a place to enthral young children. For now he'd read and pray God would provide the answers.

The answers came not in the way Max envisaged. There had been a dramatic downturn in the price of oil and almost overnight several major projects in the North Sea had been cancelled or deferred. To make matters worse, the company he worked for had been acquired by a large multi-national construction company who were seeking to enhance their sub-sea construction capabilities. Talk of reorganisation and possible redundancies were rife although Max firmly believed his skills would ensure his employment remained unscathed.

Upon arrival at work Max was met at the door and was summoned to a management meeting on the third floor. Management meetings were not unusual for Max but the timing and urgency of this one peeked his curiosity. It peeked even further as he entered the room to find it packed with all the senior managers of the company, most of his staff and most of the personnel division of the new owners' local division. The meeting was quickly bought to order and a smartly dressed American woman introduced herself. She was a consultant for the new owners and wanted to present the findings of her resent evaluations on the merger that the board had approved yesterday. "I have a list of names I'll be calling as I just want to check who is here or not" she stated. With that she read a list of names evoking replies reminiscent of Max's school days. When she'd finished she clarified if there were any present whose names haven't been called. There were a couple and they were excused. "Crikey this must be confidential," Max volunteered to a colleague.

The American woman continued, "I'm sorry to inform you that a decision has been made to make each one of you redundant effective today. As you leave the room you'll be handed a package that will provide the full details of your redundancy package and what happens next." A deathly silence filled the room filled with more than one hundred hard working men and women. The entire management of the company from the CEO down were present, as were most of his engineering division. Without speaking a word the stunned mob began to head for the door, mutely collecting their packages as they left. Max was in absolute disbelief, he'd never been fired before in his life. He's always made the decision to leave.

Jobs of almost any description were non-existent in Aberdeen and those that were now had numerous applicants, many with extensive sub-sea engineering experience. Max and Hazel discussed it at length; perhaps it was time to move on. Hazel was deeply disappointed; she loved her village, her friends, her house and the children's school. Yet without Max's income the options were scarce. With the twins having just started school, the timing could have been better but the New Zealand schools were good too. Max's redundancy package was good so the decision was made to pack up and return to New Zealand.

Auckland was experiencing a high-rise construction boom and Max had the skills - so Auckland it was. The White family settled into a lovely country home on a small block just south of the city. Max commuted to the city and the three children began attending primary school nearby. Normal life had resumed after six very enjoyable years in the glens of Scotland.

It was while returning from collecting his children from school one afternoon that Max noticed a tiny wooden church not more than a kilometre from his home. There was nothing spectacular about that church. It was painted white with a red iron roof, small and at least one hundred years old. The sign outside read "Uniting Church meets here at 10am each Sunday." Max couldn't shake it from his thoughts, the urge to go along one Sunday kept bubbling in his mind. It seemed completely opposite to the Kirks from the Scottish village – cold stone buildings filled with nothingness. That night much to Hazel's surprise Max announced to the family that he was going to go to church next Sunday and did anyone want to come. The children had never really understood the concept of church so after numerous questions it was settled that Max, Austin, Levi and Maxine would attend and Hazel would stay home and prepare lunch. Church wasn't for her.

The day arrived and everybody in their Sunday best arrived at the little church. To say the welcome they received was friendly was an understatement. "Oh my, a family," Mrs Bennett exclaimed. "We've been praying so hard for some children; the Sunday school will start again today." Everybody made their way in and sat down. The hall was tiny and barely contained twenty five seats but there were plenty to choose from. Attending that day were Mr and Mrs Bennett and three other older couples plus the Minister and his wife. Max still felt uneasy as weren't all churches breeding grounds for the devil's lies? The years of Assembly indoctrination rang loudly in his ears. I'll know as soon as the Minister starts his sermon and if he spews the lies of hell I'll calmly collect my children and head off home, Max confirmed to himself. Of course, it may not be that bad, something kept assuring Max.

The Minister's wife cranked up the old peddle organ and the little group enthusiastically sang the first hymn overjoyed at the almost doubling of their numbers. With the first part concluded, the younger Whites were ushered out and down stairs to the infrequently used Sunday school room under the caring eye of Mrs Bennett. The Minister, who was about Max's age, stood up and began his message. He read from the King James translation of the Bible and even though that version had minor variances to Max's, he'd heard it was okay. When he began his sermon Max was awestruck. He spoke of Jesus, how He so loved us, how He died for the sins of every person and that all those that believed in Him would receive eternal life. He'd never heard the gospel preached this way, so full of love and compassion but convicting and clear cut. There was no guilt but all sin was gone in the blood of Jesus if we surrendered our life to Jesus and made Him Lord of our life we would receive eternal life and live and reign with Jesus for ever and ever! Glory to God, Max thought. There were no devil lies in this Church. Max sang the closing hymn with gusto; he had found a connection with fellow Jesus lovers – finally. The last obstacle of Assembly prejudice melted away. Max felt a release he'd never experienced before.

Over the mid-day meal the three younger Whites recounted their experiences with Mrs Bennett. She'd made them milky drinks, fed them yummy biscuits and told them funny stories from the Bible and even let them colour in. "Please, Daddy, can we go back next week?" Maxine begged. There was nothing Max wanted more. "Absolutely," Max replied. "What about you, Mrs White, you coming next week too." "No," Hazel answered, "not for me, but perhaps at Easter."

And so it was that Max began attending church again. The joy it gave him to hear others, who had no concept of a privileged Assembly or an Elect Vessel, talk about Jesus in this way was incredible. He knew nothing of these people but that mattered little – they loved Jesus too and that was the link. Max had found a home. All-be-it a very small one but a church home none the less. Max reflected on the past few months, perhaps the Lord knew what He was doing after-all. What had seemed such a devastating event, being made redundant in Scotland, had lead him halfway round the earth and introduced him to others that called on the name of the Lord out of a pure heart!

Max worked on a high-rise construction project in the city, on a contract basis. It lacked the excitement of offshore oil facilities design but it paid well. The office was large and about twenty engineers and draughtsman worked together in the open-plan layout. Max got on well with his colleagues and quickly made new friends. One of his new friends was a recent immigrant from Iran named Mekmed. Although English wasn't his first language he spoke English well enough as he'd completed his engineering degree at a university in London. Over a group lunch one day the subject turned to pay rates and how they were increasing. Mekmed listened intently but Max could tell the subject troubled him in some way. Eventually Max could bear it no longer and took a direct approach. "How long have you been here now Mekmed?" Max asked. "It will be six months next week," he replied calmly. "You must be on a pretty good wicket by now," Max added. "I don't understand what you mean, wicket?" Mekmed answered. "Oh sorry, our confusing English, I meant your hourly rate. It must be high with all your experience and fancy English degree," Max teased. Mekmed sat stony faced and replied in deliberate words, "My hourly rate is zero." The group laughed; assuring Mekmed he was among friends and had nothing to fear from revealing his rate. "No, it is true," Mekmed insisted, "I am working for free to gain experience with New Zealand design. The Boss, he told me, all immigrants must train for at least twelve months before they can design here. Because I'm Muslim, and not Christian I didn't make many friends and couldn't find any work so I come for training and give my time to learn."

Max was stunned; he had no ideas but knew this wasn't right. Mekmed was entitled to at least minimum wage while he trained and his religion had nothing to do with that. The Boss, himself an immigrant, was known for driving a hard bargain but Max was pretty sure this one was illegal. Mekmed, sensing Max's anger, begged, "Please do not talk to Boss, he'll lose my job," his English rapidly deteriorating. "How do you live," Max asked. "My wife, two children and me, we live with my friend and his family, they have four bedrooms, we live in two and share the cooking place," Mekmed replied. "My friend gives me some food and we get some small money from the Government," Mekmed volunteered. The group fell silent, ashamed of their boasting of their fat salaries while this poor man was being exploited, working for nothing and eating meagre rations.

Max had never been the compassionate type or a particular fan of culturally diverse immigrants but something about this man's plight stirred his heart. Max had a friend who he'd done some work for previously who owned his own consulting business. He gave Gerry a call that evening. "Actually I've just won a new project and I am on the lookout for a good design engineer," Gerry advised. Max explained about Mekmed, six months no pay, qualified engineer, two kids, etc. "We're not a charity," Gerry explained laughing at Max's liberal dose of guilt. "Tell you what, ask him to drop over to the office and I'll have a chat with him," Gerry added. "I'm in all day tomorrow."

Next morning Max took Mekmed outside and confidentially explained about Gerry's offer. "Leave, right now," Max urged. "I'll tell the boss you had a family crisis or something." Mekmed retrieved his lengthy resume and apprehensively set off to meet Gerry. Three hours later Mekmed walked over to Max's desk, "I got job," he blurted, grinning from ear to ear. "I start tomorrow. Thank you so much Mr Max." "No problem," Max replied, "just pleased to be able to have helped. Here's my number, let me know how it goes."

Problem solved, Max continued with his life and never gave much thought to Mekmed or his friend Gerry. The compassion that had stirred so strongly on hearing Mekmed's plight had faded almost as quick once the solution was found. He was somewhat surprised when one Saturday morning, about six weeks later, when Mekmed called. "Can my wife and family drive over to your house this afternoon, I have something for you?" Mekmed asked. "Sure," Max answered, "Come for lunch?"

Max quickly explained to Hazel that a Muslim family of four were coming to lunch. Max left out the detail of Mekmed's employment woes just informing he was a previous workmate.

Mekmed and family arrived and quickly handed Hazel a large bouquet of flowers and a very large box of chocolate. "This man saved our lives," Mekmed recounted excitedly. "Thank you so much Mr Max." Max waved off the gratitude and ushered the family inside. The two girls were about the same age as Maxine and within minutes she was best friends with both of them. From a very young age Maxine had displayed an incredible ability to make new friends – a true gift from the Lord.

Over lunch Mekmed and his wife eagerly explained how the job had changed their lives. The salary was much higher than expected and Gerry had made the position permanent. They had their own rented house now, the children are in a new school and everything was wonderful. Mekmed also explained that they were Muslin and that they had first gone to their Muslin friends begging for help but none would. "But you're a Christian, Mr Max," Mekmed continued, "You help so quickly and never asked for anything. I think your God is better." Max was flattered and Hazel was a-gasp. She had no idea her husband had unselfishly done all that for these total strangers, and in total secrecy. She was quietly impressed; this was a side to him she hadn't seen before. Max didn't want to get into a deep discussion about religion so only told Mekmed that Jesus was the answer to everything in his life and strongly advised him to buy a Bible and read all about this.

Chapter 6
Obedience

129

Later that day Max reflected on his actions. He had acted that way only because he saw the injustice, he'd had no idea how much that simple phone call had changed these people's lives. Max thanked the Lord and asked Jesus to reveal himself to them and thought little more of the matter.

*"There's No Plan B
Only God's Plan"*

Chapter 7

Trees of Righteousness

Max's house had a large veranda around one side that overlooked the harbour. He loved to recline outside at this time of night. The children were sleeping, his wife was in bed reading and he was alone, sitting in the barmy night air listening to the waves gently breaking at the harbour beach below. Max had recently turned forty-seven and as he soaked in the calming atmosphere he began reflecting on the past twenty-five years. Growing up within the Assembly, Max had a plan. He envisaged maturing in the ways of his people, starting a business, getting married and raising a family. His vision quickly became a mirage though when he was unceremoniously dumped from fellowship. Since then, Max had planned very little yet somehow here he was maturing in the ways of God, married and raising a lovely family for the Lord. He hadn't started his business yet, but two out of three's not bad, he mused.

How had all this happened? He thought back to when he first left the Assembly. He had absolutely no idea what was right or wrong but mostly through experience he'd slowly built a code to live by – there were things that were just not right. That, however, only set the boundaries. As he continued in years and his experiences became refined so did his moral code. But was this righteousness he debated, or was it simply right living, or on the other hand was there a difference? Work in progress he decided, and packed that away for another time.

But what about the guidance, where was that coming from? He'd thrown a dart at a map of the world for inspiration but somehow that led him to his wife. He'd never planned it but he always had employment and money in his pocket regardless of where in the world he was. Things had sure been tight at times but never had he gone without a meal. Now that's a lot more than good fortune he reckoned. Then Max remembered that day in the waves when he'd shouted his commitment from the raging waters that he would serve Jesus for the rest of his days. He also remembered the vision he'd had nearly ten years ago of chatting in the presence of Jesus and Him telling Max he had a couple more things to do yet. Right there on his deck that night Max acknowledged the Lord's hand over his entire life. It was the Lord that had taken him out of the Assembly. It was the Lord who had taught Max by experiences what was right and what was wrong. It was the Lord that had got him into oil and gas engineering and taken him all round the world opening doors and protecting him at every step. It was the Lord who'd brought Hazel across to Canada at just the right time and caused her to stay there. It was the Lord who had given him a family of three children, restoring what had been lost. It was the Lord that led Max to South Auckland and that little old wooden Church. Now he'd led him back to Whangarei, the city where his first son was born ten years earlier.

The more Max reflected the louder his heart proclaimed praise to the Lord. *"And Jehovah, he it is that goeth before thee: he will be with thee; he will not leave thee, nor forsake thee; fear not, neither be dismayed."* Deuteronomy 31:8 [DBT] That scripture kept on echoing across his mind. So true it was and yes he had never forsaken me, ever. Even when I wasn't in a right place with Him, His love, like the rays of the sun, shone warmly on my back Max remembered. Who uses "goeth" or "thee" anymore Max thought with a start. "I have to get a different Bible."

Max and family had moved back to the Whangarei area and had built a beautiful house on a large block of land on the edge of the harbour in a small village twenty minutes from the city centre. Austin was now ten and the twins eight. They attended primary school which, conveniently, was right next door.

Across and down the road a little was the local community centre. A large sign outside provided a list of events and happenings at the centre and while out walking Max spotted a small notice that read "Christian Fellowship meets here every Sunday at 10am." Max and the three children attended the following Sunday. Hazel declined, "Church is not really my scene," she affirmed.

The little fellowship consisted of about fifty regulars plus twenty or more children that made up the Sunday school. The pastor, Bruce, looked more like a Buddy Holly impersonator than a man of God. But he sure knew how to handle a guitar and reach the high notes. Even his sermon was enlivening. The fellowship, while technically independent came under the oversight of a much larger Christian fellowship in the city and the congregation was encouraged to attend the Sunday evening service at the city church in addition to the usual morning service in the village. Compared to the little wooden church of South Auckland this gathering was a seething throng. It had a real band of talented musicians, the songs were modern and displayed from an overhead projector. Max and his young family were most impressed. They had found a new spiritual home.

A downside of building a new home is the development work of the site. Max however enjoyed the manual labour after being shut in an office most days and relished the challenge of transforming the landscape. Retaining walls were built, vegetable garden developed, a chicken coop erected and a large lawn planted. It was while manually digging the holes for the fruit trees in the orchard that it happened. Max stomped his foot down on the spade and as his did he felt something in his lower back go twang. Not wanting to leave a job half-done

Max hobbled on and finished planting the remaining four trees. Next morning however Max could barely get out of bed – serious back damage had been done.

Three weeks later Max still could hardly walk. Nothing had worked; he'd been to doctors, to physiotherapists, even ventured to a chiropractor. The net result was agony. He couldn't sit for long, he couldn't walk too far and lying in bed bought little comfort. It was Sunday morning and Max debated if he should attend church that morning but the children were keen so he hobbled across the road to his local fellowship. After the service Pastor Bruce bowled up and asked, "What's the matter with you?" "It's my back," Max complained, I hurt it three weeks ago and nothing is working." Max didn't want to talk, he needed to get back to a comfy chair and sit down. "Here, let me pray for it," Bruce requested, "I know the Lord can easily heal it for you." Max wasn't at all sure. He'd heard about faith healing, as the Assembly called it, and they had a pretty negative view of such carryings on. Never-the-less the pain was horrific so he'd nothing to lose. "Sure," Max replied. With that Bruce laid one hand on Max's head and the other on his lower back. The prayer was simple and short; Bruce simply asked the Lord to heal Max's back and quoted a scripture in Isaiah 53:5 *"But he was wounded for our transgressions, he was bruised for our iniquities: the chastisement of our peace was upon him; and with his stripes we are healed."* [KJV] When he finished he said, "There you'll be fine from now on." Max didn't feel fine but he thanked the Pastor and staggered off home.

Back home Max had propped himself up on the couch while Hazel organised lunch. He found if he leant a little to the left and stayed perfectly still the pain was almost bearable. After about 30 minutes of sitting and fidgeting for the best position, unexpectedly and without warning, suddenly Max's back went click, click, click, like some giant hand had brushed his spine realigning his vertebra. "Wow," Max exclaimed as he realised all the pain had instantly vanished. "My back has just been healed," he exclaimed loudly. Hazel and the children came rushing in to verify the news and Max explained Bruce's simple prayer and the miraculous event that had just happened. "Are you sure it's healed?" Hazel questioned in her usual sceptical manner. Max wasn't positive it was permanent either but something certainly had happened as now he was standing straight and without any pain for the first time in three weeks. "Bend down and touch your toes," someone suggested. Max obliged slowly and deliberately, returning to upright without one twinge of pain. The family stood amazed, it was an undeniable miracle. It really was true, Jesus really does heal today. Max could feel his faith rising. Hazel was shocked. She had always believed in a superior being but she had just witnessed living proof of His healing power. She tucked the thought away for another day, now was the time to celebrate.

Something changed in Max after his back healing. Somehow Jesus was even more real. The saving from the waters, the face-to-face vision in the night, that sledgehammer moment were also very real but there was something more to this. This wasn't Jesus intervening directly; this was bought about through the laying on of hands by another believer. How was that possible? Max hungered for answers. He understood the what, but not the how.

Following Bruce's encouragement Max started attending the Sunday evening services in the city fellowship. This church had a congregation of well over four hundred, three pastors and a fully equipped worship team. The senior Pastor was an outstanding teacher and uncompromising in the things of the Lord. Max felt alive as he entered the building and lingered after to soak in the presence. What was it he sensed? He had no idea but whatever it was he wanted more.

It was at one such Sunday evening service that Max truly understood the full impact of salvation – almost 40 years after asking Jesus to forgive his sins. Yes Jesus had died for his sins but that was only the starting point. He had also redeemed us and it was through Jesus that we entered God's presence as sons, joint heirs with Jesus. *"The Spirit itself bears witness with our spirit, that we are the children of God: And if children, then heirs; heirs of God, and joint-heirs with Christ; if so be that we suffer with him, that we may be also glorified together.* Romans 8:16-17 [KJV]. That is our status but the only way there was not just repentance but full and total surrender to Him. *"And whosoever shall fall on this stone shall be broken: but on whomsoever it shall fall, it will grind him to powder."* Matthew 21:44, [KJV].

Max figured he'd prefer to be broken than crushed so later that night as he sat in the moonlight on his veranda he totally surrendered his life to Jesus and made Him the Lord, the King, the Boss, of his life. For the first time in his life he finally understood what it meant to die to self and live to God. It wasn't about doing right things to obtain righteousness it was solely about having a right standing with God. Jesus had paid with His life so Max could be wholly without blame for any of his past and, since God had raise Jesus from the dead, that was proof the payment had been accepted. All Max was required to do to freely enter God's presence was to accept Jesus as his Lord and Saviour. Jesus had already done all the work. That was what righteousness was; finally Max understood. Being in right standing (righteous) gave God a legal basis to operate in his life. That revelation cleared a lot of fog from Max's brain.

While reading Matthew 6:9-13, the Lord's Prayer, one evening, Max, perhaps for the first time ever, noticed verses 14 and 15. He'd frequently stopped at the end of the prayer but the continuing words of Jesus hit home to Max that night with a thud. *"For if ye forgive men their offences, your heavenly Father also will forgive you [yours], but if ye do not forgive men their offences, neither will your Father forgive your offences."* [DBT] Seriously, Max questioned, the Fathers forgiveness of *my* sins is linked to my forgiveness of others? His mind flashed back to the Elect Vessel, Mr Belmont, Mr Davies, his own family – the list seemed endless. "Oh dear Lord," Max begged, "You didn't seriously mean all the Assembly people did you? You know how they treated me?" The Lord didn't answer Max that night but those two verses kept flashing in his mind like a giant neon sign. Several days passed and the neon lights kept on flashing. It made Max feel sick, literally. How could he possibly forgive them when the hurt was still so raw but, on the other hand, his own forgiveness from God himself was being withheld until he did forgive? What a paradox!

Eventually, Max did hear from Jesus, in answer to his complaint. Max was studying Isaiah 53:4 *"Surely he hath borne our griefs and carried our sorrows; and we, we did regard him stricken, smitten of God, and afflicted."* [DBT] As Max was reading he clearly heard Jesus repeat the words *"he hath borne our griefs and carried our sorrows"*. "You only need to forgive, Max," Jesus continued, "Surrender your hurt and sadness to me. Like the verse says I've already accounted for that."

"Of course," Max exclaimed aloud as a further realisation of the magnitude of all that Jesus had done for him swept across him. "Thank you Jesus, I love you so much," Max added in absolute sincerity. He then recounted all his hurt in a prayer to Jesus and as he did he surrendered each wound to Him and thanked Him for removing that pain from his life. As he finished up he could feel the love of Jesus rushing in, filling the holes in his heart where the hurt once sat – this feels great, Max declared. "And the forgiveness?" Jesus reminded him. With the hurt gone completely Max found it easy to forgive. All the reasons not to had vanished and with the hurt removed it seemed peculiar that he had harboured such feeling against all these people in the first place.

Max spent quite some time with the Lord that night, forgiving each one by name. The peace that encompassed him was surreal and his eventual sleep was incredibly restful. As Max continued life he found events and circumstances that fetched the memories of his Assembly hurt and the pain came crashing back. But Max remembered it was only a memory because Jesus had already borne his hurt so he again quickly surrendered the memory to Jesus and it rapidly vanished. The memories however, became less frequent with time. The lesson in forgiveness remained with Max and he not only kept short accounts with Jesus about his own short comings but he applied the same accounting to all those who did things against Max. Reviewing the day before he fell asleep of a night, repenting of any sin and forgiving any who had sinned against him became a habit with Max that remained for the rest of his time on the earth.

A few weeks later the subject of the Holy Spirit came up one Sunday evening. Max knew of the Holy Spirit and knew who He was but had never understood what He did or how to relate to Him. The preacher affirmed the scripture in Ephesians 1:13-14 *"And you also were included in Christ when you heard the message of truth, the gospel of your salvation. When you believed, you were marked in him with a seal, the promised Holy Spirit, who is a deposit guaranteeing our inheritance until the redemption of those who are God's possession—to the praise of his glory."* [NIV] This, he continued, confirms that every believer who has accepted salvation, and believes, has the Holy Spirit. This is the actual Holy Spirit of God. He pointed to Romans 8:11 *"And if the Spirit of him who raised Jesus from the dead is living in you, he who raised Christ from the dead will also give life to your mortal bodies because of his Spirit who lives in you."* [NIV] This same power of Him who raised Jesus from the dead actually lives in us? Max was stunned; this was teaching he'd never heard before. If a Spirit of that magnitude lived in him surely he'd feel it, he thought. This couldn't be about knowledge it had to be about experience.

Max's veranda was fast becoming his favourite place to reason with God and that night was no exception. If what the preacher had said about the Holy Spirit was true then this could transform Max's life and he wanted in. Unfortunately, his past kept shouting back at him – "careful, don't get involved in strange teachings!" "But this was in the Bible," Max debated. "Ah, but which Bible version," the sceptical voice answered back. "Good thinking," Max agreed and headed off to retrieve his Bible version. In the Assembly only the Darby translation was allowed as he was the founder of the Assembly movement. Although they conceded the King James Version came a close second.

Max checked the Bible verses the preacher quoted. First the one in Romans 8:11, *"But if the Spirit of him that has raised up Jesus from among [the] dead dwell in you, he that has raised up Christ from among [the] dead shall quicken your mortal bodies also on account of his Spirit which dwells in you."* [DBT] Max checked his notes from the sermon. Okay he conceded, that wording is more-or-less the same.

Then he checked the one in Ephesians 1:13-14, *"in whom ye also [have trusted], having heard the word of the truth, the glad tidings of your salvation; in whom also, having believed, ye have been sealed with the Holy Spirit of promise, who is [the] earnest of our inheritance to the redemption of the acquired possession to [the] praise of his glory."* [DBT] Max again checked his notes as he'd copied down the Scripture quotes from the overhead screen, word for word, exactly for this purpose. Close, Max conceded, but it's far from being exact. His version said *"the Holy Spirit of promise, who is [the] **earnest** of our inheritance"* The preachers version read, *"the promised Holy Spirit, who is a **deposit guaranteeing** our inheritance."* "I knew it," Max declared with glee. "That version is hieratical." He knew it and was right to be careful! "Everyone knows what earnest means," Max affirmed. "It means *doing things in a spirit of deep sincerity and conviction, or with deep feeling,"* Max stated as if confirming the obvious. "This verse is describing the person of the Holy Spirit," Max continued his debate, "It certainly doesn't have anything to do with guarantees."

Satisfied he'd spotted the errors of the preacher, Max went inside to go to bed. As he did so he noticed a half-finished crossword puzzle on the dining table and the Oxford dictionary discarded beside it. He picked up the dictionary, determined to prove his point, and located the word earnest. Sure enough his understanding of the meaning was confirmed, but then he read on. It had a second meaning, relating to old English, "A thing intended or regarded as a deposit or promise of what is to come." I never knew that, Max was shocked. He believed he understood the English language pretty well but clearly not old English. Max checked the introduction to his faithful little pocket Bible – first printed in 1890. Perhaps English may have advanced a little in the past hundred years, he decided. If that was ambiguous, what else was, he questioned. Time for an update Max stated.

Max poured over his new purchase. It stated "The New King James Version" on the title page. Gone were all of the thee, thy, thou pronouns and a quick check of Ephesians 1:14 revealed the use of guarantee in place of earnest. Max didn't take the discarding of his trusty Darby version lightly as it had been the base of his belief for all his life. However the words King James helped. He'd heard that was similar so that would do. Others used the NIV (New International Version) version proclaiming it was closest to the original intent as it was translated on a thought for thought basis not on a word for word translation like the King James. Max didn't care, he was happy to read the King's plain English for now.

Max studied all the references about the person of the Holy Spirit and His work. "Here's the thing," Max explained to himself, "if the Spirit of Him who raised Jesus from the dead was living in me, and His living there was supposed to be my guarantee of my future inheritance, then shouldn't I be feeling something? Wouldn't he know if something that powerful was living inside of him, literally?" Max was very puzzled and spent a lot of time in prayer and Bible study on the subject, but yet he felt nothing!

Disheartened, Max discussed the matter with his local Pastor Bruce. "Oh, that's simple," Bruce explained. "Let me pray and lay hands on you to receive the Holy Spirit." Bruce immediately proceeded to pray as Max puzzled as to why he needed to receive the Holy Spirit when he'd already been sealed with Him. However, Bruce seemed to know a thing or two so Max lifted his hands while Bruce prayed and spoke the words "I receive you Holy Spirit." Bruce explained, "Yes, every believer is sealed with the Holy Spirit but it also tells us in Acts 2:38 *"Then Peter said unto them, Repent, and be baptized every one of you in the name of Jesus Christ for the remission of sins, and you shall receive the gift of the Holy Spirit."* [NKJ] The Holy Spirit is a gift, but like every gift we have to receive it, unpacking it if you like, and then actually use the Spirit within us. Just like how we surrender our lives to Jesus to obtain salvation, so we have to surrender our physical spirit, soul and body to the Holy Spirit to allow Him to control us. The Spirit is rarely forceful within us; He waits to be given space. When He's got that space, stand back because then things begin to change." That made perfect sense to Max and he walked his family back home that day with a happy heart.

Later that day Max worked on removing an old tree that was in the way of his next project. As he laboured he pondered on Bruce's prayer and little speech. It made sense, why hadn't he seen that before. He decided to ask the Holy Spirit and ventured a few words. A short time later, Max suddenly felt a most unusual sensation beginning to affect him – nothing like he'd ever experienced before. It was as if someone had pierced him through the top of his back down into the depths of his heart, or was it the other way round. But not a stab of pain instead it resembled a shaft of bright warm light. Max became enveloped in the euphoria of the moment. It was the most incredible sensation of peace, joy and love flooding his body not unlike his face to face encounter with Jesus. It entered his back at about the middle of his shoulder blades and seemed to hit something inside him, near his heart, where it inexplicably splintered, ricocheted into every atom of his body. Strangely his head was completely unaffected, simply this strong awareness in his heart. At that moment a verse he'd read recently popped into his mind, *"If your whole body therefore be full of light, having no part dark, the whole shall be full of light, as when the bright shining of a candle does give you light."* [NKJ] Luke 11:36. Max knew it was the Holy Spirit answering his prayer and making His presence felt. The sensation completely overwhelmed Max. He couldn't even stand now. Max sat on the ground, out in the field at the foot of that old tree, drenched in the power of the Holy Spirit, loving every second of it. After about fifteen minutes the power level abated a little and Max was able to continue his work, but the feeling never left him completely – ever. Max definitely knew he had the Holy Spirit now!

Buoyed by the confirmation of His presence and nearness, Max began to converse with the Holy Spirit frequently whilst still praying to the Father. Unexpectedly, the words of the Bible seemed to abound with life. New meanings of verses he'd read numerous times jumped out at him. It was like he'd been reading in the dark before and someone had switched the lights on. Things began to make sense and verses began to knit in with others providing a fuller overall meaning. Bible reading was no longer any sort of chore; he couldn't wait to devour some new revelation.

As a carryover from his Assembly days Max had always enjoyed a dram or two of whiskey, on the odd occasion. Not enough anymore to get him drunk, but it was powerful stuff and little was required to evoke unforced merriment. Strangely after Max was filled with the Holy Spirit he lost his desire for the taste of the liquid amber. Max still consumed alcohol but in strict moderation, just the occasional beer or glass of wine. The desire to create euphoria by natural means had totally evaporated.

Max joined a Bible study group and a few weeks later the subject of speaking in tongues arose. Max had heard of speaking in tongues but had no real concept of it and therefore avoided it. The group leader that night had no such intentions and repeated what the Apostle Paul had said in 1 Corinthians 14:5 *"I would that you all spoke with tongues."* (Part verse) [NKJ] Max asked, "What was the reason for us to speak in tongues?" After much discussion the leader read a verse in James 3:8 *"But the tongue can no man tame; it is an unruly evil, full of deadly poison."* [NKJ] "Regardless of our efforts it's impossible for any man to control his tongue but the Holy Spirit definitely can. Thus the manifestation of speaking in tongues is a clear outward sign of the Holy Spirit operating in us," he taught. To Max that made perfect sense and when the leader suggested he ask the Holy Spirit to speak through him in tongues, Max jumped at the chance. Max for the first time spoke in a foreign language that night.

Max's walk with the Lord had morphed into a sprint. Although he'd known for more than forty years that the Lord had cleansed his sins he'd never truly experienced what it was to have a living relationship with Him. All that had changed, and Max couldn't wait to go to the next church service, Bible study group or to just read his Bible and speak with the Lord in prayer. As he drove in his car or walked along his beach Max chatted to the Father, spoke in tongues or just praised the Lord. Righteousness, as in right standing with God, bought with it a whole new level of relationship enjoyment that Max had no previous knowledge of. Was there any limit to this new found level of relationship? At the city Christian Fellowship Max really came alive. He now recognised the presence he'd sensed the first day he entered that building. The Holy Spirit operated there and the aroma of His presence lingered.

Max had been baptised as an infant at about three months old. This was the custom in the Assembly. None could explain why exactly, but it was believed that once one was baptised then they belonged to God. Max discovered that was not what the Bible said. In Acts 2:38 it states: *"Then Peter said unto them, Repent, and be baptized every one of you in the name of Jesus Christ for the remission of sins, and you shall receive the gift of the Holy Spirit."* [NKJ] The baptism was to take place after they had repented. Max checked numerous other references on baptism and each one of them accounted the act as an informed decision made by a repentant person. He couldn't find a single Scripture that suggested someone could make that decision on your behalf. He certainly had repented and given his life to Jesus, he'd even been filled by the Holy Spirit but he'd never taken the personal step of baptism. Since they lacked a baptismal font at his village fellowship it was either the harbour or to the City fellowship. Theirs was indoors and heated and as winter was approaching Max opted for the indoor event.

The evening arrived and Hazel and the family had turned out to see the man of the house go through the waters. It was to be a dedicated baptism service, with a time of worship first, a short word on the reasons and action of being baptised, then into it. Twelve were being dunked that night. Generally the Pastor would ask each one to declare their reasons for wanting to get baptised then two men would do the physical full immersion, baptising them in the name of the Father, the Son and the Holy Spirit. Following their extraction from the font the congregation would be asked if there were any words of encouragement or Prophecy.

Max was number five and when asked to declare his reason he relayed that he had been baptised by full immersion when he was an infant but he had no knowledge of that and since he wanted there to be no impediment to his relationship with Jesus, in obedience he was getting done again. With the dunking over, several in the flock rose to their feet with a word of prophecy. Almost to a man each one warned Max that the road ahead would not be easy, the devil had thought he was rid of Max but not so, and now he was mad as hell. Max gulped as that wasn't what he wanted to hear and wisely refrained from enquiring if there were any positive words out there. It was about then that Max clearly felt the Holy Spirit remind him of that scripture in 1 John 4:4, *"You are of God, little children, and have overcome them: because greater is he that is in you, than he that is in the world."* A praise of gratitude welled up in Max's heart at that moment. He didn't have to fight this battle alone.

It wasn't long before the fight began. Max was called into his boss's office; he was disappointed at Max's handling of a recent minor crisis despite a previous exemplary Record. The man was a devout atheist and it seemed he'd taken offence at something Max had said about God, so the small crisis was all he needed. He built a very personal case against Max. With the situation untenable Max resigned his position. Fortunately freelance consulting work was abundant in the city so Max took the chance to set up office from home, which also negated the twenty minute commute each day.

Next was the very grumpy neighbour who had recently purchased the vacant block of land beside of Max and Hazel's place. He first introduced himself by taking out Max's letter box while manoeuvring his bulldozer, claiming it restricted his turn into the shared driveway, despite it having been safely there for years. Forever unprovoked, the new neighbour did everything in his power to make the White's life miserable. He was well into his seventies, very wealthy having recently sold his large sheep farm. But he was also small in height, or do we say vertically challenged, and Hazel reckoned he raised his anger to compensate for his lack of altitude. Max just wished he'd leave him alone but every few days he was shouting across the fence, a new crisis to correct.

It seemed wherever Max turned, there was a problem from somewhere or some quarter and Max remembered the prophecies from his baptism and prayed a little harder for a time. The Holy Spirit however reminded him that these were all things thrown at Max from the outside. On the inside was the power and there were few obstacles there, He assured Max. He agreed and understood it was just the devil roaring, throwing dust in the air. It was tough however, especially when it spilled over onto his wife or family.

Despite the devil continuously barking at his heels like an annoying little lapdog, Max was exuberant about his walk with the Lord. The presence of the Holy Spirit made everything alive. Reading his Bible brought an inspiration every time, his prayer time was a delight, a time to chat with a friend and ask questions or make requests. Church life was never a chore. He couldn't wait to go; the privilege to participate in corporate worship and hear sound Biblical teaching of the Word inspired him. Max felt rooted in the Lord. It had taken more than forty five years Max recounted, but now I feel planted. The Holy Spirit reminded him of Isaiah 61:3 which was also the foundation of a song they frequently sang during worship. *"To provide for them that mourn in Zion, to give unto them beauty for ashes, the oil of joy for mourning, the garment of praise for the spirit of heaviness; that they might be called trees of righteousness, the planting of the LORD, that he might be glorified."* [NKJ]

Chapter 7
Trees of Righteousness

Max firmly understood he'd been planted by the Lord. It was Him that had led Max to this place and exposed the fullness of His plans towards him. Since that was indeed the case then he was certainly a "tree of righteousness." What's more it was all for the work and glory of the LORD. Max was very okay with that.

*"If You Don't Go to God's House
What Makes You Think He Will Take You to His"*

Chapter 8

Bearing Fruit

Bruce was a one man Pastor at the village fellowship and being a small autonomous church, the weekly offerings presented the only means of providing for his meagre stipend. Assisting Bruce were a small group of four elders who provided spiritual and financial guidance together with support in leading communion or worship as required. After one of the elders moved on Max was asked to take his place and thus he became a formal part of the engine room of the little fellowship. Max enjoyed the role, leading prayers, laying hands on the sick and supporting Bruce however possible and the position quickly morphed into that of assistant pastor, although never officially.

"We need you to give the sermon next Sunday," Bruce announced to Max at an elders meeting one evening. Bruce gave the word most weeks with a visiting speaker usually once a month. This week however, the guest had cancelled at the last minute, hence Bruce's suggestion to Max. Max hadn't spoken publically for years but since he was being asked he felt compelled to agree in service to the Lord. Max prayed a lot that week and asked the Holy Spirit to take charge to show him the scriptures to reference and what points to make.

The day arrived and to Max's surprise Hazel announced she was coming over to see her husband debut as a preacher. Bruce introduced Max as he prayed over him telling the congregation this was Max's first sermon and to please pray also. Max opened in prayer and asked for the Holy Spirit power to be present so that lives would be changed, as that he couldn't do that without His help. Max began and much to his surprise what flowed was a mighty word of power. It was the week after Easter and he spoke of Jesus being alive – risen from the dead, victorious with not one thing left unconquered. That same living power is available to each believer because *"if the Spirit of him that raised up Jesus from the dead dwells in you, he that raised up Christ from the dead shall also bring to life your mortal bodies by his Spirit that dwells in you."* Romans 8:11 [NKJ] We have life, we are alive with the same life that Jesus has and it's available without limit to each one of us – He is alive! Max spoke with authority, his words clear and precise and the message stirring. As he finished up Bruce jumped to his feet clapping, thanking Max, the congregation quickly joining him. "Wow, what the Lord has put in the body of Christ," Bruce concluded.

Max was as surprised as anyone at the power and ease of the delivery of the message. He knew that hadn't come from him even though he was a reasonable orator, this was to a new level and nothing he'd trained for. Even Hazel recognised this was a side of her husband she hadn't seen before. Max understood the Holy Spirit was the sole source and made sure the congratulations were diverted towards Him at every turn. On another level however, Max was pleased that he'd been able to provide a suitable vessel for the Spirit to operate through. It was further proof of a right standing with God.

Max became a regular speaker at the village church, much to Bruce's relief and spoke once or twice each month and filled in completely when Bruce was away or otherwise occupied. Max enjoyed the role of assisting; he had become an integral part of the Lord's body and this time for real. It felt good!

Max travelled considerably, mostly internationally, as he'd taken up a consulting role for railway projects. This time he was to visit India. It was to be his seventh visit there and he enjoyed observing the huge masses of people, busy about their important tasks like ants in a colony. Nobody directed the flow yet somehow each day, like a resounding symphony, the mob ebbed and flowed in perfect harmony. In addition to the observations was the food. Max didn't mind Indian cuisine but something always made him sick or gave him diarrhoea. Regardless, he was off to Hyderabad, an important client awaited.

Through a friend, Max had heard an evangelical team from the UK were to be visiting Hyderabad at the same time as him so had arranged to join them. With his week of business concluded Max linked up with the team staying at a basic church compound near the outskirts of the city. The complex was actually a large Bible college and its mission was to train local pastors who would then return to their rural villages to establish a new church. The evangelical team were there to assist with the physical church planting. The facilities were a far-cry from the luxury hotel Max had been staying at but here he was among friends, fellow warriors of Jesus and that felt comfortable. At least the food was more accommodating, it was western in origin but with a distinct local Indian twist. Max didn't get sick this time.

The team consisted of about 25 youngish people lead by a dynamic UK evangelist named Bernie. Bernie was a fiery preacher, filled with the Holy Spirit and he stirred up the best in Max. In the morning the group held a time of prayer, an advanced volley against the village to be visited that day. This was followed by an inspiring teaching by Bernie on what the Lord had laid on his heart. In the afternoon it was salvation time. About six to eight people would pile into one of the non-air-conditioned vans and drive for a couple of hours into deepest rural India – in itself a very unique experience. Much of this area had never heard the gospel of Jesus, ever. The Hyderabad Bible College provided a translator and upon arrival the group met up with the recently trained pastor who'd been allocated that village.

It was the third afternoon of rural preaching and this day Max was to lead the charge. This village hadn't been visited previously and the eager pastor, who had been established for three months, had already gained two converts in addition to his family of five. The main road through the village was tarmac but the side streets were dirt walking tracks; most were too narrow to take a vehicle anyway. The small group of Jesus believers, led by an acoustic guitarist, trooped around the streets of the small village singing hymns of praise, loudly to the Lord. The local translator and Pastor walked ahead with a megaphone inviting the locals to meet at a certain point in the village tonight and hear an important message from God. The sight of a small group of singing westerners wandering around their isolated village swiftly conveyed the message and soon several dozen children and curious onlookers followed the singers back to their starting point. Although the designated start time was still an hour away the villagers quickly began to gather. As darkness fell within the open square of the little village it was standing room only. People were sitting on fences, others were hanging out the windows of nearby houses and someone had even climbed a power pole to gain an electrifying vantage point.

The small group broke into a time of worship, praising and lifting up the name of Jesus then the newly appointed Pastor introduced Max. Max climbed the hastily prepared platform and the translator stood beside him, megaphone in hand. As Max began to speak he felt the strongest presence of the Holy

Chapter 8
Bearing Fruit

Spirit he'd ever experienced. This time the manifestation was not a consuming power, but was an authority, causing his words to flow with great force. Max's prepared message went by the way as the Holy Spirit took over, the conviction of the message incredible. Max spoke that because of sin all men had become separated from God, that there was only one true God but He so loved all the men, women and children of the world, including this small village in India, that He'd sent His only Son to die, paying the penalty of our sins so we wouldn't have to. Then on the third day He rose again and now lives at the right hand of God. Salvation is available free to everyone that acknowledges they're a sinner and surrenders their life to Jesus as their Lord and Saviour.

Max climaxed his message with a great utterance, "Who will confess they're a sinner and take Jesus as their Lord and Saviour? Raise your hand now?" To the amazement of the small preaching team, and especially Max, at least one hand of every person present shot into the air and they surged forward to take the sinner's prayer. That night more than 250 souls dedicated their lives to Jesus and filled in a response form to say they wanted the Pastor to contact them and that they intended to attend his new church. The young, newly trained pastor sat on the nearby steps weeping loudly praising the name of Jesus thanking Him for the miracle of his instant church.

As the rest of the team helped coordinate the thronging responses Max still strongly under the Spirits Power called out the offer to pray for the sick or injured. It was then that the miracles began to multiply. The lame, the lepers, the sick, the blind, all came forward and were immediately healed. An old man approached, barely able to see, led by a young boy who told the interpreter he was almost blind and wanted to see. Max began to pray and while still in full flow the man began shouting loudly. Max stopped and looked around for the interpreter but he was nowhere to be seen. The man kept talking loudly so Max supposed he wanted more prayer so started to pray again. The man's silence didn't last long as Max tried to continue praying for his sight. Twice more the scenario repeated itself when Max finally noticed his language man returning. "What's he shouting about?" Max asked. "Oh, he says his eyes are great now, he can see perfectly, but would you please quickly pray for his knees as they're very sore too?" Max looked into the man's eyes and all the white covering his pupils had completely vanished, he certainly could see again. Not wanting to agitate the man again Max quickly bent and prayed for healing in the knees. And of course Jesus obliged with those too. The man skipped away unassisted, loudly proclaiming he was blind but now he sees.

A young woman approached Max holding her ear, obviously in severe pain. Max didn't need any translation and laid his hand against the side of the woman's head and was just about to pray when suddenly the woman screamed and jumped back waving her hands in the air. Max was certain he'd somehow thumped the wrong spot and had obviously hurt her badly. She was putting on a show, indeed. "Did I hurt her?" Max asked the interpreter. "No, not at all," he replied, "she's been in agony for three weeks with stabbing pains in her ear and head and as soon as you put your hand near her head everything went and she has no pain and can hear perfectly." "Praise the Lord," Max shouted.

Next up was a young lad about ten; he'd brought his little five year old brother along for prayer. "What do you need prayer for?" Max asked kindly, remembering his young sons back home. The translator began laughing and said, "He wants you to pray for his brother so that he grows up immediately to his same height so he can play cricket against him." Max laughed too and recalled a motto of one of his old work colleagues, "Miracles I can do immediately, the impossible takes a bit longer." Never-the-less Max prayed a hearty blessing over both the lads, asking the Lord to allow them to grow up knowing Him and that He would grant understanding to the brothers wish.

It was nearly midnight and finally the crowd had disbursed and the van packed ready for the two hour trip back. As he sat in the van the presence of the Holy Spirit lifted and Max became consumed with utter exhaustion. The past six hours had floated by and he'd never once felt tired or even thirsty. He fully appreciated whose power had been driving him and quickly fell into a restful sleep.

Max stayed on at the camp for another week and even though they went out evangelising each night there was never a repeat of the first preaching. He never understood exactly why but knew the Holy Spirit was in control of all things. Max returned home buoyed with life and a rekindled enthusiasm for the Word of the Lord, certain perhaps that this might be a new calling on his life. Although there were several other invites for international ministry something always came about to block his attendance. Clearly the Lord had other plans and that was fine with Max.

The city Christian Fellowship had a very dynamic youth pastor named Luke. He had been leading youth for some time under the guidance and programs developed by previous leaders. But Luke wasn't content with merely entertaining these youngsters with the hope they may get a glimpse of the ways of the Lord. He wanted to tell them the gospel of Jesus, uncompromised, unabridged. He presented his plan to the church elders who, while they admired his enthusiasm, weren't at all confident that children as young as 13 were ready to learn about sin, its consequences and God's redemptive plan. But Luke was persistent and asked only for three months to give it a trial.

It was to be a church service dedicated to the youth, thirteen to thirty. It would be held on a Friday night, the music would be loud and the preaching direct, warning strongly of sin but how to be rid of it and enter the love of God and be filled with His Spirit. It would be called Zeal Church. *"For the zeal of thy house has consumed me,"* Psalm 69:9 [NKJ]. Any person in the city regardless of their background, denomination or upbringing was invited. Luke spread the word around the schools and various church youth clubs and Friday night arrived. By start time the church hall was filled with at least 70 young people. There were no games or entertainment but they went straight into loud, hard praise and worship of the creator God. Next came Luke's forty minute uncompromising word, "everyone had sin – what is sin – Jesus died in your place – God wants you to live for Him – Accept Jesus as your Lord and Saviour." Nine souls came to Jesus that night.

Next week, the word was out and at least 250 young people packed the auditorium – Zeal Church was born, the three month trial already forgotten. Austin had heard reports from those older than him of the wonders of Zeal Church and couldn't wait until he turned 13 and attend too. It was with much glee then that Austin finally waved goodbye to his two younger siblings that first night his father drove him in to attend. Austin, Levi and Maxine had been regular attendees at the village Christian Fellowship Sunday school for several years. They had each matured well in the knowledge and understanding of the gospel message but none had taken the step to surrender their lives to the Lord. Max didn't fret. He could see the progress and provided they were kept near the Lord's fire they would catch alight sooner-or-later.

Austin had been attending Zeal for several months and Max had observed a maturing in him. While at the Sunday evening service, Max happened to cross paths with youth Pastor Luke. "Great news about Austin," Luke exclaimed as he shook Max's hand. "What news?" Max questioned. "Didn't he tell you, Austin came forward and gave his heart to Jesus last Friday night?" Luke announced. Max was very surprised; Austin hadn't mentioned a thing on the journey home in the car that Friday night. Hazel had often noted that about Austin, if it didn't involve others directly then he felt no reason to share. She'd been informed several times by others of Austin's achievements that he'd never bothered to mention to his loving parents. This time, however, it was a big event and Max couldn't constrain himself as he burst into Austin's room later, requesting all the details. Austin however was unperturbed and simply confirmed the facts to his father. He did volunteer it did feel pretty good. Max praised the Lord and thanked Him for His grace.

Edged on by their elder brother's accounts of Zeal, Levi and Maxine couldn't wait and the day they turned 13 they were there too. Before long they too had accepted Jesus as their Lord and Saviour. Max was over joyed when Levi announced the news. He was much more open than Austin and couldn't keep a secret, even when he tried. His siblings had long abandon telling him what had been purchased for others as a birthday or Christmas present. The classic occurred when his mother, whose alarm clock had broken, had recently asked to borrow Levi's clock to wake her for important occasions. Levi was returning to the car with rest of the family from a Christmas shopping assignment when Hazel met them. She'd been shunted off to complete her own tasks while Dad took the children to buy for their mum. Levi was under very strict instructions from his brother and sister not to mention a word concerning what they'd purchased for their mother. Levi assured them he would most definitely oblige – he could keep a surprise when he had to. Barely ten minutes had passed when poor Levi bursting with expectation and pleasure, blurted "You won't have to use my alarm clock any more mum." Immediately Austin and Maxine jointly, harshly and very loudly condemned their brother's total lack of confidentiality. "But I didn't tell mum what we had bought," Levi pleaded, and technically he was right but, technical or not, his mother now clearly knew what awaited her on Christmas Day.

Thus so it was that Max and Hazel learned that their three teenage offspring had each made a commitment to follow the Lord. Max thanked the Lord and intensified his prayer for Hazel's salvation also. She had been asking questions, she's seen the changes in her husband and her children. The realisation hit her that Christianity wasn't just a doctrine it was about having a relationship with a living Saviour that she could interact with. She was more than curious. About this time someone invited Hazel to attend an Alpha course with her. The Alpha course is an evangelistic course which seeks to introduce the basics of the Christian faith through a series of talks and discussions. The program ran for ten weeks and consisted of a full sit down dinner then a thirty minute teaching DVD followed by a free and frank question and answer secession. Hazel enjoyed the time. Not only did she get to meet a lot of new people but she got to ask a lot of the questions she had about God, Jesus and the Holy Spirit. While Hazel didn't make a commitment to Jesus during the course it did plant a lot of seeds and she was keen to hear more.

A visiting Pastor Will, from the city Fellowship, had spoken at the village church that morning and Max invited him back for Sunday lunch. Hazel and Max liked Will and his wife; they had also been the leaders of the Alpha course Hazel had attended. Hazel wanted to talk as she trusted Will and liked his uncomplicated answers. The two talked for a couple of hours during which time she made the decision to give her life to Jesus. Max was a very happy man and he guessed Jesus was too.

Hazel didn't stop there. She also asked Will to baptise her. Austin, Levi and Maxine had all been baptised at the City Fellowship over the past year or so and the pressure was on Hazel to complete the numbers. Summer had arrived and the harbour was always warmer after the New Year so an early February immersion was scheduled.

Chapter 8
Bearing Fruit

The Day finally arrived and the summer sun danced across the waters of the bay. Following the morning service the whole village fellowship descended on the secluded bay to witness the event. Bruce had agreed to assist Will and the two of them, together with Hazel, waded out some distance from shore in the warm calm bay until the water was about waist height. Max and one or two others followed to witness close at hand while the remainder of the congregation waited on the beach. Hazel simply stated, when ask her reason for baptism; that she wanted to follow Jesus and be obedient. "I baptise you in the name of the Father, the Son and the Holy Spirit," Will recounted and with Bruce's help took Hazel down and up through the water. Back on the beach there were several words of encouragement spoken over Hazel.

There was one other young woman, also from an Alpha course, who got baptised that day. And once she was also back at the beach, songs of praise were sung and the formalities concluded. The little gathering sat under the trees on that private beach and enjoyed a celebratory lunch.

Max was truly grateful to the Lord for showing his family the way of Jesus. When He'd asked Max those years ago back in Scotland, what about his family's salvation Max had no idea what to do. He reflected back and while he'd actively encouraged his wife and family to seek the Lord he had never seriously pushed. All he'd done was to lead by example and get himself in a right place with the Lord. Max hadn't developed a plan, he simply acted in obedience. Now the fruit of his life had matured and his whole family had become Jesus followers. Perhaps that was one of the couple of things Jesus told him he had to go back for during his encounter vision. What was the other thing? Max had no idea but knew that Jesus did, so he'd just stick close to Him and sooner-or-later he'd find out.

A few weeks later Max dropped his offspring off for their weekly Bible study at a friend's home. Zeal Church had recently started these as a way to allow for more in-depth teaching and provide an environment where these young believers could ask questions. Austin, Levi and Maxine were hungry for more and eager to learn. After seeing them off, Max visited with a friend for a couple of hours and he was surprised upon returning to find them still going. After waiting for about half an hour he went to check, expecting to find them engrossed perhaps in a game or competition of some kind. He was somewhat surprised to discover his eldest son lying inside, by the front door slain in the Holy Spirit. Several others were also in the same state while others were speaking in tongues. The presence of the Holy Spirit hit Max as he entered the room so he just sat quietly and let the sensation envelope him. It was another hour before the presence lifted enough to allow the young group to disburse but Max didn't mind. It was a great joy to his heart to witness his children baptized with the Holy Spirit of the living God. "Glory to Jesus," he sang.

Chapter 8
Bearing Fruit

After Bruce celebrated his seventy-sixth birthday he began to speak more frequently about retiring from his Pastor's role. Max and the other elders could see the burden the position put on him and brought up the matter one evening. Bruce was keen but his wife Betty was dead against the idea. Bruce in his diplomatic manner suggested he think about it during his up-coming eight week sabbatical in Australia. He would pray about it and in the interim he suggested the Fellowship invite Pastor Will from the City Fellowship to take care of things in his absence with the idea of him continuing in the role if that was the way Bruce felt the Lord was leading when he returned. Max and the other elders readily agreed that Pastor Will would certainly be a great asset to the Fellowship.

Pastor Will was indeed well accepted and the little Fellowship enjoyed his clear teaching method for the retreat period. Upon Bruce's return he recounted to the elders that he felt God had given him a vision of him constructing a building and having now laid the concrete floor he was to hand his tools to another person standing by to complete the next stage. Bruce sensed it confirmed what he felt in his spirit about stepping down and said he would formally resign at the next elders meeting. A couple of weeks later Bruce signed his letter of resignation and Will was confirmed as the new village Christian Fellowship Pastor.

The following Sunday Max was a little surprised not to see Bruce and Betty in attendance but assumed they'd been called away somewhere. Pastor Will had a stirring message on his heart and was about to reach the main point in his sermon when suddenly the door burst open. It was Sandra, a long term fellowship member and good friend of Bruce's wife Betty. "What are you doing standing up there?" she shouted to Pastor Will. "What do you mean? I'm preaching the word, like I was asked to," Will replied calmly and diplomatically. Undeterred Sandra continued loudly, "I've just come from Betty and Bruce and they are terribly upset. Betty says you forced Bruce to resign so you could take over the Fellowship."

Will was taken aback, as was Max. He now knew why Bruce and Betty weren't there; obviously Betty didn't support her husband's decision to give up the prestige village position. But this was not the time and place for such discussion. Max leapt to his feet and as calmly as he could muster suggested Sandra could discuss this with the elders of the fellowship later as Bruce had formally resigned and Will had been appointed as the new permanent Pastor. Sandra was not eager to leave it there and following several more verbal eruptions stormed out, slamming the door behind her. Somehow Pastor Will managed to compose himself enough to finish his message. In closing he suggested that in the light of Sandra's comments it would be a good idea for the whole church to meet one evening during the coming week to clarify the situation. After discussion it seemed that Monday night at 7.30pm was the most suitable.

Chapter 8
Bearing Fruit

That Monday evening all the adults assembled at the allotted time. Bruce and Betty came along but Will thought it better if he stayed away to avoid it getting personal. Max opened in prayer then invited each of the other elders to give their account of events surrounding Bruce's resignation meeting. These generally concurred with the facts that Max understood and felt the meeting was going well.

George had recently joined the fellowship. He'd lived in the area for years and had been a Christian most of his life. He lived a hippy type of lifestyle on a small lifestyle block in the next bay with his wife and five children. He had recently lost one of his young sons tragically in a boating accident and that had stirred him to rekindle his relationship with the Lord. After much prayer he'd alighted on the village Christian Fellowship and made it his home church. Unfortunately, George was also a talker and a proficient expounder of his own understanding of all things. This naturally included how to change church Pastors and heal rifts. Observing a small break in proceedings George fearlessly entered the fray, advising, suggesting and organising the proceedings. "It would be best if Pastor Will stayed away for a week or two while the church waited on the Lord for guidance." George advised. The small group quickly agreed as that seemed the best method of avoiding any further confrontation. Max however did not but he was one against so many and conceded he too would wait. What are we waiting for, Max mused, "Lord we don't like the one you sent, please send someone else?" Wisely Max held his tongue.

The following Sunday arrived and neither Pastors Bruce nor Will showed up and after a time of worship Max prayed quietly for guidance on what to do next. He need not have bothered as George skilfully morphed his closing prayer into a stirring sermon walking over to stand behind the pulpit as he did so. George recounted the tragic account of his young son dying in his arms. It was a truly moving experience and garnered sincere sympathy from most present that day. Max couldn't help wondering though, how much of that was about George and how much was about Jesus.

The following Sunday Bruce was still a no-show and miraculously George assumed the pulpit standing again. This time he was more prepared and gave a word strong on encouragement but it lacked much Godly substance. After the service Max stood, thanking George for filling in and suggested the church should meet again this week to further the discussion on the position of Pastor. Wednesday evening proved the date most suitable this time.

Wednesday evening arrived and the little meeting room at the community centre was packed. George had invited a number of his Christian friends to attend as they apparently had now joined the fellowship. Bruce and Betty were also in attendance and Max left it to one of the other elders to open proceedings. George had come prepared and allowed no dissension. He believed, and his new friends heartedly agreed, that it wasn't necessary to have formal Pastoral leadership in a church and that more would be gained if the fellowship sat in a circle and discussed topical issues. "That's what we'd do at home, so why not in Church?" George concluded. Bruce said nothing and Max asked George for a scriptural reference of his church model. George undeterred quoted a couple of vague Bible verses that had little to do with church function and continued with his discourse. He recommended to rescind Pastor Will Pastoral offer and that the Fellowship try his model for a time. Pastor Bruce said nothing as did his wife but Max could see she was not happy. Not willing to stir that pot Max pointed out that the Elders of the church had been appointed to order the smooth running and operation of the fellowship and that such dramatic change should be worked through by them with prayer and fasting. Considerable comment ensued, mostly disparaging, and Max was told in no uncertain terms that a fellowship dominated by one or two was no longer tolerable. It was at this point that Max opened his Bible and read from Psalm 127:1 *"Unless the LORD builds the house, they labour in vain that build it: unless the LORD keeps the city, the watchman wakes, but in vain."* [NKJ] "I believe it is the Lord who builds and him who appoints," Max concluded.

George and his cronies feigned outrage. "Max was saying he was the Lord!" they cried. One of two tried to intervene but George was determined to go for the kill. It was either him or Max and he had the vocal mob. Finally Max had taken all he could bear and stood to his feet. "Sorry my friends but if this the way this Fellowship is headed I can no longer be a part of it.

There are some things which are just not right." Max recalled. Without waiting for an answer, Max quickly headed for the door. Outside the room Max stood to gather himself. He had a great calm in his spirit but massive grief in his heart. At that moment the door opened and a couple of his close friends hurried out and over to Max. Overcome with emotions Max wept loudly. "The devil has taken hold of this Church," Max advised his friends between tears. "We know," they answered, "We're not staying either."

And so it was that Max left the village Christian Fellowship. He'd been kicked out of a church once before but this time was very different, Max had left this church of his own accord. Either way, however, Max's pain was very real. Next day Max phoned Pastor Will and explained what had happened and he wasn't the least bit surprised. He'd got the distinct impression during the few weeks he'd pastored the little fellowship that contentment was to be maintained at any cost. It mattered not where the Lord was leading; the goal was doing church to make one feel nice. Now from the outside Max fully understood and agreed.

His next call was to Gerry, the senior Pastor of the City Christian Fellowship. Max had been in regular contact with Pastor Gerry throughout the process, leaning heavily on his spiritual guidance. Max explained the events of the past evening and told Gerry he was now looking for a good church home and could he please recommend one. Gerry laughed

Chapter 8
Bearing Fruit

heartily and told Max that his Fellowship would be privileged to count Max among its members. Max had found a new church home. Pastor Gerry was an outstanding teacher filled with the Holy Spirit - the Bible rightly formed the base for everything he did.

*"Under the Same Management
for Over 2000 Years"*

Chapter 9
Man's Culture

"Hello its Dad here," the voice at the other end of the phone said. Max hadn't spoken to his father since his ill-fated visit with him nearly ten years prior. "Oh, hello Dad," Max tried to sound cheery but just hearing his voice stirred a deep pot of emotions. "We would like to come for a visit," his father continued. Max knew his father lived 600 kilometres away and he would not be making the 16 hour round trip for any type of social visit. More information was needed. "Sure, I'd love to see you," Max replied then asked, "Who is, we?" "Oh you remember Jason, Niles's brother? He is keen to drive me up. I'm too old to drive that distance these days," his father answered. "We just want to come by and see how you are and meet your family." Max knew Jason all right; surely he wasn't a priest these days? Nice guy but he had almost zero charisma. But if that meant some time to chat with his Dad then why not. "That'll be lovely," Max replied. The two chatted for a short time and set a date that worked for them.

"Grandpa's coming to visit in a month," Max announced at the dinner table that night. "Really," Hazel questioned, "I was talking to mum this afternoon and she never mentioned it." "Not your dad," Max responded, "mine. He apparently wants to come up and see how we are." "I doubt that," Hazel stated. "He wouldn't be allowed, unless they've changed all their laws." Max agreed it was indeed a puzzle but he didn't care, it would be good to see his father again, even if it involved having a security guard 'priest'. Austin, Levi and Maxine were blasé about finally meeting their 'other' grandfather but were, of course, keen to know if he'd be bringing presents! Max doubted his father was visiting to be a grandfather.

Saturday afternoon, about four weeks later, Max, Hazel and their family sat across the room to his father and the obligatory security priest, Jason. He seemed relaxed and Max was genuinely please to be finally sitting in the same room with his own flesh and blood. "We've been discussing your case at our local meeting," his father began. "We feel we were too hasty in withdrawing from you at that time and we wanted to come in person and say on behalf of all the brethren that we're very sorry. Also the Assembly has made a decision that you're no longer withdrawn from."

Max was stunned and his mind flooded with a million different responses. So the mighty Elect Vessel, who was so close to God Himself, had taken twenty five plus years to realise a small group of his little flock in rural New Zealand had made a monumental mistake! Before Max could compose an appropriate response his father added, "It was your youngest brother that really pushed for this and kept bringing it up in the Assembly. Finally we asked the Elect Vessel about it and when he heard your case he completely agreed." Max was still lost for words and somehow his brother's push to get the Elect Vessel's approval was not helping. Not too much had changed in the Assembly it seemed and still closely paralleled Joseph's authority in ancient Egypt; "*I am Pharaoh, and without you shall no man lift up his hand or foot in all the land of Egypt.*" Genesis 41:44 [NKJ] Max chewed things over in his mind for a time and finally, much to his father's relief, Max spoke. "Oh, so this means that there are no longer any barriers between us and that we can now enjoy a meal or cup of tea together?" His father was prepared for that one and quickly answered, "No, you would have to be accepted to come and break bread again before we can do that." "But I do break bread at the church I go to now and I know that I'm very much a part of the family of God. You don't have a monopoly on who does or doesn't break bread." Max was feeling angry now and he didn't want this get-together with his father to end that way.

There was a short pause as the two visitors struggled to retrieve the required answer from their programmed memory banks and it was Jason that succeeded first. "There is only one Lord's Table, you realise," Jason stated. "The Assembly is the Lord's true Church and He has placed the Elect Vessel with us for guidance. We know through him that only those that are part of Christ's Assembly will make it to heaven." Max agreed with part of that as he and his family clearly knew salvation was possible in none other than Jesus Christ. However salvation was dependant on us surrendering our lives to the Lordship of Jesus Christ and had very little to do with joining a specific church group. There was so much Max wanted to say but clearly they only saw their doctrine through the eyes of the Elect Vessel. Max had learned to use the Bible as the foundation of his faith. "I use my Bible for my guidance," Max replied. His words hit home. The visitors also believed that the Bible was the Word of God. They were, however, completely inapt in when it came to any variation between the Word of the Bible and the words of the Elect Vessel. In their foggy mind that situation simply didn't exist. Max however had experienced hundreds of examples of that conflict and placed zero credence on the Elect Vessel's teachings.

Suddenly the ruse of telling Max he was no longer withdrawn from became meaningless. It was just a ploy to try and tempt him back to his old ways in the Assembly and Max wasn't about to take his family back into the dark ages. It was time to end the conversation. Max stood up and said, "Excuse me a minute I've got something to show you." He disappeared up the hall and returned a few minutes later with his now rarely used Darby translation of the Bible. This was the version of the Elect Vessel. Max opened it at Joshua 24:15 and read *"And if it seem evil unto you to serve Jehovah, choose you this day whom ye will serve; whether the gods whom your fathers that were on the other side of the river served, or the gods of the Amorite, in whose land ye dwell; but as for me and my house, we will serve Jehovah."* [DBT] "Sorry Dad," Max continued, "In this house we have decided to follow the Lord, or Jehovah as this version reads. Jesus was the one that died for my sins, not the Elect Vessel and we all have made the decision to follow Him alone."

His Father acknowledged the deliberate calmness in Max's voice and determined there was no way his oldest son was ever going to return to Assembly life. He could continue to talk but that would only lead to an argument and he hadn't really come to debate with his son. He'd delivered his message – his reason to visit – so now was the time for what he'd really come for. After a long pause Max's father finally said, "Its nine years now since your mother died. She would have loved to have been here to see you and all her lovely grandchildren." And with that the formal part of the discussions terminated and the informal part began. For the next two hours Max and his father talked about everything. Max showed him around his harbour-side home and talked about Hazel, Austin, Levi and Maxine. Max enquired about his mother's death as he'd never been able to attend the funeral. He asked about his brothers and sisters and their children, their jobs and where they were living. The two could have gone on for days as there was much to discuss but finally Jason appeared and announced that they had better be on their way as they had a big trip ahead of them.

After a final round of memento photos it was time to say goodbye. Max gave his father a big hug for the first time in twenty five years. He wished he could do that every week or so but he knew that was silly thinking. Just as his father was getting into the car he handed a book to Max and said, "Here's a little gift I bought for you." Instantly all the grandchildren's eyes lit up, was it their turn now? Max took a look at the book, "The moral Glories of the Lord Jesus Christ" by C. A. Coats, first published 1910. Max knew of CAC as he was known in the Assembly; he was one of the founding fathers before the Assembly leadership became exclusive. Max feigned delight and thanked his father and held up the old book for the benefit of his children, whose gleeful anticipation subsided rapidly. "That book was a real help to me anytime I was going through a tough patch," his father said as Jason started the engine. As they waved goodbye Max put the book on the hall table where it remained unread for the next year.

Max enjoyed attending the city Christian Fellowship. Jerry, the Senior Pastor there was an ardent man of God and had a very deep and clear understanding of God's Word. Max enjoyed sitting under his teaching and had learned a lot about the Holy Spirit and His work, what it means to relate to God the Father, holiness, worship and sanctification, just to name a few. It was not just doctrine but living reality. Church was an experience of collectively entering into the presence of the Lord to worship Him in spirit and truth and hear a Word inspired by the Holy Spirit. Max knew he was growing in his knowledge and understanding of Jesus and that his knowledge wasn't just understanding in his mind but experiential knowledge. Bit by bit he was really beginning to truly understand who God really was and what it actually meant to 'walk' with Him.

Max delighted in gaining insight into scripture and applying those scriptures into his life. He felt he was ahead of the pack in a lot of his understanding and was always keen to share his experiences. It was while at his home group one evening the subject turned to the armour of God as described by the apostle Paul in Ephesians 6. Max had recently been studying this and the Spirit had revealed to him exactly what the sword of the Spirit meant. Verse 17 says, *"And take the helmet of salvation, and the sword of the Spirit, which is the word of God:"* [NKJ]. It was the Word of God, as in scripture. In any situation we can stand on the Word of Scripture and use it as a sword of faith to fight our situation. Max had discovered its' power, had applied it to his own circumstances and had recently witnessed it in action. So at his study group Max, keen to expound on his new found understanding, quickly began unpacking the scripture. "This sword of the Spirit is nothing more that the word of the Bible," Max stated, glowing in the depth of his knowledge. The little group looked at Max expectantly and Deborah said, "Yes, and…" Max was a little surprised Deborah needed more as he thought he'd been fairly clear. "No, it was just that," Max reiterated. "We each have our own sword with our Bibles that we can use to apply God's word to any situation." Deborah was still a little puzzled as to the point of Max's revelation and answered, "Yes, of course. That's a fundamental principle which has certainly been a huge factor in my spiritual walk over the years." Suddenly the penny dropped and Max realised that while the revelation may have been new to him, other Christ followers had understood and practiced it for ages. Max shut his mouth tight and decided to do more listening that night. Alone that night he repented of his arrogance and asked the Father to help him appreciate more his fellow workers in Jesus.

A few weeks later Max was looking for a key to a gate that someone had given him recently to gain access to a private beach along the bay. While doing so he came across the abandoned book his father gave him during his last visit. After locating the key Max sat down to try and understand why his father felt that particular book should be an influencer in Max's life. Hazel was out at Saturday morning sports with the children, the house was quiet, now was as good a time as any.

First, Max surveyed the title "The moral glories of the Lord Jesus Christ" – an extremely lofty and highly esteemed title, he thought. He began reading but the further he progressed into the book the more discouraged he became. It certainly very ably expounded, page after page, on all the marvellous characteristics and moral attributes of the Lord Jesus but not once did the words draw him any closer to Jesus, but in fact seemed to do the opposite. It portrayed a Man that was extremely wonderful and glorious, far removed from the like of any earthly man. A person of such outstanding attributes, those that were impossible for any man to attain to.

Max put the book aside for a moment and tried to get his head around why a superbly factual account of our Lord and Saviour would have that effect. Then it dawned on him. The book was purely a descriptive narrative of a person who undeniably was wonderful, marvellous and outstanding in moral characteristics but left no means for anyone to be reconciled with that standard. Dear old Mr Coats certainly had an extremely knowledgeable theological understanding of the marvellous character of our Lord Jesus but it was purely observed. Yes, the description certainly did glorify the greatness of our Lord Jesus and every word was absolutely true.

Max remembered that God did not reveal His righteousness to us so we can observe it. He does so to allow, or should he say, desires, us to experience it. Picking up his Bible he opened it at John 17 and began to read. *"These words spoke Jesus, and lifted up his eyes to heaven, and said, Father, the hour is come; glorify your Son, that your Son also may glorify you: As you have given him power over all flesh, that he should give eternal life to as many as you have given him. **And this is life eternal, that they might know you the only true God, and Jesus Christ, whom you have sent.**"* [NKJ] [Emphasis added] Max understood the meaning of the word translated as 'know' in that verse. It did not mean knowledge; it enshrined a deep personal understanding of someone, obtained through long term experience of being with that person – Experiential knowledge. It wasn't about understanding from man's culture or view point but what is obtained from God's view point.

Max discarded the book where it belonged, in the rubbish bin. He knew his father meant well but walking a Christian life wasn't solely about knowledge. He didn't want that kind of teaching lying about in his house.

"My wife and I would like to pop round for afternoon tea sometime, if you are available?" Pastor Jerry asked Max one Sunday morning after church. It was a big church and Max was delighted the senior pastor was available to actually pastor his flock. The convenient date for Jerry was the next Saturday about 2pm. Max quickly confirmed.

Jerry's wife June was a motherly type with a distinctive caring personality and a bubbly persona. June had a unique ability to strike up a conversation with anyone, anywhere, and within three sentences could turn the conversation to that person's relationship with Jesus. Her well known opening phase was, "Did anyone ever tell you that Jesus loves you?" Many a soul had opened up and turned to Jesus as a result of that statement. Max always felt challenged by her words, 'Did anyone ever tell you.' He definitely appreciated that Jesus did love him but how many others had he told that Jesus loved them too? Surely that was a primary obligation for every Christian but how infrequently it was done, Max mused.

Gerry, June, Hazel and Max enjoyed a pleasant cup of tea that Saturday and set the world aright on numerous topics. Eventually the subject evolved to the seasonal bloom, during which, June and Hazel decided first hand observation was best and disappeared outside. Having manlier topic in mind Gerry and Max remained indoors.

Hazel was keen to move to be near her ageing parent in Timaru when the children left home for university. Max was not averse to the idea but he was keen to ensure it was the Lord's will for them to leave the area they'd been planted in for the past twelve years. Alone with Gerry, Max opened up about the subject, asking him what he thought the Lord's mind might be on the subject. The move would also involve a career shift and Max had some thoughts on that also, so the extent of his vision of the future was somewhat more complex than a simple location shift. After bearing his soul Max asked Gerry what he thought and sat back waiting for an in-depth briefing from the Lord on his longer term future. To his surprise Pastor Gerry replied, not with a prophetic announcement, but simply asked Max if he had peace in his spirit about this. Max understood what that meant but not why. Sometimes though he reflected that when he schemed about certain plans he'd felt his insides turn into knots, but he felt very calm anytime he discussed or thought about this move. "Actually I do feel great peace when discussing this," Max finally answered. "But why do you ask that?

"Firstly," Gerry began, "for the record I have peace in my spirit about your plans too. From my experience I've learned to listen to my spirit. The Bible tells us in Romans 8:16 that *"The Spirit himself testifies with our spirit that we are God's children."* [NIV] If the Spirit of God dwells in us then our own spirit becomes linked, or entwined, with Him. When something we're planning is right and Holy Spirit agrees then that brings peace. If, however, it is not His Will, we will feel a check in our own spirit regarding it. Least that's what I've found from my own experience," Gerry concluded. Max was fascinated, he'd never heard that teaching before but it was absolutely practical, very simple and made complete sense. "Thanks, that's so interesting," Max replied. "It certainly makes hearing from the Lord much more of a reality," he added. "True," Gerry said, "we really complicate things when sometimes it's just not that difficult." Max immediately tucked the teaching into his life skills bag under the tag of 'very useful items'!

Gerry and June eventually departed with Hazel enlightened about several of her favourite flowers and Max with a lot more clarity about understanding how to interpret the Lord's guidance. "Very fruitful afternoon," Max remarked, and Hazel agreed.

Austin celebrated his eighteenth birthday and his mother made an extreme effort to ensure it was one he'd always remember. He had enrolled to attend university and study history. He'd always been a strong follower of the classics and this was a passion close to his heart. Max was excited. He liked the idea of his eldest son attending university as he'd never been allowed when he was that age and always regretted it. It took Max years after leaving school to obtain his qualifications. Austin's mother on the other hand was not so enthralled. Her eldest son leaving the nest meant the tearing of her loving strings of motherly control. "I'll be okay mum," Austin assured her and deep down Hazel knew he would be, but what if he wasn't? And so it was that the White family began to come of age and flit the nest.

Finally it was orientation day at the university followed by immediate induction. Austin was confident as Max and Hazel went with him to inspect his lodgings. Austin's room was situated on the 2nd floor of the Halls of Residence and beyond the adjacent towering transmission tower was the peaceful view of the grassy farmlands beyond. Hazel fussed ensuring Austin unpacked properly and understood where the bathrooms etc. were located. Austin attempted to assure his mother he was eighteen and quite capable, but to no avail. "Mothers are supposed to do that," Max advised. With the mess hall located Austin advised that orientation was about to begin and that was students only and, with barely a glancing wave, Max and Hazel's eldest son disappeared into the throng of students entering the assigned lecture hall. "He'll text us if he needs anything," Max promised his son's apprehensive mother.

Days passed and nothing was heard from Austin. Several texts had been sent but none returned. Hazel was certain he'd fallen on hard times and was desperately trying to etch out a living while living under a bridge somewhere. Max, while less worried, did acknowledge it had been a while and picked up the phone and rang Austin's cell-phone number. Surprisingly a happy and healthy sounding young man quickly answered. "Just thought we'd give you a call to see how everything is going?" Max said. "It's just that we hadn't heard from you in a while." "I did text a couple of weeks ago." Austin assured his father. "No, everything is fine here, classes are going well and I've got heaps of new friends." He sounded content and happy so Max passed the phone over to Hazel. A much relieved Hazel later announced that "He has promised he'll be home for mid-semester break in about three months."

True to his word Austin did arrive for a week during the month long semester break and filled in the family on all the details. "Is there such a thing as opposite to being home sick," Austin asked. "No," Hazel answered sternly. "Well there is, because that's how I've felt ever since I arrived there," Austin continued confidently. "It's good to be home but I truly never really missed you guys at all." That explains an awful lot, Hazel thought. "What about Church," Max asked, "You manage to get there sometimes? "Heck yea," Austin answered, "I go every

Sunday, usually to both services and we have a college Bible study group every Wednesday. It's really cool." Max was relieved but he had bathed the situation in a lot of prayer so was not totally surprised. Max recounted the proverb, *"Train up a child in the way he should go: and when he is old, he will not depart from it."* Proverbs 22:6 [NKJ] Once again, Max reflected, the word of God is so true.

"What about drink and drugs, do you see much of that?" Max asked. "Heck yea," Austin answered enthusiastically, "Lots of students drink. It's not actually allowed in our hall of residence but some still do. One student got kicked out because a group were caught drinking in his room." "Have you tried it?" Levi asked. "Yea I had a glass of beer once but it's so expensive. Some students spend almost all their allowance on booze. I've decided I'm not going to waste any of my money on alcohol through my whole time at university," Austin announced. Max was impressed even if his son's reasons were mostly financial. He reflected on his own experiences that his son was now learning for himself. 'There are some things that are just not right.' Praise the Lord!

True to his word Austin never touched a drop of alcohol throughout his three years at university and seldom did even years later. Max never discouraged drink in the family home and freely consumed the occasional glass of wine or beer. If any of the children wanted a drink they were encouraged to do so at home as part of normal family life. Much better there in a controlled environment than them experiencing it without bounds among their friends as their father had done.

Austin disappeared as quickly as he came and his communications were no more frequent but at least Max and Hazel understood he was getting on with life.

Seemingly before their time the two youngest offspring were also off to complete their education. Levi went to Canterbury to study physics and Maxine to Southland to study nursing. Each was different in how they approached leaving home. Levi, who had always been more of a family boy, was seemingly much more upset about leaving his latest girlfriend than his own flesh and blood. Maxine, always the social one, made twelve best friends within the first day of arriving at her hostel.

And so it was that Hazel and Max found themselves rattling around in the empty family home. Hazel's parents lived in Timaru and were now elderly. Two of their children were already in the South Island so now was the time to move closer to loved ones again. Moving house, after more than a decade in the same spot, was a monumental task. "How did we accumulate so much stuff?" Max asked nobody in particular. The decision was made to sell off most possessions as they displayed the obvious results of raising an active family and buy new in Timaru. "The cost of dragging this old junk all the way is just not worth it," Hazel decided.

A massive garage sale was held and to Max's surprise most of the stuff sold. The Salvation Army became the recipient of the remaining few unwanted items. What was left was professionally packed into an interisland truck ready for the 1,500 kilometre journey. Deborah, Max's friend from their Bible study group, had arranged a leaving party at her home for Max and Hazel a couple of nights before departure. Much to their surprise the place was packed. Max was impressed by how many close friends he'd accumulated in his time in Whangarei. They both had a wonderful time reminiscing, advising details of their new venture and what their offspring are currently up to.

After a time Deborah announced the meat was ready to barbeque. And a small group of willing men assembled around the small flame grill at the side of the house. The area was poorly lit so one of the assembled ventured off to find a solution and another returned some dishes back to the kitchen. Max watched as the remaining enthusiast prodded and turned the meat seemingly unsure of how to proceed. Finally he said "You've always been renowned for your barbequing capabilities Max. Why don't you lead the way?" Without waiting for a confirmation he handed Max the thongs and disappeared into the darkness. It was true that Max did enjoy cooking outdoors and was very good at it; he did feel that this was perhaps one occasion when he might be excused from duty. However, he said nothing and spent the next hour cooking up a feast for the fifty or so invited guests. He was joined periodically by inquisitive onlookers urged on by the pangs of hunger but mostly Max cooked alone. Max envisaged 'what would Jesus do,' as was the current saying, and quickly decided it was not a chore he'd been landed with. His duty was to cook the meat to perfection to ensure all the guests ate well at his farewell party. Decision made he went about his task in earnest. Max acknowledged that there was a time in his past that he may not have felt quite the same about being abandoned to cooking duties on such an occasion but life had mellowed him. Or perhaps he really was more Christ like than he once was.

Max's father had recently moved to a small town an hours drive North of where Max and Hazel lived. Before setting off to the far south, Max and Hazel took the short trip north to visit with his ageing father. He lived with Max's younger sister who had never married and he seemed genuinely pleased to see his eldest son again. Once seated inside Max was very surprised when his sister asked if they wanted a cup of tea. Was this a new edict, Max wondered. He quickly got his answer when Max questioned his sister why she wasn't having one too. "We'll have ours later," she stated pointedly. Max and Hazel sat drinking their tea meanwhile chatting away happily to their hosts about family and old times. How absurd, Max thought.

Max's father offered to show him the garden and the two of them wandered around discussing the art of growing plants in the clay ridden northern soil. Eventually his father said, "We pray for you daily Maxwell, that you'll come back to the Assembly and break bread." "Dad I do belong to God's

Assembly, I do take communion regularly. You need to focus your prayers towards the unsaved." Max replied. "Yes, but you don't have the teaching of the Elect Vessel," his father stated as if it was a clincher. Max had had enough; he was like a broken record. "Sorry Dad but I think it's time Hazel and I got on our way." Max's father's goodbye sounded more final than previous but it had been nice to meet again as they both knew his final days were at hand.

Six days later Max and Hazel arrived at their new home in Timaru, with the furniture truck containing all their treasured possessions, close on their tail. Max had secured a job in the city as the result of an earlier visit and he started work the next day while Hazel set about organising the house and replenishing the furniture.

Finding a good church didn't prove quite as simple. Not that there was a lack of churches, far from it. Finding one that both Max and Hazel would enjoy together was the challenge. Every Sunday for the next several months, Mr and Mrs White visited a different gathering. None seemed like home and this soon began to concern Max. Was he being too fussy? He wanted a church like the one he'd left, one where the Holy Spirit had full sway. Unfortunately, these seemed few and far between in this southern city. Eventually they decided on the Hope Fellowship which Hazel liked because the people were very friendly. Max liked the teaching of the Pastor but didn't see much outworking of the Holy Spirit. "The Lord will guide me," Max decided. "He has always done so in the past, why would he stop now?"

Hazel's parents lived in a small town about 30 kilometres west of Timaru and most Saturdays were spent visiting with them and doing the odd task that had become too difficult for the ageing pair. Her father was almost ninety and, while in reasonable health, was showing his age. During a conversation one afternoon the topic of faith in Jesus came up. Both Hazel's parents were un-churched but had been brought up in Sunday School as children. Hazel's dad was a reasoning person and never made rapid decisions but when he decided on something it was usually permanent. "So do you believe in Jesus?" Max asked him. "I believe in a superior supernatural being," he replied. "So why not Jesus?" Max asked. "I used to go to Sunday School as a kid and the teacher there told us that we must give all the glory to God and take nothing for ourselves. Who does He think He is demanding all the glory?" Hazels' father exclaimed. Max was flabbergasted. He hadn't heard that argument before and it was certainly not something he'd ever want to speak out loud. However, he now knew where Hazel got her previous superior supernatural being belief from.

Max wanted to shout, "Well, of course He gets all the glory. He created us and is supreme over all things, He's God of the universe, omnipresent, omnipotent – shall I go on!" However, he constrained himself. He didn't want to start an argument. "You're going to meet your creator God one day soon," Max answered. "That's good," Hazel's dad replied, "I have quite a number of things to ask Him. "What about your eternal salvation?" Max continued. "If He turns out to be real I'll talk to Him about that then," he replied. Max couldn't believe what he was hearing. Here was a man only a short time away from meeting his creator and completely from his own understanding he'd devised a scheme to negotiate his way into a possible eternal life. Hazel's dad made it clear the debate was finished and changed the subject. Max, however, decided to intensify his prayer for the man. While there is life there was hope.

About a year later Hazel's dad was diagnosed with aggressive cancer and died a few months later. Max wasn't able to be at his bedside at his death since he was travelling for his work but Hazel reported he was in a coma for about 24 hours before he died. He tossed and turned a lot and mumbled frequent undistinguishable garble for the first hour or so but he was quiet and still for the remaining hours, Hazel reported. Perhaps, Max thought, the Lord had allowed his negotiation time during that period after all. Certainly not a risk he'd like to take and he only hoped his negotiations had been successful. Meeting with the Lord during those hours before death in such lingering situations are not unusual. There had been dozens of reported cases over the years of people who had died for a short period but had been revived and lived. Many of these told of their very real encounters with Jesus or Hell. Max however was at peace. He had warned the man to get right with God.

*"You choose –
Smoking or Non-Smoking"*

Chapter 10
Church Culture

"There's someone on the phone for you," Hazel called to Max. "He says he's your brother!" His interest peaked as he hurried over to take the call. "It's Dad, Maxwell," his youngest brother stated bluntly. "He's very frail and mostly bed-ridden now and we don't think he'll last much longer. We wondered if you wanted to come up and see him before he died and say your goodbyes. He's at our sister's house. Do you have her number?" Very too-the-point Max thought but avoided going down that path. This probably wasn't very easy for him either and besides they hadn't spoken in about 15 years. "Ok," Max replied, "give me her number and I'll make arrangements to get up there."

Max and Hazel had settled into Timaru and had begun to really enjoy the city, its' culture and sunny weather. It was too far to drive to his father for this short visit so it was decided Max would fly and go alone. However, because of work and other immediate commitments it was nearly eight weeks later before Max finally arrived at his sister's house. "How is he?"

Max asked. "Still lingering on," his sister advised. "He keeps asking when you're coming so he'll be pleased to see you."

Max was ushered into his father's bedroom. A wizened-up old man that slightly resembled his father lay in the bed. His face lit up as Max entered. His sister explained that his voice was very weak but his mind was sharp and clear, so watch out. Alone with his frail father Max sat on the edge of the bed, holding his hand looking at his now expressionless face. Max's mind flashed back to all the good times they'd had together in his youth. Milking the cows together, feeding out to the cows in winter, taking the milk to the factory, fishing.... There were so many and Max was pleased that despite their differences over the years no earthly man could rescind those pleasant childhood memories.

Max's father lifted his head slightly and began to whisper something. "It's hard to say goodbye," he croaked. Max laughed, "Dad this isn't goodbye, we'll see one another again. You know I love Jesus with all my heart and I know that you do too. That's all that matters now. I'm going to Heaven and so are you; we'll see each other again there. This is not goodbye; this is just farewell for now." His father didn't say anything for quite a while but Max could see him aligning his thoughts and finally he said, "Yes I know Maxwell, we will see each other again. We do both love Jesus, don't we?" Yes, thought Max, breakthrough; and it only took thirty six years! Joy flooded his heart as he bent over and kissed his father while saying,

"Farewell Dad, see you on the other side." His father didn't reply but Max could see contentment in his eyes.

Max had barely returned home when his brother was on the phone again. "Dad died last night," he said, genuine sadness in his voice. "He went downhill fast," Max replied. "It was like he'd been holding out to see you Maxwell," his brother continued. "He'd been the same for weeks but as soon as you went he began to deteriorate." "Wasn't anything to do with me," Max added, laughing. His brother laughed too and added, "No I didn't mean that. The official cause of death is age related; he was eighty seven!" His brother paused for a moment and added solemnly, "You won't be allowed to come to the funeral. You understand that, Maxwell?" Max had anticipated that and had no intentions of going anyway. He'd said his goodbyes in person. "Yea, I know that," Max replied. "I'm okay about it though." Max and his brother signed off and now with both parents gone none of his brothers or sisters ever spoke to Max again. The exception being Max's older sister who had also left the Assembly many years since. Max had a good relationship with her and they spoke often and spent time together when and as they could. That era is finished now, Max declared, as he determined to get on with life and serving the Lord.

Max had been in the South for a couple of years when he was presented with an interesting business opportunity. It involved ownership of a mining development, exactly what Max was eminently qualified for. It involved a lot of money but, at the encouragement of a workmate, Sean, a fellow follower of Jesus, the decision was made to venture forth. Neither Max nor Sean had the funds necessary to complete the project so a number of local investors were brought in to provide the funding for the first phase. Max was keen to ensure he made Godly decisions in running the company so he added a well-known national Pastor, Bevan, to the board of directors in addition to himself and Sean.

Sean's church was heavily into the prophetic and a few months after the founding of Max's company they held their bi-annual prophecy conference. This was the first such conference Max had attended and a strong array of renowned prophets had been invited from around the country as guest speakers. Sean had been to several and warned Max to expect the unexpected as God was sure to move. Much to his surprise he did, or so it seemed. Word was out about Max's new venture and words of knowledge and prophecy around Max and his venture flowed thick and fast. Max was delighted, certain his new venture, which carried considerable risk, was assured of a very healthy future. Bevan was the speaker of an afternoon session and he called out Max and prophesied for about 15 minutes on all the things the Lord was going to do with the millions earned from the business. He detailed under 'Thus says the Lord' a list of several specific dates and events to watch out for and ended with a warning to Max the devil was out to get him.

Chapter 10
Church Culture

The conference closed and Max went about his blessed business confident he was working for the Lord for the benefit of the Saints. Several months passed when, at a board meeting, Sean turned up with his local pastor in tow – a close friend of Bevan, the other company director. Max, as Chairman, was a little surprised as he'd not received advanced warning of the visitor. With the agenda business concluded Max called for other business at which point Bevan leaned forward and tabled a complaint from Sean against Max. Sean's pastor was there as a witness as this is God's business after all, Bevan advised. It transpired Sean felt personally aggrieved that he hadn't been allocated more shareholding in the company. His sole shareholding, as agreed, had come to him as a commission for bringing in the bulk of the investors but his cash contribution was small. In addition to the investors and Sean's shareholding, Max held the majority balance. He'd put in every penny he had and more, but the bulk of his equity was reserved for dilution by new investors that would be required for a future stage as the mining project progressed. Plainly put, there just weren't any addition shares to gift to Sean.

Max tried to explain the situation but the other three had come with a fixed mind and were determined to see Sean's shareholding increased, perhaps even to a point of being the controlling interest. Max couldn't believe what he was hearing. Bevan was the very prophet who had spent fifteen minutes proclaiming the blessings of the Lord over Max and the company in front of several hundred witnesses.   Now, apparently, the Lord had abandoned Max because of greed and he was to give most of his blessed shareholding to Sean, regardless of legalities or practicalities. With the meeting going nowhere Max called an end to proceedings asking his fellow directors to attend a new meeting the same time the next day.

The next day's meeting disclosed the break had only served to harden resolve. It was three against one and they were determined to get their way. Max was continually reminded this project was a God project and he was working for the Lord not himself or the investors. Somehow Max was beginning to doubt that. During a break Max went for a walk and prayed aloud to the Lord as he walked, laying out the situation, asking for guidance. As he walked the Lord reminded him of Pastor Gerry. Did Max have a check in his spirit about this? Actually, yes he did – a massive one. Here were three fellow Christians trying to seriously enrich themselves and they were doing it in the name of the Lord. Max, clear of thought, went back into the boardroom. "The answer is no and this meeting is over," Max said firmly as he hastily ushered them out. He locked the door behind them and went home for the afternoon.

Hazel was working and Max had the house to himself. He cried out to the Lord, trying to understand what was going on. Someone had kindly typed up Bevan's 'Word of the Lord' prophecy from the conference so Max retrieved it and began reading. What hit him most was the statement at the beginning, "Thus says the Lord." Was it really the Lord, he asked himself? At the end of the document Max noticed Bevan had finished with; "This is declared in the name of the Lord. And like the prophets of old if my words fail to come to pass then the Lord has not spoken." Max got out his Bible and found a verse in Deuteronomy 18:20-22 *"But the prophet who presumes to speak a word in my name that I have not commanded him to speak, or who speaks in the name of other gods, that same prophet shall die.' And if you say in your heart, 'How may we know the word that the LORD has not spoken?'— When a prophet speaks in the name of the LORD, if the word does not come to pass or come true, that is a word that the LORD has not spoken; the prophet has spoken it presumptuously. You need not be afraid of him."* [ASV]

"Of course," Max reflected. What parts of his prophecy have come true? Fortunately Bevan had mentioned several specific dates with vague events that were to happen on those days. Max went back through his diary to two of the dates that had already passed – nothing. Even the days either side were devoid of anything significant. This man was blatantly lying in the name of the Lord God. Perhaps he did it in his enthusiasm and just wanted to encourage me, Max wondered. He picked up his Bible again and looked at other verses where the Lord talks about false prophets. The Bible was full of warnings on the subject A couple in Jeremiah stood out. Jeremiah 23:16 *"This is what the Lord Almighty says: "Do not listen to what the prophets are prophesying to you; they fill you with false hopes. They speak visions from their own minds, not from the mouth of the Lord."* Then further on in verse 21 he noticed. *"I did not send these prophets, yet they have run with their message; I did not speak to them, yet they have prophesied."* [NIV]

Max's thoughts flooded back to the conference he'd attended. It had been crammed with a variety of prophets speaking sometimes spectacular miracles over the lives and circumstances of innocent individuals. Max repented for even having set foot in the place and asked the Lord's forgiveness. Max recounted to the Lord what he'd heard and how wrong he believed it was as it simply didn't align with the Word of the Bible. Max heard Jesus reply, he just said sadly, "I know."

One of the things that had intensely puzzled Max arising from that conference was the strong theme that apparently Jesus was giving individuals the power to create great wealth as His Church needed the money. The time was now to walk in the blessings of the Lord. The inference was the more money you earned the more blessed you must be and the more serviceable to the Lord you were. Max looked up the verse in Haggai 2:8 that read *"The silver is mine and the gold is mine,' declares the Lord Almighty."* [NIV] Why would the Lord ask me to create my own pile of gold Max questioned, when he owned it all anyway. The Bible talks a lot about living in trust and faith. If he was content to trust Jesus regarding his eternal salvation he certainly was prepared to trust him about gold and silver.

The fog in Max's mind began to clear but much confusion remained. He asked the Holy Spirit for clarity of understanding of the Word and vowed to be very cautious listening to prophets in the future.

The next weekend Max reclined to kick back and watch a little TV but since reality TV was the only programming on offer he flicked over to an International Christian Network. A well-known tele-evangelist was holding forth about tithing. He based his message on Galatians 6:7, *"Do not be deceived: God is not mocked, for whatever one sows, that will he also reap."* [ESV] "Whatever you sow into this ministry God will bless. It will grow and multiply and as the Lord says in Malachi 3:10 *"Bring the full tithe into the storehouse, that there may be food in my house. And thereby put me to the test, says the LORD of hosts, if I will not open the windows of heaven for you and pour down for you a blessing until there is no more need."* [ESV] "There you have it," he declared. "God is asking us to put him to the test with your tithing and his Word is clear. What you will reap is a huge multiplication of your seed money to the point where your bank account won't be able to contain any more." The fiery preacher continued on for his allotted twenty five minutes urging the viewers to sow wisely, don't sow into any ministry, God knows the good ones and He will guide you. He concluded urging the viewer to give until it hurt, don't worry about what you will eat and drink. Once you've tithed, your seed will sprout quickly and you'll not only have your food but your new car, your new job, your new wardrobe.

Max knew about tithing and felt convicted. For years he'd always given faithfully. Generally it was about a tenth of his income but also if he saw someone in need he helped out as he could. He had always had enough to get by and had rarely gone without but this took tithing to a whole new level. Max got out his credit card and dialled the free call number on the screen. The automated system took his $1,000 donation with ease, following which an operator came on the line asking for his address details to send the evangelist's latest book.

Ten days later Max sat down to read "Financial Wisdom – Your twelve steps to the full blessings of the Lord." The book was full of outstanding wisdom on careers, dating, depression, dreams, enemies, self-confidence, victory and many more – it even had two whole pages on the 12 facts you should know about the Holy Spirit. The main section however was reserved for keys and pointers about money, giving, goal-setting, ideas, mentors, time-management, problem-solving, miracles, seed-faith, work and success. Max consumed this new-found teaching with a passion, certain that the results of its wisdom and his recent financial seed would manifest the blessings of the Lord in his life imminently. He was confident the millions needed for his business venture was a forgone conclusion and he sat back and waited. After all he had God on his side.

The weeks past and the miraculous blessings of copious funding never materialised. Max wondered if perhaps he wasn't giving enough or wasn't praying sufficiently. He encouraged others from his church to join him for weekly prayer meetings at his business to usher in the blessings of the Lord as his capacity alone seemingly was insufficient for such a massive project he'd been handed. He searched his Bible daily searching for any scripture that indicated possible financial blessing and declared his faith in those scriptures. Almost every speaker on the various Christian TV networks preached financial prosperity as the greatest blessing for the saints today. He drank in the teaching of each tele-evangelist, positive he was on the cusp of imminent breakthrough if only he gave a little more or prayed a little harder.

Meanwhile, the previous directors, Sean and Bevan, had resigned their positions and set about advising all in sundry that Max White was not to be trusted. They spoke with the shareholders of Max's company and recommended they check every detail of their investment as, while they couldn't point to anything specific, there surely will be deceit there somewhere. One shareholder took their words literally and asked the Financial Regulators, the Tax Office and the Fraud unit to get involved. After an extremely invasive and very public two year investigation they announced that they had found that, while Max may have made some poor business decisions, he'd done nothing against the law and he and his company was given the all clear. It was too late however, the damage had been done. No new investor wanted any association with a tainted company and the receivers were the only option. Max lost every penny he had ever earned and went into retirement with his sole income a meagre government pension.

In retirement Max quickly found his life had swung overnight from not having enough hours in the day to having many more hours than tasks. Hazel worked full-time in the city so with the house to himself Max spent hours each day in prayer, reading his Bible and seeking guidance from the Lord. What puzzled him particularly was that the Lord hadn't come through with the blessing he so desperately sort after. Instead of the promised millions he now had nothing. He wasn't in poverty but it would be very fair to say money was tight.

Max asked Jesus to search his heart to reveal if there was any un-judged sin in his life. He'd heard one of the tele-evangelists preaching strongly on ancestral curses. Was it a sin my fathers had done that gave the devil access and allowed him to hinder his blessings. Max poured out his thoughts before the Lord. He went over his actions with Sean and Bevan asking to be shown of anything he done against them. Jesus was silent about that but he did remind him about forgiveness. Following his leaving the company, Sean in particular, despite being a fellow Christian, had deliberately set about to hurt Max but little did he know that as a result of his upbringing Max was an expert at receiving hurt. While the sticks and stone thrown at him did hurt momentarily the long term effects were negligible. Never-the-less Jesus was right; he did have to openly forgive them. Max immediately repented of his unforgiveness and forgave both his brothers in the Lord plus the many other people who had recently railed against him. A strong sense of Peace embraced Max as he remained in the presence of Jesus, searching his mind of all others requiring the same treatment.

As the days passed Max meditated more on the reason why he hadn't been a recipient of the Lord's financial blessings. The teaching in the church everywhere seemed to focus on knowing Jesus and receiving his blessings. The blessings had to be manifested in your life now and if you believed in Jesus and had invited him to come into your life then they were certain. Max's life expressed the opposite. Was he not in right standing with God?

One afternoon Max relaxed watching a teaching on YouTube by a trusted pastor on Hebraic Hermeneutics. He'd never heard of the subject before and curiosity got the better of him. First, he checked the dictionary for a technical explanation on the title and found it meant "theology that is concerned with explaining or interpreting concepts, theories, and principles relating to understanding the Bible." The teacher, David Nathan, was Jewish and had been raised an Orthodox Jew until he became a born again believer in Jesus in his early twenties. This gave him a very unique understanding of the Bible and in particular the Old Testament. Understanding God's written word in its original language frequently provided a much clearer viewpoint to understand its true intent. Max had visited Israel a few years previous and had discovered that countless terms and phrases lost all intent when translated into English, especially when the translation was metaphoric.

One point David explained, that was of major importance when reading any scripture, was to understand the context. Most Christians, he said, had formed a very dangerous habit of reading a Bible verse in isolation and applying their own presupposed assumption of its meaning. Often a different understanding became plainly apparent when the verses either side of a subject verse were included. He also pointed out the Bible usually repeated itself in other places, particularly when important doctrines were at stake. Max had experienced such an out of context scenario years prior when he reflected on verses the Elect Vessel used to support his 'doctrines.'

A corner stone of the Assembly teaching was not eating with those that did not adhere to the Elect Vessels teaching. In 2 Thessalonians 3:14 it says, *"But if any one obey not our word by the letter, mark that man, and do not keep company with him, that he may be ashamed of himself;"* [DBT] The Elect Vessel taught this was a Biblical edict that anyone who disagreed with him (as the direct descendant of the Apostle Paul) for any reason was to be completely shunned. However, if the verse is read in context of that whole chapter it's talking about people who are busy-bodies, don't work and go round scrounging meals from their friends. When read in context, this becomes common sense rather than some arbitrary callous rule. It wasn't a decree requiring every believer to religiously adhere to every word the apostle Paul wrote or be shunned.

Armed with this new understanding Max decided to apply it to the reaping and sowing teaching he'd learned from the tele-evangelist. He read the verses in Galatians 6:6-10 to give context. *"Let the one who is taught the word share all good things with the one who teaches. Do not be deceived: God is not mocked, for whatever one sows, that will he also reap. For the one who sows to his own flesh will from the flesh reap corruption, but the one who sows to the Spirit will from the Spirit reap eternal life. And let us not grow weary of doing good, for in due season we will reap, if we do not give up. So then, as we have opportunity, let us do good to everyone, and especially to those who are of the household of faith."* [ASV]

Max meditated before the Lord about this verse and asked the Holy Spirit for clarity. Slowly he began to see the meaning. First, he determined that the plain reading of the text showed that Paul was indeed including cold hard cash but he wasn't pushing for his own enrichment. The financial giving was to be sown everywhere there was a need, especially to the needs of other Christians. He also makes it clear that those who work full-time in the ministry should be compensated by the ones being pastored. 1 Corinthians 9:11 clarified the point considerably. *"If we have sown spiritual things among you, is it too much if we reap material things from you?"* [ASV]

Second, Max noticed the verses were devoid of any magic consequence resulting from the sowing. The Spirit reminded Max of the difference in nature between the physical seed, the plant and the fruit. What is planted rarely looked anything like the mature fruit. If Max were to plant tomato seeds he wouldn't expect a massive bunch of tomato seeds to suddenly pop out of the ground. It was all about the fruit not the duplication of the seed. Why then would the tele-evangelist suggest otherwise, Max debated? A dozen reasons flooded his brain including several that are unprintable. He had been duped, no other word for it. What a fool he'd been. He repented before the Lord for listening to the voice of man and not that of the Holy Spirit and forgave the Tele-Evangelist.

In addition to money Max noticed the scripture spoke of our sowing to our spirit. The Holy Spirit challenged Max on that point; what was he sowing into his life, was it things of this world that would perish or was it things that were eternal? Eternal life is the culmination and everything that is to strive for. Money is not going to be any use to us in that life.

Max recalled he had regularly heard similar money blessing teachings in various Churches he'd attended over the past few years. Undoubtedly there was an unhealthy focus on receiving the earthly blessings – now. Many churches were simply becoming bless-me-up clubs. The thinking seemed to be that Jesus was attached to an individual and if a blessing was needed then this could be obtained from a favourite Pastor who provided the most motivational pick-me-up. Suddenly the concept weighed in on Max. It felt so foreign. His relationship with Jesus was based on him coming to Jesus and accepting Him as his Lord and Saviour. He had surrendered his life entirely to the Lordship of Jesus and understood completely he had been redeemed. He had died to his old self and the things of this world. Why had he been so focused on what he could get back from Jesus now, in this earthly life, over the past few years? Max repented of the human application of God's Word and prayed at length, in the Spirit, for the state of the Christian Church.

Max read the verse in Matthew 6:33 *"But seek first the kingdom of God and his righteousness, and all these things will be added to you."* [ESV] Jesus had been talking about our earthly needs, food, drink, clothing etc. in other words our earthly requirements. His conclusion to that; we were to seek the Kingdom and his righteousness first. That obtained, all the other necessities of life were provided automatically as required. Max decided that was good enough for him and determined that with the Spirit's help he would do just that. He knew 'His righteousness' could only be obtained through the redemptive work of Jesus from the cross. It was a state of being righteousness, redeemed (past tense) by Jesus not of obtaining to, righteousness. "Help me Holy Spirit," Max asked.

Listening to a trusted Bible based teacher Max first heard the term 'Seeker Sensitive Churches,' and set about to understand the term. The teacher was clear he disapproved of such churches, which peaked Max's curiosity further and he began some research.

He found that Robert Schuller (1926-2015) was probably the man most responsible for establishing the Seeker-Friendly, Purpose-Driven church model. After Schuller established the Crystal Cathedral and his T.V. Show "The Hour of Power" two young pastors took his ideas and implemented them on an even larger scale: Bill Hybels and Rick Warren. Both of these men had learned about growing a church directly from Schuller and have built massive churches in the USA. Indeed, there are now many mega-churches with well-known pastors riding a wave of popularity in the evangelical world. The movement claims millions of conversions, commands vast resources, is gaining in popularity, and appears to be attracting millions of un-churched people into its fold. The movement has witnessed massive growth particularly in the USA and many English speaking countries.

Max read that the big problem with the Mega-Church doctrine is that it's a watered-down and neutered message focused on meeting the "felt needs" of people. The true Gospel message is that Jesus Christ gave His life as a sacrifice for our sins to fully redeem us, thereby restoring our relationship with our creator God. Jesus didn't die on the cross to give us purpose or make us successful. The true and complete Gospel is essential so that people can hear the Word of God and can understand the weight of their sin; it's only from that point that people have the opportunity to repent and have their sins forgiven. The deception is that the message confuses people into thinking that becoming a Christian is simply "accepting" Jesus so that He can make you more complete, or more satisfied.

Basically, the seeker-sensitive church tries to reach out to the unsaved person by making the church experience as comfortable, inviting, and non-threatening to him as possible. The hope is that the person will eventually believe in the gospel. The concept enshrines the idea to get as many unsaved people through the door as possible, with church leadership willing to use nearly any means to accomplish that goal. Theatrics and musical entertainment are the norm in the church service to keep the unsaved person from getting bored as he may with traditional churches. State-of-the-art technology in lighting and sound are common components.

Expertly run nurseries, day care, adult day care, community programs such as English as a Second Language, and much more are common fixtures in the larger seeker churches. Short sermons, typically 20 minutes at most, are usually focused on self-improvement. Supporters of this movement will say that the single reason behind all the expense, state-of-the-art tech gear, and theatrics is to reach the unsaved with the gospel; however, rarely is sin, hell, repentance, spoken of, nor is Jesus Christ as the exclusive way to heaven rarely reiterated.

The seeker-sensitive church movement pioneered a new method for founding churches involving demographic studies and community surveys that ask the unsaved what they want in a church. A kind of, 'if you build it they will come,' mentality. The reasoning is that if you give the unsaved better entertainment than they can receive elsewhere, or 'do church' in a non-threatening way, then they will come, and hopefully, will accept the gospel. The mind-set is to hook the un-churched person with great entertainment, give him a message he can digest, and provide second-to-none services. The focus of the seeker church then is not Christ-centred, but man-centred. The main purpose of the seeker church's existence is to give people what they want or meet their felt needs.

Generally, the gospel presentation is based on the idea that if you will believe in Jesus, He will make your life better. Relationships with your wife or husband, co-workers, children, etc., will be better. The end result of the message the seeker church conveys to the unsaved person is that God is like a great cosmic genie, and if you stroke Him the right way, you will get what you want. In other words, if you profess to believe in Jesus, God will give you a better life, better relationships and purpose in life. Basically, the movement is a type of system centred on giving unbelievers whatever they want. The result is that people make a profession of faith, but when the circumstances of their lives don't immediately change for their material good, they forsake Christ, believing He has failed them.

But, Max thought, what does God have to say about all this? Is it possible for a movement to be successful from a human perspective, but be unacceptable to God?

The concept it seems is based on the premise that there are many people out there who are seeking God and want to know Him, but the perception of the 'traditional church' scares them away from faith in Christ. Yet is it true that people are truly seeking God? Max saw that, surprisingly, Scripture taught the exact opposite! The apostle Paul tells us in Romans 3:11 that *"no one understands; no one seeks for God."* [ESV] Clearly there is no such thing as an unbeliever who is truly seeking for God on his own. Furthermore, Ephesians 2:1 tells us, *"And you were dead in the trespasses and sins."* [ESV] Someone who is dead in sin cannot seek God because he doesn't recognize his need for Him, which is why Paul speaks in Romans 1:22-23 about the ungodliness and unrighteousness of men. *"Professing they to be wise, they became fools, and changed the glory of the incorruptible God for the likeness of an image of corruptible man, and of birds, and four-footed beasts, and creeping things."* [ESV] Max could clearly see from the Word that all unbelievers reject the only true God and that they form a god around what they want (a god in their image or the image of something else), a god they can tame and control.

Max was stunned. He knew some of these churches and visited several. He began to look more closely at the church he attended. It was growing fast and had many similar attributes to some of these. His suspicions were confirmed a few weeks later when he attended a special service at his church just prior to Christmas. Many unsaved were present and the Pastor gave a very stirring word reading from John3:16. *"For God so loved the world, that he gave his only begotten Son, that whosoever believeth on him should not perish, but have eternal life."* [ESV] The speaking was powerful on the message of the single verse. "God so loves, God gave his son. Eternal life is achieved by believing on the Son. All we had to do was to believe on the Son and we would have everything," the Pastor declared.

Max reflected later on the twenty minutes and eight seconds long sermon. Is that really 'the whole' gospel? He asked himself. If God loved us so much and since He is the almighty God why couldn't he just let us into eternal life? Why did he have to give his Son? And was it just a simple case of believing. Max looked up James 2:19 which said, *"You believe that God is one; you do well. Even the demons believe—and shudder!"* [ASV]

Max knew full well what the gospel meant and he knew the Pastor fully understood as well. But to teach those who didn't yet know Jesus Christ that all you had to do was to believe seemed to be missing out a lot of very important stuff. What about sin? Why did Jesus have to die? Doesn't the sinner have to acknowledge he's a sinner to gain repentance? What about redemption, and the power to live a life in right standing with God by the Holy Spirit? Max felt there was so much missing from the Pastor's message. He doubted anyone could truly be born again as a result of just believing in the Son without repentance. Then it struck him – wasn't that the seeker church message? Dear God, why did you plant me here? Max asked.

Max expanded his prayer to include his church but, since he had no idea how or what to pray about it, he prayed in the Spirit. He committed it to the Lord and continued to attend asking Him for guidance.   Max marvelled how subtle the slant on the teaching was. Unless he'd been recently thinking about the seeker movement he wouldn't have noticed the Pastor's sleight of hand. Max knew the full meaning of the John 3:16 verse but doubted the unsaved could come away truly transformed, or indeed transformed at all. How subtle that devil is, Max thought as the verse in Mark 13:22 came to mind. *"For false christs and false prophets will arise and perform signs and wonders, to lead astray, if possible, the elect."* Lead astray even the Elect? Max decided he needed to stay close to the Lord and read His Word. That was the staple in his life that he knew would remain.

*"Time is Horizontal
Eternity is Vertical"*

Chapter 11

Sanctification

"More cake, Dad?" Maxine asked. "No, can't eat another thing," Max replied. He felt bloated but also very content. Austin, Levi and Maxine, together with their wives, husband and children had all descended on the Timaru family home for the occasion of Max's seventieth birthday. Hazel had excelled herself with a magnificent fruit cake, Max's favourite. Levi and Austin had manned the barbecue and Maxine, together with her brother's wives, had cooked up a storm in the kitchen. "You guys trying to kill me through over indulgence," Max complained light-heartedly.

Joking aside Max did feel blessed. It had been a long path but God's love had never, ever, come close to failing him. He'd restored family back to him and allowed Max to enjoy not just his own children but grandchildren too. "Praise the Lord" Max exclaimed.

As he'd done for much of his life Max began the next day with a simple request of the Holy Spirit, "Good morning. Reporting for duty, Lord, what would you have me to do today?" As he'd grown in the Lord he'd realised that righteousness – being in right standing with God – wasn't something to achieve. He didn't have to do things to become righteous because the blood of Jesus, at the cross, declared his sin penalty paid in full thereby fully restoring a perfect relationship with God. So it was that morning as he read the Word, that he noticed as if it was the first time he'd seen it, the verse in 1 John 3:10 *"By this it is evident who are the children of God, and who are the children of the devil: whoever does not **practice righteousness** is not of God, nor is the one who does not love his brother."* [ESV – Emphasis added]

"So, Holy Spirit," Max asked, "If righteousness is a state, what I've been made? How on earth do I practice it?" The paradox kept revolving in Max's mind. The Scripture was also pretty clear on the importance of practicing righteousness – whoever doesn't do it is not of God. Max liked the way John wrote; he was a very black and white person who left little ambiguity. Max grabbed his phone and typed 'Meaning of Practice' into the Google search line. The first point he discovered was that 'Practice' was both a noun and a verb. It's not only an action I do or take but it's also describing something I am. The search showed up two principal meanings.

1. The process of repeating something many times in order to improve performance.

2. The actual application or use of an idea, belief, or method, as opposed to theories relating to it.

Max meditated on the meanings and slowly the Spirit began to make things clear to him. The illustration of going to the doctor came to mind. A doctor, or any professional, is said to be practicing his profession. This doesn't mean he's practicing in order to get better at it over time (hopefully). No it means he, or she, has achieved a certain level of competence, knowledge and experience and is free to apply those skills to everyday life. A doctor is who he is, rather than what he is striving to be. So it is with our walk with God, Max reckoned.

In studying the 1 John 3 chapter Max noticed it spoke in verse 9 about practicing sin. *"No one born of God makes a practice of sinning, for God's seed abides in him; and he cannot keep on sinning, because he has been born of God."* [ESV] Interesting thought Max, so since I'm born again I cannot keep on sinning? Clearly that doesn't mean I'm not capable of sinning, Max debated. He'd experienced sin since he'd been born again and on more than one occasion. So applying the same reasoning to this as he did to practicing righteousness, Max understood it was about his state of being. If he was made righteous and was in right standing with God then it meant he no longer lived in a state of sin or wrong standing with God. It simply wasn't possible to have a foot in both camps; one was either righteous or unrighteous.

The more Max meditated on the thought of remaining in that righteous state the more he appreciated the work of the Holy Spirit. I still physically live in a world whose prince is the

Devil, Max stated to himself as he recalled the verse in Ephesians 2:1-2, *"And you were dead in the trespasses and sins in which you once walked, following the course of this world, following **the prince of the power of the air**, the spirit that is now at work in the sons of disobedience."* [ESV] Yet how it is possible for me to live in a constant state of righteousness while living in this sin filled world, he debated.

Slowly the haze began to clear as he reread the 1 John 3:9 verse again, *"for God's seed abides in him."* Max knew he had been sealed with the Holy Spirit of God when he was born again and the Bible refers to that seal as a deposit, or in other words, a seed. Max looked up the reference in Ephesians 1:13-14 *"When you believed, you were marked in him with a seal, the promised Holy Spirit, who is a deposit guaranteeing our inheritance until the redemption of those who are God's possession—to the praise of his glory."* [NIV] Ok, so if the Holy Spirit is functioning within me then according to 1 John 3:9 I won't be making a practice of sinning, Max reasoned. So does it follow that if I'm not practicing sin I must be practicing righteousness? The scripture in 1 John was clear, there is no state of limbo; it is either a practice of sin or righteousness. Absolutely, Max concluded. So, Max summarised, the Spirit is the sole key to him living a life here on earth now, practicing righteousness.

Ok, Max decided. I understand that but in a day-to-day setting what does that actually look like? The thought challenged Max and since he had the time he continued on with a more detailed study. The verse in 1 John 3 made it clear that the practicing of righteousness resulted in the evidence that such a one was a child of God. *"By this it is evident who are the children of God;"* Max recalled the scripture in Romans 8:14 *"For all who are led by the Spirit of God are children of God."* [NLT] Max marvelled for a moment how all scripture linked up. Paul the writer of Romans describes the same event that John the disciple of Jesus reiterates in his epistle. So, if I'm led by the Spirit then I'm a child of God, redeemed and practicing righteousness. That much was clear to Max.

"How am I led by you in my everyday life?" Max asked of the Holy Spirit. Max didn't hear any thunder or even an audible voice but he did receive a strong urge to take a look at his own life, how it had matured over the years.

Max recalled his days in the Assembly when the Holy Spirit was allotted a brief mention during the 'Breaking of Bread' service on a Sunday morning. This was usually covered off by a senior brother standing to his feet and thanking the Spirit for His presence and work. Once that was accomplished the service quickly moved on to praise of the Father. The Holy Spirit was known and indeed acknowledged but there was no intimate relationship with Him. I guess, Max figured, they really didn't need the Spirit because they had their Elect Vessel – poor things!

Chapter 11
Sanctification

During those years Max reflected, he knew of the Holy Spirit but knew nothing about Him and, because of this ignorance, was actually a little afraid of Him. Goodness, how stupid of me Max thought. His mind drifted forward to the time years later when he received the Holy Spirit and was baptised in Him. The change that had created in his life was dramatic, but had he been led by the Spirit for all those past 25 years? Probably not, Max answered himself honestly as he reflected on how it was that the relationship had developed. The secret he believed was when he truly began to surrender himself to the Holy Spirit as he accepted the fact He permanently dwelt within him.

The surrender process Max recalled wasn't easy. No sooner had he surrendered some part to the Spirit then he wanted, or more correctly, took it back. The Holy Spirit was always gracious and politely waited for Max to make a mess of things and ask the Spirit for guidance on sorting out the mess. Yep, Max acknowledged, that's pretty much how it went. Speaking in tongues was probably my first breakthrough, Max decided. That speaking had developed over the years from initially a brief utterance under the Spirit's power to at times a heart wrenching outpouring to the Father of an unknown burden. Max recalled a recent period, lasting several weeks, when during his morning prayers, his crying out in the Spirit was so intense he found himself weeping as he pleaded with the Father on an issue his heart was desperate to relay through the Holy Spirit within. Max never found out what that desperate situation was only that intensity passed and the burden lifted, replaced by peace.

For many years Max had begun his prayer time following a similar pattern. First he would go over his recent history and repent of any sin in his life, asking Jesus to cleanse any new stench of sin from his soul to maintain a clean house for the Holy Spirit to dwell in. Not that he continually regurgitated his past sins, he knew Jesus had forgiven and forgotten those it was only if there was any new sins he'd committed. It seemed to Max that the closer he got to the Holy Spirit the more things he found necessary to cleanse from his life. It would be fair to say that at seventy Max was less inclined to commit overt sins, physical actions, but he was continually challenged on the condition of his heart. Jesus spoke of things done in our heart being the same as if we'd actually committed the sin. Matthew 5:28 gives the account. *"But I say to you that everyone who looks at a woman with lustful intent has already committed adultery with her in his heart."* [ESV] Not that Max had a particular issue with heart adultery but the same rule applied even if one thought his brother a fool as Matthew 5:22 confirms. *"But I say to you that everyone who is angry with his brother will be liable to judgment; whoever insults his brother will be liable to the council; and whoever says, 'You fool!' will be liable to the hell of fire."* [ESV] So it was that with the Spirit's clarity Max found plenty to repent of on a daily basis.

Forgiveness was also a daily part of his prayer life. Max would go over recent things that people had said or done and regardless of the level of hurt he made a deliberate point of forgiving them. The result of unforgiveness was just too great, Max reckoned. The blood of Jesus therefore was always on active duty within Max, purifying his heart to allow the Holy Spirit unfettered freedom within him.

After this initial cleansing portion at the start of his prayer time Max then turned to the Holy Spirit and stated aloud his surrender to Him. While he repeated it daily, ritual like, the action of surrendering his spirit, soul, body, mind, will, emotions, eyes, ears, tongue, hands and feet were very real to Max. How else can the Holy Spirit have control if I never submit to him after I've unnecessarily taken back command?

Surrendering his mind, will and emotions to the Holy Spirit, was something he felt strongly about. Max felt particularly challenged by the writings of Paul in 2 Corinthians 10:5. "*We destroy arguments and every lofty opinion raised against the knowledge of God, and take every thought captive to obey Christ.*" [ESV] Max had previously heard teaching on this verse with the emphasis on the fact that 'we' had to take every thought captive. The teacher informed that we have to retrain our brains to think differently and only allow the approved thoughts to get through. "How on earth can I do that on my own," Max questioned, but the teacher was adamant that with enough training we can achieve it. "We need to discipline our thoughts," the teacher insisted. Max was unsure why Jesus had removed all sin from his life through His work on the cross but unfortunately when it came to controlling our thoughts we were on our own?

Something didn't smell right and Max determined to fully understand what the right meaning is and asked the Holy Spirit to reveal the truth to him. The Spirit didn't answer with a lengthy divine revelation as Max secretly hoped, but just encouraged him to read the verse in context. Max looked up the reference again and read 2 Corinthians 10 from verse 3 to verse 6. *"For though we walk in the flesh, we are not waging war according to the flesh. For the weapons of our warfare are not of the flesh but have divine power to destroy strongholds. We destroy arguments and every lofty opinion raised against the knowledge of God, and take every thought captive to obey Christ, being ready to punish every disobedience, when your obedience is complete."* Well that sure clarified it, Max decided. How dangerous to take verses in isolation, he remembered. So let's be clear;

- Firstly this is a war

- We don't wage war according to the flesh

- We have weapons to wage this war

- Our weapons are supercharged with divine power

Max couldn't be certain for anyone else, but he definitely knew his mind was a battleground of competing thoughts especially when it came to the things of the Lord and calling it a war was spot-on. Weapons Max knew about, and the sword of the Spirit was one of them. The point that made things clear to Max was the statement that it was the divine power of the weapon we use that destroyed arguments, lofty opinions and took every thought captive. The Lord never intended we take these thoughts captive by our own power. I have His Holy Spirit dwelling in me and He certainly is that divine power. These thoughts, arguments and opinions are destroyed when my obedience to Christ is complete according to the last verse, Max observed. Max checked the Greek translation of the word for obedience. It was hupakoé which conveys the meaning of submissiveness and compliance. That sounds like surrender to me, Max decided, and he thanked the Spirit for this clear revelation.

It was for this reason that as a part of his daily surrender to the Holy Spirit that Max always asked the Spirit to take all his thoughts captive and only release to his brain for action or to his heart for storage or ruminating on, those thoughts He approved of. Max envisaged that might be an extremely busy task at times given the copious volume of creative thoughts that frequently leapt into his mind from seemingly nowhere. Definitely a job for divine power Max reckoned; clearly he had no personal ability to do it.

The result of the thought captivity process soon became evident to Max. He found that while the volume of thoughts seldom abated he did notice a strong prompting when anything a bit dodgy made its appearance. The things that did reach his heart to ruminate on did not create anxiety or fear, peace was always the result. Max remembered that peace was a fruit of the Spirit. *"But the fruit of the Spirit is love, joy, peace, patience, kindness, goodness, faithfulness,"* Galatians 5:22 [ESV]

"Ah, so that's how it works," Max said as he finally understood by seeing the evidence in his own life. Max was subtly reminded by the Holy Spirit of his initial question that sparked his lengthy reminisce – "That's how you're led by the Spirit," Max was reminded. It seemed so clear now as he looked back on his walk with the Holy Spirit over the years. He was a son of God; he was led by the Spirit of God. Max felt a contentment cloak him as he pondered on the thought. He was still living in this evil world surrounded by sinful filth yet with the help of the Holy Spirit it was possible to live a godly life, one in-keeping with the standard required by our God. Truly in the eyes of the Father he was clothed in fine linen. "Praise the Lord," Max declared.

A few days later Max was again reading the Word when a verse in 1 Corinthians 1:2 caught his attention. It mentioned sanctification. *"To the church of God that is in Corinth, to those sanctified in Christ Jesus, called to be saints together with all those who in every place call upon the name of our Lord Jesus Christ, both their Lord and ours:"* Max had heard the term plenty enough but what did it really mean in terms of being applied to his life? Out came the Google search which gave the meaning as, 'set apart, made holy.' "Oh, Holy Spirit," Max begged, "I know I've been made holy and set apart by Jesus but does my life really reflect that?"

In reply, the Spirit challenged Max to take a look at understanding redemption. "But I asked about sanctification," Max protested. The Holy Spirit didn't reply but repeated the urging to understand redemption. Again Max found himself Google searching the meaning of redemption – "The action of regaining or gaining possession of something in exchange for payment, or clearing a debt." "Ok, that was pretty much what I understood it meant, but why are you pointing towards it?" Max asked. Quickly Max was reminded he hadn't asked about the meaning of the word but about what it means for his life.

Max took a look at the dictionary meaning again – The action of regaining possession of something in exchange for payment. Max had frequently heard preachers speak of God's plans for the redemption of his life as in the action of saving or being saved from sin, error, or evil. However, was God's redemption plan just to save me from something or was it so I can regain something? Interesting question, Max decided. If we were to regain something then what was that and how does it affect my life now?

Max noticed the word 'redeem' means to buy out or to pay a ransom. Apparently the term originated specifically in reference to the purchase of a slave's freedom. Applying this term to the death of Jesus on the cross meant that if Max is 'redeemed' then his prior state must have been one of slavery. Max read in Matthew 20:28 that *"Even as the Son of Man came not to be served but to serve, and to give his life as a ransom for many."* [ESV]

Ok, Max agreed, I understand that Jesus paid the price for my release from slavery and that His death was a literal exchange for my life. Then Max read in Colossians 1:13 -14 *"He has delivered us from the domain of darkness and transferred us to the kingdom of his beloved Son, in whom we have redemption, the forgiveness of sins."* [ESV] So, Max mused. My first state was in the domain of darkness. Because Man sinned in the Garden of Eden, God cursed mankind because they disobeyed him and believed the lie of Satan. Ok, so that's how I got into the domain of darkness; Max certainly believed and appreciated that. Jesus, through His death had paid the price of Max's ransom. But Max knew that Jesus didn't remain dead, He rose again on the third day. When Jesus rose He was victorious, the power of Satan's stranglehold over mankind was forever broken.

Max felt urged on to fully understand what the Holy Spirit was saying to him. So far his little Bible study hadn't really revealed anything new to him. He had a strong appreciation of all that Jesus had accomplished for him on the cross. Max knew what it meant to live a life in the Spirit but clearly the Spirit was trying to show Max that there was something more and it related to being transferred into the Kingdom. He picked up his Bible again and began reading Romans 6. Verses 5-11 stood out to him.

"For if we have been united with him in a death like his, we shall certainly be united with him in a resurrection like his. We know that our old self was crucified with him in order that the body of sin might be brought to nothing, so that we would no longer be enslaved to sin. For one who has died has been set free from sin. Now if we have died with Christ, we believe that we will also live with him. We know that Christ, being raised from the dead, will never die again; death no longer has dominion over him. For the death he died he died to sin, once for all, but the life he lives he lives to God. So you also must consider yourselves dead to sin and alive to God in Christ Jesus." [ESV]

For so much of his life Max had focused on what Jesus had achieved through His death on the cross and rightly so, he believed. However this verse in particular was pointing to what had been achieved through His resurrection. Slowly a light began to shine a little clearer in Max's mind. Verse 5 of Romans 6 kept revolving in his mind. It said Max would be *"united with him in **a resurrection like his"**.* "Ok' you've got my attention, Holy Spirit," Max said. "Please help me to understand what that actually means for me now?" Things became a little clearer to Max when he got to verse 22 in Romans 6. *"But now that you have been set free from sin and have become slaves of God, the*

fruit you get leads to sanctification and its end, eternal life."
[ESV] The fruit of being a slave of God is sanctification and
eternal life. Now we're getting somewhere, Max declared, as
he saw his study begin to tie back to his original question on
Sanctification.

Max began to summarise what he'd reviewed.

- His old self, my sin nature, was crucified when Jesus
  died.

- He had been ransomed by Jesus and was no longer a
  slave to his sin nature.

- He had been united with Jesus in a resurrection like
  Jesus'.

- By His resurrection he had been transferred in the
  Kingdom of Jesus.

- He had become a slave of God.

- The result of being a slave to God matures as
  sanctification.

"Ok," Max queried, "a slave? I thought I was a son of God,
blessed and living the good life in the Kingdom?" Max read the
verse again but the words didn't change, it still read slave. Out
came his phone and another Google search resulted in the
meaning of 'slave'. The result surprised Max somewhat. Yes, it
could mean forced to do hard labour without pay and all those
other intolerable things that men had imposed on their fellow

man. However, it became clear when he read more carefully that the real meaning is "a person who is the legal property of another." Max definitely had no problem with becoming the legal property of the living God! Further, applying that new found meaning to his previous state, of being a slave to sin, caused Max to shudder - he had been the legal property of the dominion of the devil. Oh, thank you Jesus!

The true magnitude of the redemptive work of Jesus began to become clear to Max. When God created man at the beginning of time He was the legal owner of man. God created man for His own pleasure to enjoy his company. Man sold out to the devil in the Garden of Eden and Satan became the legal owner of man and thereby man became subject to the same eternal fate as him – torment forever in the pit of hell. God in his mercy sent Jesus to pay the ransom for man's redemption when He died on the cross. If any person surrenders their life to Jesus, thereby causing their old sin nature to be crucified, then the ownership of that person is legally transferred back to God because God accepted Jesus' ransom blood offering and He raised Him from the dead (Romans 8:11). Those who have identified with the death of Jesus are also subject to the same resurrection power which brings that person back under God's ownership and right standing with God (righteousness) together with the ability to live a Godly life. The Holy Spirit gives that ability to live that life now, even though we still physically live in these earthly bodies. The previous sin nature still exists but it has lost its power over those who have died with Jesus in this way.

Max understood now. Jesus didn't just save him, He completely restored him back to what God fully intended when He first created man. Max thought about the idea of God walking and talking with Man in the cool of the day in the Garden of Eden. How incredible that would have been. Quickly the Holy Spirit reminded him that he too has exactly that relationship with God right now. By living a life free from the effects of sin Max was sanctified or set apart as holy, he had right standing with God and had been given a place in heavenly places. Ephesians 2:6 confirms that, *"and raised us up with him and seated us with him in the heavenly places in Christ Jesus."* [ESV]

Just as a member of a government has a seat in the house so in the same manner Max had a seat in heavenly places – in the very realm where God lives. And what was even better, Max didn't have to compete for it; all he had to do was completely surrender to the Lordship of Jesus Christ and receive the gift of a redeemed life. "Thank you Jesus for the cross and thank you Holy Spirit for allowing me to understand the full extent of my redemption," Max exclaimed.

This true understanding of exactly who he was in Christ wasn't totally a new thought to Max as he had understood the basics of that for years. But when he added the fruit of living a life pleasurable to God the effect of sanctification became real.

It absolutely was not what he'd done or achieved that mattered, it was who he now was in God's eyes. Since God was his legal owner Max rested with a renewed assurance that nobody could snatch him out of God's hand. He felt safe and secure in that confidence.

A few weeks later Max attended his regular Sunday church. Bringing the word that day was one of the younger Pastors who was a gifted presenter and enjoyed adding mild theatrics to make his point. It certainly helped to retain the interest of the congregation. This week he engaged the assistance of his young son and his much cherished leather jacket. The title of his message was 'Our Covering'. Explaining that his young son, though very endearing, did have a mischievous side and in the past, when caught in the act of doing something wrong, he'd run and grab his father's leather jacket and throw it over himself in an attempt to hide from the impending discipline.

He called his son to the stage and threw his leather jacket to throw over him 'as a covering' explaining that's how God looks at us. He doesn't see us, or who we are, he sees the covering over us. That covering he explained is Jesus when he lives in us. God only sees Jesus and therefore accepts us.

To give a Biblical base he used Romans 13:14 *"Rather, clothe yourselves with the Lord Jesus Christ, and do not think about how to gratify the desires of the flesh."* [NIV] And also Galatians 3:27, *"And all who have been united with Christ in baptism have put on Christ, like putting on new clothes."* [NLT]

Later that day Max pondered on the message and listened to it again the next day on the on-line podcast. In the light of what Max has just been studying about redemption, this message seemed to be more about atonement than redemption. The message was completely unbiblical in a Christian context as there is a very big difference between atonement and redemption.

Max wasn't in the business of correcting Pastors' messages but in this case what he'd said had gone completely unchallenged and it was contra to what the Bible taught. Max prayed a lot asking the Lord to rectify the message but the Holy Spirit kept on prompting Max to do something about it. Max gulped and sat down to compose an email which went something as follows:

"I'm prompted to take issue with the content of your message last Sunday about "Covering." In a Christian context your message is completely unbiblical. The issue is the very big difference between atonement and redemption.

In the Old Testament sin was atoned (covered) by the blood of animals. Atonement could not remove the sin but it covered it over so God could accept His people and maintain His holiness. It wasn't permanent and underneath the covering was the same sinful nature. This is the reason God made Adam and Eve those nice leather clothes in Genesis 3 – they resulted in blood being shed. Had it been able to remove their sin then there would have been no need for Jesus and the cross.

Chapter 11
Sanctification

In the New Testament under Jesus Christ we are redeemed. This simply means that the death of Jesus has paid the price of a ransom, releasing us from bondage to sin and death (our old sinful nature). Our sinful state is not covered over; we are released from its power. We become a new creation in Christ Jesus. How can we be born again if we're just covered over? God takes away our heart of stone and gives us a new heart. God said to Samuel that He didn't look on the outward appearance but on the heart.

To suggest a Christian is simply covered in Christ (as per your leather jacket illustration) begs the basic question, what's underneath? It does not deal with our sinful nature which would remain concealed under the covering of Christ. On that basis where could the Holy Spirit dwell in such a body and how could a believer possibly walk a life pleasing to God without the Holy Spirit, simply by being cloaked in Jesus?

I'm sorry, but there is major error in this teaching and my spirit has been burning within me after hearing an experienced and knowledgeable Pastor put forward such a concept of salvation in a church setting. It has nothing to do with what I believe or think or anyone else for that matter. The Word of God is the test and what you taught at length on Sunday simply does not match what the Bible teaches, that is what I meant by unbiblical.

You may respond that you quoted from the New Testament and, yes, it does talk about being clothed in Christ in two places; Romans 13:14 and Galatians 3:27. These verses however must be read in their entire context. Romans relates to us putting on Christ as a part of other teaching in Romans about putting off our fleshly nature. Galatians specifically talks about being baptised in Christ – fully immersed in Him. It's about complete and total surrender to Jesus.

As I'm sure you're aware, there is a trend in some circles to teach that we invite Jesus into our life to obtain salvation. That is, of course, a totally unbiblical teaching which can never result in salvation because it never deals with the sinful nature for which Jesus died and redeemed us from. The only possible path to salvation is through total, complete and utter surrender to Jesus Christ making Him the Lord, the King and Boss of our lives. Suggesting we can just accept a covering of Jesus over our life to obtain salvation feeds directly into this "adding Jesus" mentality which again I stress is unbiblical."

Max sent the email off and in reply the pastor suggested they discuss the matter after the early morning prayer meeting later that week. The Pastor together with the Senior Pastor approached Max after the prayer time and suggested that terming the message unbiblical perhaps was a bit strong. Max had no intentions to debate that and simply asked to be shown the New Testament scriptures that support atonement as a Christian principal. Max had learned long since that God's word spoke for itself and was the final authority on every word of doctrine.

Chapter 11
Sanctification

No Biblical references were forthcoming as Max well knew, so he reiterated his understanding of redemption verses atonement. After a brief discussion the Senior Pastor concluded that he understood what Max meant now and acknowledged that Max was absolutely correct in asserting the difference between redemption and atonement. "We'll discuss it and see how the message should be modified when it's given again," the Senior Pastor concluded.

Max wasn't quite done. "While I've got you both," Max began, "Is there any chance we can have more teaching sessions in our church." Max was very serious, there appeared to be a very strong need for some sound Biblical given the lack of basic understanding even by some of the pastoral staff. The Senior Pastor's reply was swift and curt, "We tried that for twenty years and it resulted in very little church growth. Since we changed to encouraging uplifting messages church attendance has multiplied." Max was shocked at the answer but simply said, "Okay then," and made his way out of the building. He was horrified to hear the Senior Pastor confirm that the leadership of the church he'd attended for years was solely interested in bums on seats; a congregation itching to have their ears tickled as the apostle Paul put it in 2 Timothy 4:3. *"For the time is coming when people will not endure sound teaching, but having itching ears they will accumulate for themselves teachers to suit their own passions."* [ESV] "Dear Lord, please do not allow this," Max cried as he drove back home.

"Jesus said "I will be back"
way before Arnold did"

Chapter 12
The Lamb's Wife

So why is it you go to church?" the stranger asked. Max had been walking a popular coastal track near the city and had stopped to admire the view. It was a stunning day and the calm bay glistened as the sun skipped gracefully across the ripples awakened by the soft sea breeze. The hills beyond where obscured by a hazy blue, typical of the settled weather for that time of year. Max enjoyed walking as did Hazel, so it was that the Whites found themselves chatting with another retired couple while absorbing the brilliance of the late summer day.

The question burned into Max. He'd attended church since he was born, except for the few years after leaving the Assembly. So why was the question so hard to answer? All Max could come up with to give an answer to the stranger was, "I like to meet and greet my fellow believers and because I deeply love my Lord and Saviour I enjoy giving praise to Him." The generic answer seemed to appease the questioner and the topic quickly moved on. Not for Max, it disturbed him. Why hadn't he been able to answer such a simple question more genuinely? Perhaps he was losing it – he was seventy-five years old now! No, it wasn't an age thing, Max decided; it just wasn't easy to articulate to an unbeliever why he'd faithfully attended church all those years.

Max enjoyed going to Church. He enjoyed worshiping Jesus and the Father, empowered by the Holy Spirit. Sure, the music had moved on a bit, perhaps for the best, compared to the old hymns he'd sung during his assembly days. The art of worshipping his creator God in a collective setting was an unexplainable experience, one that went way beyond thankfulness and honour. The feeling was of total peace, love and joy, standing in the presence of the Father, honouring Him, together with the One who made it all possible. Not as an intruder but as one truly knowing he belonged there. It was a time when other likeminded men and women would join in doing the same. The power of the collective embellished the atmosphere. Myriads standing in the presence of a Holy God; each one without blame, redeemed and set free by the blood of Jesus. Yes, Max decided, that's why I go to Church.

The thought, however, wouldn't alight so a week later Max began a study on what the Church is today and is it exactly what Jesus intended? Max had no idea where to start on such a mammoth subject so after asking the Lord's help he spent the next hour praying in tongues. That bought a great peace to his heart but didn't really answer any questions except now he felt strongly compelled to ask why there are so many different denominations. "But that wasn't the question I asked," Max protested. However the compulsion remained and Max felt led to read 1 Corinthians 1 and the paragraph starting at verse 10 leapt out at him. *"I appeal to you, brothers, by the name of our Lord Jesus Christ, that all of you agree, and that there be no divisions among you, but that you be united in the same mind and the same judgment. For it has been reported to me by Chloe's people that there is quarrelling among you, my brothers. What I mean is that each one of you says, "I follow Paul," or "I follow Apollos," or "I follow Cephas," or "I follow Christ." Is Christ divided? Was Paul crucified for you? Or were you baptized in the name of Paul?"* 1 Corinthians 1:10-13 [ASV]. That seemed to indicate to Max there should only be one church, yet in the small city where Max lived there were at least twenty different fellowships or denominations of various sorts from the ultra-conservative to the extremely liberal. "Why was this, Lord?" Max asked.

Max had read several books, over the years, on the great fathers' of the reformation; how they had identified the false teachings of the established Roman Catholic Church. And since the leaders of that Church had flatly rejected the concept their century's long traditions could possibly be wrong, these great reformation fathers had begun their own denominations. Max had no problem with that as it was clearly the right option at the time given the decay of the established church. Salvation was only through the blood of our Lord Jesus Christ; it could not be purchased, as in indulgences. There was no doubt these men were godly and led by the Holy Spirit as what transpired was a fire of revival that continues to this day.

Abandoning an organised church structure unfortunately gave way to a perceived right that anyone could question anything. As the Bible was translated into the language of the people, more and more believers had access to the Word of God. Those led by the Spirit were clear on how to interpret this Word and teach their flock of faithful followers. Others however while very learned theologians, unfortunately taught from their own understanding of God's Word and hence division resulted. Division, as Paul put it in 1 Corinthians 1, Max decided was perhaps a bit of an understatement as he'd read of many who were ostracized and some even burnt at the stake having been labelled blasphemers simply because they disagreed with the teaching of a particular leader. As a result and over time the surviving 'blasphemers' drew on their support base and started their own separate congregation and, thus, sects and denominations were born.

Max reflected that today things had matured to such an extent that seemingly anyone could go out and start their own church, promoting their own brand or flavour of 'Christianity'. If the preacher had a strong personality or was a gifted speaker their initial flock could quickly morph into thousands. The reverse was also true, Max observed of the church attendees. Church hopping, as he termed it, really was a thing. Many Christians, if they disliked their Pastor, the message or even just others in their congregation, would simply move on to another church. So plentiful was the choice that decisions could be made on the style of music, the pastor, the length of service, service times, the venue or the age group of others attending. The list seemed endless. No wonder, Max concluded, that the church leaders had engineered their churches to accommodate the wants of the people. They were afraid of offending their flock, with the resulting loss of numbers and of course revenue, to such an extent that they watered down God's Word by leaving out the challenging bits and focusing solely on the good parts – love and blessings and fellowshipping together.

Max read the verse in 1 Corinthians 1:12-13 again. *"What I mean is that each one of you says, "I follow Paul," or "I follow Apollos," or "I follow Cephas," or "I follow Christ."* **Is Christ divided***? Was Paul crucified for you? Or were you baptized in the name of Paul?"* [ESV] [Emphasis added] The Jesus Max knew certainly was not divided. Max was grieved when he pondered on the divided state of the present day church. In the 1,900 plus years since the Apostle Paul wrote to the Corinthians it seemed that not a lot of progress had been made. If Paul was grieved then Max could only surmise how the Holy Spirit felt about the situation now.

Max talked through his questions of the divided body of Christ with a close friend who pointed out what Paul said in 1 Corinthians 12:12-13 *"For just as the body is one and has many members, and all the members of the body, though many, are one body, so it is with Christ. For in one Spirit we were all baptized into one body—Jews or Greeks, slaves or free—and all were made to drink of one Spirit."* [ESV] His advice was that, as the verse indicated, all these various denominations were just different members of the same body. They each have a specific function but they all work together for a common cause, bound together with one Holy Spirit. Max wondered how the Assembly ruled over by the Elect Vessel would fit into that scriptural setting. Or, for that matter, the churches who believe the gifts of the Spirit ended when the Apostles died out, or those that believe in ritualistic worship or the infallibility of their leader. Clearly, Max concluded, there were a few flaws in his friend's argument.

Max continued reading to place the verse in context with the subject of the whole chapter. Verse 4-6 helped his understanding *"Now there are varieties of gifts, but the same Spirit; and there are varieties of service, but the same Lord; and there are varieties of activities, but it is the same God who empowers them all in everyone."* 1 Corinthians 12:4-6 [ESV] The subject of the chapter was spiritual gifts. Undoubtedly there certainly are different gifts of the Holy Spirit and each person has different abilities and characteristics. Some are musicians, others are prayer warriors, teachers and administrators. However is Paul talking about churches or individuals? The Holy Spirit is given to individuals not to whole congregations, that much was certain to Max in accordance with his understanding of the Word. Paul removed all doubt when Max read verse 27.

"Now you are the body of Christ and individually members of it." The body of Christ – His Church – is one but made up of many parts. All those parts, however, do not operate in isolation to each other but are all linked in one body.

The scripture was plain to Max. It wasn't the Lord's Will to have a multitude of denominations based on theology - man had created that. Of course Max understood that not all Christians lived in the one city or even one country. They were scattered all around the world in every time-zone and due to physical constraints naturally it was impossible for them to gather as one. Obviously that was the case in the Apostle Paul's day too Max understood, so perhaps it was all about the wider body of Christ and not just the individual gatherings in the city where Max lived. Also Max knew the Holy Spirit was God so no doubt He had the power to bring all the individuals together regardless of where they lived or what time they attended worship. The point is, Max decided, that each Church, regardless of location, is subject to the same Holy Spirit, governed by the same Word of God and worship the Father in spirit and truth.

Max couldn't put the subject to rest and over the next few days he wanted to understand what exactly the church was meant to be. He looked up a verse in Ephesians 5:26. *"Husbands love your wives, as Christ loved the church and gave himself up for her, that he might sanctify her, having cleansed her by the washing of water with the word, so that he might present the church to himself in splendour, without spot or wrinkle or any such thing, that she might be holy and without blemish."* [ESV] Ok, Max decided, that much is clear. The Church belongs to Jesus Christ – not to charismatic Pastors. He paid for it with His life which demonstrates a very substantial love. If He loves His church that much then He's definitely going to bring it to fruition. He's going to present it to Himself without spot or wrinkle – holy and without blemish.

Max felt deeply challenged by that. He knew what sanctification was as he'd done a deep study on that a few years back. This verse told how Jesus was sanctifying His Church by the *"washing of water with the word."* The Word, Max knew, was the Bible and Jesus wanted all in His Church to allow His Word to wash over them. "How do I do that, Lord?" Max prayed. Quickly Max was reminded of a function of the Holy Spirit that Jesus taught in John's Gospel 14:26 *"But the Helper, the Holy Spirit, whom the Father will send in my name, he will teach you all things and bring to your remembrance all that I have said to you."* [ESV] Ok, so let me understand that Max asked, "I read the Word and even if I don't remember it all it will be like it is washing over me. You, Holy Spirit, will at times bring to my remembrance things I have read as and when I need to apply that to my life." The realisation of that struck home to Max as he recalled countless times the Holy Spirit had, at exactly the right time, dropped a verse into his mind which provided a clear understanding at that very moment. Often these were verses he had no remembrance of but because he'd read them, often many times, their washing over him had soaked in somewhere which allowed the Spirit to bring it up again at the appropriate moment. Despite his age and life experience Max marvelled at the simple way all of God's Word meshed together and made practical sense. "Praise the Lord!" Max exclaimed.

Max didn't want to leave it there; he was keen to understand how the Church would be presented without spot or wrinkle. Later that day Max picked up his grandson's well used tee-shirt. How he'd got it in such a state was not forthcoming but the dirt was well ground in. "Looks like you've been dragged through a swamp backwards," Max fake-scolded his endearing grandson. "We better get this cleaned up quick, before Grandma gets home." He collected it up together with several other items in a similar state and threw them into the washing machine and dialled up the 'heavy duty' cycle. The young grandson was fascinated with mechanical machinery of any type and washing machines were no exception. Max lifted the lid allowing his young kin to peer inside. The rotors thrashed back and forth forcing the clothes to lurch uncontrollably in the soapy water. Max couldn't help appreciating how violent but controlled the operation was. No doubt the intention was to remove the dirt completely.

As the young and old heads studied the thrashing clothes and swirling water of the machine doing its job, the Holy Spirit reminded Max that getting the dirt out is not always a pleasant task. It's the same process when it comes to ironing out the wrinkles. Max marvelled how he'd obtained such a deep spiritual revelation while sharing a mechanical moment with his grandson. "Thank you Lord," Max acknowledged. "I'm removing the spots from within the Church," the Holy Spirit relayed in reply. That did not feel like a pleasant procedure, Max decided.

Max contemplated the process further and asked if the spots were on people within the Church or was it things in the Church that represented the dirt. Max was reminded to read Ephesians 5:26 again. *"Christ loved the church and gave himself up for her, that he might sanctify her, **having cleansed her** by the washing of water with the word, so that he might **present the church to himself in splendour**"* [ESV] [Part of Verse and emphasis added] Max saw the cleansing was in the past tense. When Jesus died on the cross He cleansed all those truly part of His Church. That cleansing is done. Max believed that perhaps the spots were contamination that had occurred from outside influences as Jesus was building His Church in a fallen world until the presentation takes place. But is that right Lord, or is the dirt from somewhere else?

Max sensed the Holy Spirit was trying to tell him something so he began to listen intently. Max read 2 Thessalonians 2:3 *"Let no man deceive you by any means: for that day shall not come, except there come **a falling away first**, and that man of sin be revealed, the son of perdition;"* [KJV] [emphasis added].

What day was that? The previous verse tells us; *"the day of Christ,"* The day Jesus Christ returns to claim His Church. So, Max reflected, before Jesus returns there is going to be a falling away. "What does that mean, *Falling away?*" Max queried. Max understood when he read John 16:1 *"I have said all these things to you to keep you from falling away."* Jesus was talking to His disciples in that verse and clearly while He didn't want them to fall away it certainly sounded possible for them to do so if they moved away from Him.

In case there was still any doubt in Max's mind he read in Hebrews 3:12 *"Take care, brothers, lest there be in any of you an evil, unbelieving heart, leading you to fall away from the living God."* [ESV] This was written to the 'brothers' a term the apostles used when addressing those in the church and the falling away was from the living God. Max also read in Matthew 24:24 the words of Jesus, *"For false christs and false prophets will arise and perform great signs and wonders, so as to lead astray, if possible, **even the elect**."* [ESV] The elect, Max knew was the Church – those approved of God.

Putting the pieces together Max reflected on what he had observed. Not everyone in the Church was going to be a part of the finished article. The spots and wrinkles were going to be removed and when Christ returns the Church will be glorious. "Dear Lord, I want to be sure of being a part of that spotless Church, when Christ returns," Max pleaded. "Help me to live a life sanctified and serviceable to the master." Max turned to 2

Timothy 2:21 and read *"Therefore, if anyone cleanses himself from what is dishonourable, he will be a vessel for honourable use, set apart as holy, useful to the master of the house, ready for every good work."* "Now that's what I'm talking about," Max stated.

"So what do I do, Lord?" Max asked. Quickly the words of Jesus in Mark 13:5-6 came to mind; *"And Jesus answering them began to say, Take heed lest any man deceive you: For many shall come in my name, saying, I am Christ; and shall deceive many."* [KJV] Take heed, or watch out, as other translations of the Bible put it. Many are going to come in the name of Jesus and deceive many! Max was sobered at the thought as he recalled the various deceptive teachers he'd believed for a time over the years. How easy it was to get caught, he reckoned.

One thing puzzled Max. Right from the time of the apostles there had been false teachers and those falling away from the faith. What was unique about this 'falling away'? It must be an obvious event as Paul had listed it as a sign of the return of Jesus Christ to claim his bride. "What is this, Lord, and how will I know?" Max asked. In reply Max's attention was led to the book of Daniel. Max read Daniel 11:32 *"And such as do wickedly against the covenant shall he corrupt by flatteries:* **but the people that do know their God** *shall be strong, and do exploits."* [KJV] [Emphasis added]. But that was fulfilled at the time of the Maccabees, wasn't it? Max questioned. "Yes, but keep reading," was the reply. Max read verse 35 *"And some of* *them of understanding shall fall, to try them, and to purge, and to make them white, even to the time of the end: because it is yet for a time appointed.*" [KJV] "Okay," Max conceded, "That is clear; it is referencing our time also — *the time of the end.*" It also sounded a lot like washing — making them white. Max understood the meaning of that word 'know' in the original language. It had far deeper connotations than just knowledge of. It involved a deep intimate understanding built up by an experiential knowledge of the person. Max liked the idea of knowing God in that context — God the Father, God the Son (Jesus Christ) and God the Holy Spirit. Max further resolved his deliberate intention to walk every day led by the Holy Spirit.

The Holy Spirit wasn't done with the subject though and drew Max to the parable Jesus told of the ten virgins. He looked it up in Matthew 25 starting at verse 1.

"Then the kingdom of heaven will be like ten virgins who took their lamps and went to meet the bridegroom. Five of them were foolish, and five were wise. For when the foolish took their lamps, they took no oil with them, but the wise took flasks of oil with their lamps. As the bridegroom was delayed, they all became drowsy and slept. But at midnight there was a cry, "Here is the bridegroom! Come out to meet him." Then all those virgins rose and trimmed their lamps. And the foolish said to the wise, "Give us some of your oil, for our lamps are going out." But the wise answered, saying, "Since there will not be enough for us and for you, go rather to the dealers and buy for

yourselves." And while they were going to buy, the bridegroom came, and those who were ready went in with him to the marriage feast, and the door was shut. Afterward the other virgins came also, saying, "Lord, lord, open to us." But he answered, "Truly, I say to you, I do not know you." Watch therefore, for you know neither the day nor the hour." [ESV]

Max knew there had been copious teachings on this parable over the years, but the real point was often discarded. Max went on to YouTube and watched a teaching by David Nathan on the subject. David was one of the soundest teachers of the Bible he knew and he enjoyed the fact he didn't embellish the story but simply explained what it meant through the reading of the plain text. First David explained the characters in the account. The bridegroom of course was none other than Jesus Christ. The Bride was the Church and the ten virgins all members of the bridal party or members of the Church. The oil he explained typifies the Holy Spirit and he is described this way in numerous references throughout the Bible.

The intriguing part of the parable was that all ten virgins were together and were all expectant of, and waiting for, the return of Jesus. The sad thing was they all grew weary and slept. Perhaps, David suggested, the Church has got so busy doing church they had forgotten the real cause of being together. The wakeup call went out and everyone was stirred into action. The five wise ones, filled with the Holy Spirit, were clear on what to do as their lamp (Spirit guided life) lit the way for them. The five foolish however, without the Holy Spirit, didn't have the resources within to see the way to follow the Bridegroom and went off to find those resources elsewhere. When the foolish ones believed they were finally ready to go in, it was too late. Jesus had already come back and had retrieved His bride.

Incredibly the five foolish represented fifty per cent of the church. Half missed out on going in because they neglected or perhaps rejected the ministry of the Holy Spirit to live their lives by. They were doing all the same things as the wise virgins but totally by their own resources, 'buying' it from those who 'sell'. The astounding conclusion is that the Bridegroom tells these foolish virgins *"Verily I say unto you, I know you not."* No doubt all the virgins knew exactly who the bridegroom, Jesus, was but the fact was Jesus never knew them. "There's that same intimate word 'know' again" Max recounted. "And it was a reciprocal relationship."

Max had heard other teaching on this parable over the years with varying interpretations. One teacher went as far as to denounce the wise virgins; "How mean of them. Why wouldn't they share their oil with their friends?" Max plainly understood, however, from the scripture that the Holy Spirit was given individually and it was personal. There wasn't a verse he knew of that described Christians sharing the Holy Spirit. God was liberal in giving freely of His Spirit as Max saw in John 3:34 *"For he whom God has sent utters the words of God, **for he***

gives the Spirit without measure." God 'gives' His Spirit, no buying involved, Max observed, and He's given without measure. It seemed clear to Max there was no reason for any believer to live without the Holy Spirit.

"How can this be?" Max asked. "Perhaps up to half the church living without the Holy Spirit, when Jesus returns?" The concept seemed abhorrent to Max. Yet the parable was plain. Max was led to ponder on the prevalent teaching of the Church over the past ten years. What was the main focus? He recalled some of the themes of the church he attended – Always only Jesus, Jesus Unlimited, Kingdom Now, Loving Jesus, At Home with Jesus. "Nothing wrong with any of those," Max stated. "Anything that glorifies Jesus is okay with me." As soon as Max had uttered that statement he felt a strong check in his spirit. "Uh, what was that, Lord?" Max queried. Quickly Max felt the Holy Spirit say, "Those were the themes but what was the focus of the messages each week?" Max thought about it and began to reflect on the substance of the church teaching. They were always strongly uplifting, motivational and encouraging, teaching that if we ask Jesus into our life we will live a blessed life. Through Him we can obtain all the blessings, we can pray and ask for His help for everything we need in our lives. He can do exceedingly abundantly above all that we can ask or think – expect answers, Jesus loves you. Max couldn't point to anything specific in any of those that were doctrinally incorrect. It was absolutely true, Jesus was the giver of life and through Him we have everything.

Max knew the Spirit was leading him somewhere but he wasn't certain yet of just where. I'll sleep on it and it'll be clearer in the morning, Max decided. About three the next morning Max was woken abruptly from a restful sleep. A phrase thundered in his head, "They're obsessed with the gifts and have forgotten the giver." Suddenly it all made sense. The preaching at churches all over the world focused on souls asking Jesus to come into their lives as doing so would enable them to live a blessed and plentiful life – now! With Jesus in their life everything became possible. They could have that job, that car, that house, that lovely husband or wife. Repentance, redemption or sanctification were rarely mentioned. The emphasis was on asking Jesus into your life – to 'share' your life with Him. The message of total surrender (dying to self) to Jesus was long discarded as an obtuse relic from the past. Jesus was my friend, not my Lord.

Max got out of bed and reclined in his favourite prayer chair and started to pray. Firstly he repented of having any part in such teaching. Not that he'd ever taught it but by his silence he'd condoned it. He cried out to the Lord to provide a way for these people to get to know the Giver, to really know what it is to have a living relationship with Jesus. He prayed that the full truth would be told in all the churches. He prayed that the outworking power of the Holy Spirit would be clearly seen and the supernatural unleashed. As Max ran out of prayer topics he reverted to tongues and continued on until daybreak.

There is just one question Max asked the Father as he prayed. "I can see what the church taught has definitely diverted the focus away from the divine, to that which perishes, but how will that cause the great falling away?" The answer came back in an unexpected way. Max found himself vividly recalling a recent news article he'd read about the God of the Christian Church being Jesus. Max had enjoyed the article; he believed that, according to scripture, Christ Jesus is the head of the Church. "What do you mean by that?" Max asked. Max was again reminded of the answers, within the article, of several people the writer had interviewed. They had all said that, "Jesus was their God." Max still wasn't clear of what the Spirit meant as he knew that Jesus was indeed God. John 1:1 made that beyond doubt, "*In the beginning was the Word, and the Word was with God, and the **Word was God**.*" Max knew that the Word referenced there was referring to Jesus. His deity was undeniable. Suddenly the penny dropped. They weren't saying Jesus wasn't God they were saying that Jesus, in the singular, was their God.

Max thought for a moment on what the seemingly insignificant difference might be and asked the Lord for further clarification. Max was reminded of a song they had frequently sung in Church which had the phrase "Jesus our God." Max for some reason never felt comfortable with the term of calling Jesus 'Our God.' Slowly however, as he pondered on that term again, he realised that it wasn't what the term implied it was what it denied. If Jesus was our God what place did the Father or Holy Spirit have? Jesus wasn't God in His own right; He is one with the Father and the Holy Spirit. Max check John 10:30 again just to be sure and it still said *"I and my Father are one."* [KJV] Max checked Romans 8:9 which made it very clear about the Holy Spirit's deity *"But ye are not in the flesh, but in the Spirit, if so be that the **Spirit of God** dwell in you. Now if any man has not the **Spirit of Christ**, he is none of his."* [KJV emphasis added] Paul calls Him the Spirit of Christ and the Spirit of God. At last it was crystal clear to Max. Jesus cannot be considered in isolation of the Father and the Holy Spirit. Certainly it was impossible for us to give Jesus too much honour or praise, given all He's done for us. But that's not the point; He isn't 'our God', we serve a triune God, Father, Son and Holy Spirit.

Max's mind swirled with detail on the subject and gradually lots of what had been happening around him began to make sense. The focus in the secular world was One World Order – one government, one economy and one religion. Max hadn't paid a lot of attention to it because he knew from the scripture that it was the devils plan to bring in a counterfeit government at the end of time with the Anti-Christ at its head. But this new revelation demonstrated exactly how cunning and subtle the devil is. He knew he couldn't drag away vast numbers of Christians into his darkness simply by enticement. No, his plan is always by deceit and lies. By years of twisting a core anchor of Christianity he'd managed to entice millions of believers in Jesus to reject the Father and the Holy Spirit and His power. All he had to do was to manipulate the scriptures to have Pastors focus singularly on Jesus and the gifts available through Him. He had created this illusion to such an extent that millions of believers in Jesus were happy to call Jesus their God - singular.

The devil's closing argument, with this deceit, is when he has respected Christian leaders stand up and declare that the Christians have Jesus as their God, The Jews have Yahweh as their God and the Moslems have Allah as theirs but the end result of each of them is heaven; so there's no real differences in religions just alternative means of getting there. The theory was that no one way was better than the other - it came down to what you really believed was best for you. The end result, they claimed, was always heaven – whatever you believed that meant to you!

That teaching wasn't new to Max; he'd heard it for years but now for the very first time he could see that millions of Christians all around the world had bought into this lie. These Christians all knew of Jesus but Max doubted many of them really knew Him in an experiential way. Jesus made it extremely plain in John 14:6 *"I am the way, and the truth, and the life. No one comes to the Father except through me."* [ESV] Dramatically the realisation became clear to Max; this was the great falling away. It had started. This was one of the great signs of the return of Jesus for His Church. He was about to claim His prize, His bride which He'd given His life to redeem. Only those that were without spot of wrinkle were a part of His bride.

Stirred up by the flames of his recent revelation Max made a determined effort to speak to every person possible, Christian or non-Christian, to warn them to be ready for the coming of the Lord. There would be no second chances he warned, once the day of grace had ended.

Max felt for the Pastors of his church. They were good people, he knew they loved Jesus and they honestly believed they were preaching the truth from the pulpit. Unfortunately they had been blinded to the subtle wiles of the devil. He had enticed them to magnify Jesus singly and they had not stressed the need for radical repentance or who the Father is and how or why we worship Him. It had been years since they'd taught on the Holy Spirit and how to use His power to understand scripture and live a pure life. Instead they implemented systems and programmes, developed by men apart from God, which they believed were making their churches more acceptable to the masses, inoffensive and inclusive. They had implemented teaching programs that bypassed the Holy Spirit, determining spiritual gifting based on the believers natural ability. Max remembered he tried to warn his Pastor a few years back but was told they'd tried doing teaching sermons but that didn't result in much church growth. Max prayed for them, in fact he prayed for everyone. He wanted to see all his friends and acquaintances make it to the wedding supper as the Lamb's wife. However he now understood that many who profess Jesus will not go in.

Chapter 12
The Lamb's Wife

The verse in Matthew 7:22-23 hit home to Max. *"Many will say to me in that day, Lord, Lord, have we not prophesied in thy name? And in thy name have cast out devils? And in thy name done many wonderful works? And then will I profess unto them, I never knew you: depart from me, ye that work iniquity."* It's not about what we have done Max concluded, it's all about who we 'know'. "Thank you Jesus," Max prayed.

*"The lost and found is located inside
come on in"*

Chapter 13
The Time of the End

Max watched the live stream of the international news as he ate his lunch. His planned walk for the day had been cancelled, it was raining. The usual murders, road accidents and natural disasters ensued, followed by a predictable response by a leading Politician. "And now to International news," the newsreader continued. "The Jerusalem Accord, initiated by Saudi Arabia, was signed today by Israel, the European Union, Russia, Great Britain, eleven Muslim countries and several other nations." Max sat bolt upright, he didn't even know there were any talks on-going. Unfortunately that was the limit of the interest of the news channel and they moved quickly onto the next gripping international scandal.

Max quickly Google searched 'The Jerusalem Accord' and several articles were presented which Max read hurriedly. Efforts to find a peaceful solution to the Jerusalem problem, as it had been termed in the Press, had been greatly intensified since the recent devastating Middle East war. During the early 2020's Iran rekindled its threats against Israel with a vengeance. As a part of the ceasefire agreement that ended the long running Syrian civil war, Iran, with the blessing of Russia and Turkey had vastly expanded its military bases in Syria under the guise of playing peacemaker between those for and against their leader Bashar al-Assad. The effective result was that Assad had become a puppet of Iran who soon had free reign throughout the country.

Iran built massive missile storage facilities and re-established Syria's once thriving chemical weapons programs churning out enough deadly toxins to kill half the world's population on a daily basis. Fearing an Israeli backlash Iran petitioned the United Nations requesting an international force be stationed in Damascus to assist in peace keeping operations and hopefully diminish Israel's determinations. As a deterrent to Israel Iran built massive barracks to house this UN force coincidently adjoining its sprawling missile and weapons factories. Iran also insisted that the peace keeping forces be predominantly Shia Muslims which included mostly countries to the South of Russia - Kazakhstan, Kyrgyzstan, Tajikistan, Turkmenistan and Uzbekistan. Russia played an arm's length big brother role to maintain its influence in the region and Turkey, keen to be accepted as a player in the region, provided the bulk of the numbers.

As time progressed Iran couldn't resist lobbing a few conventional missiles over the fence into Israel. In-keeping with their standard protective policy Israel responded with typical disproportionate firepower and wiped out one of Iran's major missile production facilities on the outskirts of Damascus. An unfortunate consequence of the attack was a massive chemical blast caused by various munitions stored near the factory. The resulting explosion and fire instantaneously engulfed the massive barracks housing the sleeping UN multi-national peace-keeping forces, killing about seven thousand military and civilian personnel.

The international outrage from the bombing was instant and exceptionally vocal. Disregarding the insane logic of housing so many innocent lives in such close proximity to such a dangerous fire ball, the Press sided wholly with Iran. In their eyes Iran was simply doing its job keeping the peace and next minute Israel turns up and destroys thousands of innocent lives. The fact Iran had, in an unprovoked attack, killed twenty five Israeli civilians when it indiscriminately fired off half a dozen missiles, was totally ignored. Israel was the villain for responding. Strangely the Sunni Arab nations were remarkably silent. Lead by Saudi Arabia they were far from enthused with Iran's presumptive role in war-torn Syria.

The response from the UN Peacekeepers was rapid. Righteous indignation prevailed and the UN Security Council was powerless to oppose them. Every country that had lost citizens in the raid contributed massive amounts of military equipment and personnel. The city of Damascus swelled by millions as the coalition readied for a massive assault on the tiny nation of Israel. Coordination was scanty. Russia tried to use its military muscle to influence a logical plan of attack but every general and two-bit commander was determined to show Israel she could not mess with Shia Muslims. Under the cover of darkness one night a small group of fanatics raided a chemical missile plant, stole five of them and fired them off via a mobile launcher vaguely in the direction of Israel. Three were shot down by Israeli defences and landed harmlessly on the Syrian side of the border but two went a little further with one making a direct hit on the sleeping Northern Israeli town of Qatsrin, population 7,200. Thousands of its innocent citizens never awoke that next morning and many hundreds more suffered horrendous effects from the lethal chemicals unscrupulously rained upon them.

Iran realising they had inadvertently poked an angry bear in the eye with a sharp stick quickly went on the offensive; completely disregarding the fact that the firing had not been officially sanctioned. Israel was reminded that missile was only a down-payment and that she should prepare to have thousands of such projectiles rain down on her. The Nation of Israel would now be wiped from the map, was the official edict from the Iranian President.

The Israeli response was to warn governments of all the millions of UN forces to leave Damascus within 48 hours or face the full force of their military. They advised that Hitler had tried to exterminate their people once using gas and they renewed their vow that would never happen again. In defiance however not one single solider was allowed to move from Damascus and Iran's reply was to fire off a dozen chemical projectiles into Israel one hour prior to the advent of 48 hour deadline. Israel's missile defence system fortunately was at the ready and miraculously intercepted all of them. Immediately the Israeli Defence Forces determined the facts and implemented their long held plan of last defence. Moments later three powerful nuclear missiles impacted the vast city of Damascus. Millions died and the entire city and all its myriads of weapon warehouses and factories were destroyed. The world reeled in shock and Iran, Turkey and the South Russian States quietly retreated from the world stage.

That was almost one year ago exactly and Max remembered well that day as he read in his Bible the prophecy in Isaiah 17:1 *"An oracle concerning Damascus. Behold, Damascus will cease to be a city and will become a heap of ruins."* [ESV] From the day Damascus had been established in about 2500 BC, some 4500 years ago, it had been a thriving city but now it was destroyed just like the prophet described. Remarkable how God always fulfils His Word regardless of time passed.

Following the Damascus bombing the world reaction was strangely muted. Few openly sympathised with Israel. Russia, however, loudly accused the United States. While Russia didn't have many personnel based in Damascus at its demise, it had supplied much of the high-tech military hardware and was somewhat embarrassed that it's much hyped missile defence system didn't detect a single incoming nuclear projectile. Russia's beef was that the USA was at fault because it had helped the Israeli's develop the undetectable missiles – she had acted irresponsibly. In reality it was the Israeli's themselves that had developed the incredible technology and sold it to the Americans. Never-the-less the USA had become the world villain and in the opinion of many had to now endure punishment for allowing the loss of millions of lives.

Eventually China, edged-on by Russia and strongly encouraged by the European Union, announced its long stated ambition to end the US dollar's status as the world's reserve currency. The replacement would be e-Dollars controlled by one single central bank to be located in the neutral territory of Switzerland. They claimed that since the vast majority of all transactions were now completed electronically; physical currencies should be a relic of the past. Because China now operated the largest economy internationally and governed the bulk of world trade an overwhelming majority of nations quickly agreed and signed the new e-Dollar reserve currency accord. Except for the United States who vowed to do everything humanly possible to fight it.

At stake with the USA was trillions of dollars in loans that had to be converted to e-Dollar with cold hard cash. They simply did not have the reserves. In addition they had for decades operated their international trade at a substantial deficit to its trading partners, made possible only because of the US dollar reserve status. The Federal Reserve simply issued more currency to balance the books. With that reserve currency status removed the USA had to pay all its trading partners in cold hard cash – namely e-Dollars. No payment – no imports!

Overnight the US economy descended into free-fall as domestic existence took precedence over all else. In one foul swoop China had eliminated the global power-house economy for, in its opinion, their meddling in international affairs. Max remembered reading about the 'Kings of the East' in Revelation 16. Perhaps this was the stirring of their beginnings. Not that it was the fulfilment of that chapter yet Max believed, because he hadn't heard anything about the Euphrates River being dried up. Max tucked away the term under the heading of "Watch for more to come."

With Israel's protector, USA, side-lined by its devastating internal economic woes many were ready to condemn the tiny nation. However its' protector rose from an extremely unlikely source – Saudi Arabia. While the Saudi's would never come right out and say it they were delighted that Israel had terminated the rising threat of their prickly neighbour, Iran. They quietly supported Israel while it negotiated its' way through the labyrinth of international consequences following its sacking of Damascus.

Unbeknown to most and certainly to Max, intense negotiations had been on-going for some months on the status of Jerusalem, the stated capital of Israel but also claimed by the so-named Palestinian people. That status also included the ownership of the Temple Mount area where the Jewish Nation desired to build its' third Temple but it also housed the Dome of the Rock and the Al-Aqsa Mosque claimed by many Muslins as the third most holy mosque in the world. However it transpired that view was predominantly held by Shia Muslims and as the Saudi's were Sunni this was far less a problem. The Saudi King had appointed Abdul El-Hashem to lead the negotiations and he had done so with great gusto and diligence. Abdul El-Hashem was born in Turkey, a Sunni Muslin who now lived in Qatar and was a close personal friend of the Saudi King. Abdul, now in his mid-forties, had risen in power not by his personal wealth but by his cunning ability to lead and influence those in authority. He counted as close friends more than two dozen prominent international leaders. Strangely it was also widely reported that he'd been killed in the Damascus nuclear bombing but obviously he was very much alive now. A dead man resurrected, one report claimed. Max recalled the scripture Revelation 13:12 *"One of the heads of the beast seemed to have had a fatal wound, but the fatal wound had been healed. The whole world was filled with wonder and followed the beast."* [NIV] Could it be, he wondered?

It was this Abdul that had concluded the successful agreement with Israel. The agreement provided for the return of a portion of the Temple Mount to Israel providing them with unfettered access and the right to build and worship within their sector. The agreement was to be a trial for seven years at which time it would be reviewed and possibly expanded as agreed at that time. He had named the document the 'El-Hashem Jerusalem Accord'. Endorsing parties to the agreement included some thirty-five countries including all the member states of the European Union, Russia, Great Britain, eleven neighbouring muslin states and, of course, Israel. The United States had been consulted but due to its 'domestic problems had not been accepted as a signatory.

Max was breathless as he read. This surely was the Man, the Agreement! He flicked open his Bible and read from Daniel 9:27 *"And he shall confirm the covenant with many for one week:"* [KJV Part of Verse]. Max knew the meaning of one week was a period of seven, meaning seven years. So who was the man that Daniel was talking about? The rest of the Daniel verse explained it further as Max read on, *"and in the midst of the week he shall cause the sacrifice and the oblation to cease, and for the overspreading of abominations he shall make it desolate, even until the consummation, and that determined shall be poured upon the desolate."* [KJV] The same person who confirms the seven year covenant, or agreement, with many is the same guy that's going to invade the temple three and a half years into it. "On that basis could this be it, Lord," Max asked, "Is this Abdul El-Hashem the Anti-Christ"? Max was encouraged to check things from the Word. He read what Jesus said in

Matthew 24, what Paul wrote in 2 Thessalonians and the references to 1260 days in Revelation. He didn't want to jump to conclusions so took the advice of Jesus – Watch. He decided he would do just that, if Abdul El-Hashem was 'the Man' then it would quickly become apparent.

The Internet immediately became alight with a myriad of doomsday preachers proclaiming the pending end of days as the Anti-Christ. This was followed by almost as many counter-preachers saying he certainly was not the Anti-Christ as the Rapture of the Saints must occur before the tribulation begins and the Anti-Christ was the one to bring the tribulation. Max wasn't sure on either count, preferring to wait and watch, although if his suspicions were correct then the pre-tribulation rapture preachers had it wrong. Max read 2 Thessalonians 2:3 again. *"Let no man deceive you by any means: for that day shall not come, except there come a falling away first, and that man of sin be revealed, the son of perdition;"* The revealing of the son of perdition was described in a similar era as the falling away and he'd already seen the beginning of falling.

The Israelis wasted no time at all and immediately began construction of The Temple of God on the land they'd been allocated. Max checked the information on the building and its progress and he was astounded as he read that the building of the front courtyard was being deferred as it encroached into an area claimed by the Muslins as a courtyard for their mosque. Max quickly checked the temple described by the Apostle John in Revelation 11:1-2 *"And there was given me a reed like unto a rod: and the angel stood, saying, Rise, and measure the temple of God, and the altar, and them that worship therein. But the court which is without the temple leave out, and measure it not; for it is given unto the Gentiles:"* [KJV] Max tucked the information away in his confirmations bag.

A few weeks later Max read a news report about a group of Arab activists that had been burnt to death in the city of Jerusalem that week. Apparently they'd been protesting against two men dressed like beggars who'd been prophesying doom outside the entrance to the Temple Mount for several weeks. In their efforts to deter them they'd taken up rocks and began heaving them towards the strange prophets. No sooner had they fired off the first rock than the whole group had been engulfed in a massive fireball. Max checked his Bible again and read in Revelation 11:3 *"And I will give power unto my two witnesses, and they shall prophesy a thousand two hundred and threescore days, clothed in sackcloth."* Then he read in verse 5 *"And if any man will hurt them, fire proceedeth out of their mouth, and devoureth their enemies:"* [KJV] Okay Max decided, all this is beginning to get a bit too coincidental, "I'll admit this must be the seven year tribulation period. The Lord's return is imminent".

Debate raged amongst various international ministries who had strongly held the belief in a pre-tribulation rapture. They claimed that any international events occurring couldn't possibly be the end-time tribulation period as the Bible was clear we could be kept from God's wrath and that we had not been appointed to wrath. Max agreed that the Bible was clear that we would be saved from God's wrath as stated by the Apostle Paul in Romans 5:9. *"Since, therefore, we have now been justified by his blood, much more shall we be saved by him from the wrath of God."* [ESV] However Max understood there was a vast difference between man's tribulation and God's wrath.

Max read where Jesus spoke about tribulation in Mark 14:19-20 *"For in those days there will be such tribulation as has not been from the beginning of the creation that God created until now, and never will be. And if the Lord had not cut short the days, no human being would be saved. But for the sake of the elect, whom he chose, he shortened the days."* [ESV] But who was this elect or who are the chosen ones? Many preachers dismiss this verse as saying that it referred to Israel and that God needed to bring tribulation to Israel to refine them so that the chosen may become obvious. Perhaps, Max wondered, but then he read in Revelation 12:17 speaking about the Anti-Christ *"Then the dragon became furious with the woman and went off to make war on the rest of her offspring, on those who keep the commandments of God and hold to the testimony of Jesus."* [ESV] Max knew enough to understand that the dragon was the Anti-Christ controlled by the devil and the woman was Israel but that those who hold the testimony of Jesus were definitely the Church. At some point there is coming tribulation inspired by the Anti-Christ and that is coming on the Church too. The difference was, Max believed, that this was wrath of man, inspired by the devil, and wasn't God's wrath. The church throughout its' history had been subject to man's wrath so why should the current day Church be shielded from it. Particularly so, Max reckoned, taking into account the current luke-warm, half-hearted condition of many Christians. Max was satisfied that 'yes' this guy was definitely the long anticipated Anti-Christ and was not to be trusted.

The weeks rolled on accumulating into a year and very little more seemed to occur, or so it appeared to Max. If this was the time of tribulation then it wasn't unbearable so far. Generally most countries had accepted the new e-Dollars and the USA was still deeply mired in economic turmoil but the earth was still rotating and the sun even rose each morning. Max had always been a fan of electronic banking so the switch by New Zealand to a cashless society hadn't impacted his life to any extent. "These new e-Dollars don't buy any more than the old dollars!" Max protested to his family who'd gathered in Timaru for a festive Christmas celebration. "Just wait until you have to get a chip to be able to access them," Austin warned. Austin had meant it as a joke but the ensuing laughter wasn't boisterous as the White family knew well the implications of such an event. Max felt a wrench in his heart as he momentarily pondered the future.

What delighted Max the most was the massive outpouring of the Holy Spirit that had swept across the nation and also, he had heard, around the world. It had begun in the youth outside the mainstream ministries. Hundreds of young people up and down the country were regularly meeting together, not for games or social engagement, but just to praise Jesus and give glory to the Father. The presence of the Holy Spirit indescribable, His Power and peace filling every person present to the max.

The movement had morphed out of the traditional Wednesday night youth gatherings where entertainment in a Godly environment was the emphasis. For these young people, that wasn't enough, they wanted to experience this God they'd been told about. They demanded their leaders teach them how to worship by entering through the Spirit into the presence of the living God. They demanded to know what it really meant to be redeemed and transformed by the blood of Jesus. As a result the Holy Spirit found conditions He could thrive in and the effect was immediate and miraculous. Because these young believers were not steeped in years of religious traditions or the mainstream rigid comprehension of God's Word the raw power of God Almighty throbbed in their hearts. Healing the sick was common place, dead were raised to life, spirits of depression and anxiety were cast out.

Words of knowledge became a massive evangelistic tool that the Holy Spirit used to great effect in everyday settings.

Young people under the power of the Spirit of God would receive words of knowledge about strangers they had never met. In shopping malls and supermarkets walking up to unknown persons asking them pertinent questions only that person could have known – how was their sick mother, what they did when they couldn't sleep at 3am, and so forth. The openings these questions evoked was incredible as they explained that it was the Holy Spirit as they continued to recount where the person lived the names of their children, brothers and sisters. Hundreds were coming to the Lord Jesus daily.

The mainstream churches, however, weren't so excited; they had programs and systems in place and didn't want these young people disrupting their one hour and twenty minute services. For this reason they 'encouraged' them to do their type of church on a Wednesday evening or in some cases on a Sunday evening. The youth didn't care; they took any opportunity they were offered to praise the Father and rejoiced as souls were being saved.

Max, despite his age and uncertainty about their choice of music, loved it. It was the praise and worship that made it for him and he longed to soak up the feeling of standing in the presence of the Father, pouring out his worship, made possible by the blood of Jesus. Max also noticed that many others his age and younger had joined the Wednesday and Sunday gatherings abandoning the traditional morning services. He also saw that the move of the Holy Spirit was infecting all those that attended. The attendance at the meetings swelled to thousands and frequently these gatherings went on for two or three hours. This was the Church that was clearly speaking the Gospel of the Kingdom. Max reflected on the verse in Matthew 24:14 *"And this gospel of the kingdom shall be preached in all the world for a witness unto all nations; and then shall the end come."* [KJV] The whole world certainly was taking notice.

Meantime, outside the Church, the devil was also stirring. The world press were besotted by the flamboyant Mr Abdul El-Hashem. He had brought peace to the Middle East, something which had eluded many great peacemakers for the past seventy plus years. Using this freely provided platform Abdul expounded on his program to transform the world so that the rights of every citizen could be truly realised. Religion was the fundamental cause of most wars for as far back as history records, he claimed. Ideology was the other, his manifesto continued. There should be no more capitalism, communism or fascism. Neither religion nor ideology should take precedent. If world peace is to be achieved then there must be an urgent melding of the two. He urged all governments and religious institutions to come together to create this unique, once in a lifetime opportunity, of absolute peace. Imagine no more war or destruction, ever, he preached.

Abdul's words were very persuasive and resonated with the vast majority of the citizens of the earth. Many however were sceptical but their voices were quickly drowned out by a world press single minded in its endeavour to promote this captivating man and his unique manifesto. Behind the scenes Mr El-Hashem became very busy. He set up an army of ardent spellbound followers whose sole determination was to help create a path to implement his ideas. El-Hashem had chosen his team well and many were bureaucrats from the United Nations, top ranking officials who had strong connections to their various national governments. Max was stunned at how quickly his message was filtering through to the world governments quick to jump on the bandwagon of the popular press message of the moment.

In addition to his work at the UN, Abdul El-Hashem had also met with the Pope and connected into his organisation for the promotion of one world religion under the banner – we all serve the one God. Allah, Yahweh, Jesus, Buddha, Shiva, Krishna or Lakshmi were just a different path one could take to get to heaven – or so he preached. The Pope had been actively working on just such an arrangement for the past twenty plus years and had strong commitments from the majority of Muslim groups, many mainstream Christian organisations and several of the well-known tele-evangelists. The Pope and the leaders of these religious groups, while not necessarily backing El-Hashem directly, embraced his manifesto with gusto. They used every opportunity to tap into the theme of the combined world press to urge all people, regardless of their pathway to heaven, to show love and demonstrate tolerance towards all mankind.

Abdul El-Hashem's next move was to lobby the UN to establish an international structure to allow the operation of his all-inclusive manifesto and take advantage of the seemingly spontaneous international acceptance of it. The new structure which he was determined would not be called a government but 'The Manticore' – A Persian legendary creature which had the body of a red lion with wings, a human head with three rows of sharp teeth and prominent horns, bat-like wings, a trumpet-like voice and a tail of a scorpion. He left out the description that the mythical Manticore also shot venomous spines from its tail to paralyze or kill its victims. His reasoning, which went unquestioned, was that since most nations identified with animals as national symbols (the Eagle in the USA, the Bear in Russia) this combination animal would encapsulate the fact of unification. He proposed that he would be the interim head of the Manticore to oversee its implementation. Max looked up Revelation 13:2 *"And the beast that I saw was like a leopard; its feet were like a bear's, and its mouth was like a lion's mouth."* [ESV – part of verse] Max marvelled at the description of Scripture that so adeptly described this new organisation.

The new organisation would require a source of income and he proposed a financial transaction tax. This could be easily managed by the new Swiss central bank with the advent of the new e-Dollars. The cost per transaction would be very small at less than 0.01% per transaction (one cent per every one hundred e-dollars). Economist had calculated that on a volume of over three trillion e-Dollars of global transactions per day this would result in revenue of about fifty billion e-Dollars annually for the new Manticore organisation. Mr El-Hashem confirmed that would be enough since they would only be providing oversight not services.

Thus the fledgling Manticore was established, exceptionally well-funded and with a charismatic Mr Abdul El-Hashem as its head. Operating under the authority of the UN all governments around the globe were encouraged to pledge their support to the Manticore and allow its officials to implement humanitarian projects within their countries and regions in order to obtain the stated goal of world peace. The uptake, while cautious initially, quickly became an avalanche as the majority of the worlds 197 independent nations conceded their ultimate authority to the Manticore. The organisation of united religions headed by none other than the Pope himself quickly pledged its' support and cooperation to work strongly with the Manticore. Finally world peace was within the grasp of mankind and war would now be but a distant memory.

Abdul El-Hashem divided the world up into ten regions and sought nominations from talented and loyal individuals to head up each region. Elections were held in each region by electronic voting to select the popular choice for the position of Regional

Pacifier. Each Pacifier would hold the office of President of The Manticore for a period of one month on a rotating basis. Following the elections the Pacifiers would vote for one of their own to be appointed to the permanent position of Commandant – that of overall responsibility of the Manticore. Abdul El-Hashem, keen to be duly appointed by the people, put his name forward for the Middle East region. Unfortunately two of the regions, one in North Africa and the other in Central Asia could not agree on the final outcome of the vote and various groups threatened to take up arms against the others. This flew in the face of everything the Manticore stood for so Abdul El-Hashem stepped in assuming the position of Pacifier for those areas until the tensions subsided and fresh elections could be held sometime in the future. Once the results of the remaining eight other elections were final the Pacifiers voted to select the Commandant and much to the delight of the press and the surprise of nobody, Abdul El-Hashem was elected unopposed.

Max and many of his friends followed all these international events keenly. What amazed them the most was the complete accuracy of the Bible prophecies. The events of the past few years were straight from the pages of Revelation, even to the naming of the organisation after a frightening beast. Similarly with the ten regions, or ten kings, that reigned for one month and that El-Hashem had taken control of a total of three of these regions, just as the Book said he would. Max read Revelation 17:12 *""The ten horns which you saw are ten kings who have not yet received a kingdom, but they receive authority as kings with the beast for one hour.*" [KJV] These ten regional Pacifiers certainly had been given authority as if they were kings of their regions but they did not actually have any kind of kingdom, just an allocated one. Also their one month rotating leadership was for a short period, as in one hour. Incredible, Max exclaimed.

The rise of Abdul El-Hashem, from a complete nobody to the head of all the worlds' governments and religions, had taken only three years. The power centralised in his group was mind-blowing as was the ease with which he'd achieved it. Given his reported death and regaining of life story many held him to be a Messiah type figure, the return of Jesus some claimed and others believed he was the twelfth Imam, The Mahdi. Max new full well this was the Anti-Christ. Unfortunately a large number of Christians disagreed with Max as they strongly held the belief that the rapture of the saints would occur before the Anti-Christ appeared. Besides, when he appears there would be great tribulation, they claimed. They saw no reason to change and went about church as normal, certain that if they had Jesus in their lives they would live a fully blessed life. By contrast the youth Spirit empowered movement multiplied in strength and the Lord added to them daily those that were to be saved.

It had taken three and a half years but finally the new temple in Jerusalem was completed and the Red Heifers as prescribed by the Law of Moses to sanctify the temple were finally available, having been grown and groomed in strict accordance with the Law. The Levite Priests were prepared, dressed in their strict priestly garments and animal sacrifices were set to begin. A Red Heifer in accordance with Numbers 19 was to be slaughtered outside the camp, or in this case, the city, and burnt. Its blood was to be kept and used to cleanse the temple, making it holy and acceptable to offer burnt offerings to the Lord.

Much was publicized about the temple dedication and as many Israelis as possible were encouraged to come to Jerusalem and celebrate the dedication. Unfortunately, it was only the devout orthodox Jews who attended in large numbers along with thousands of animal-rights protestors from all around the globe. The slaughter of any animals whether part of religious law or not was inhumane in this day and age and must not be allowed to proceed, they claimed.

The Red Heifer ritual began with it being ceremonially led outside the city limits and upon reaching the allotted field was immediately slaughtered and its blood captured in a large stone jar. The Israeli police had done a great job of keeping the crowds at bay but once the news of the slaughter was repeat broadcast on social media and every possible television channel around the world, all hell broke loose. The thousands of protestors rushed the Israeli police protecting the newly dedicated temple. Firing into the air at first the police were quickly overwhelmed and survival instinct erupted as some saw their colleagues being dragged off, stomped on and hurled over the edge of the temple mount walls. The situation was out of control on all fronts but the police held the superior fire-power and after several hours eventually regained control. The cost had been horrific; 15 Israeli police dead and many more severely wounded, but on the protestors side the count was 123 dead and hundreds more, gravely injured.

The Israeli government had had enough and called in the IDF (Israeli Defence Forces) who stood guard day and night in large numbers, dispersing the crowds anytime a small group of protestors formed. The temple priests were allowed to continue with their God ordained sacrifices on a daily basis. Unfortunately the damage was done and massive rallies were held in Tel-Aviv and many major cities around the world. The crowds, angry at the death of so many innocent animals, and of course some of their zealous members, raved on to anyone and everyone possible. Riots broke out in several cities causing millions of e-Dollars in damages.

Finally El-Hashem had had enough; the Manticore could not allow the destruction of its core principle – peace. Dissension will not be tolerated. Freedom of religion was allowed only within the rights as dictated by the leader of the Manticore's URO (United Religions Organisation). The Pope delivered his group's consensus findings to El-Hashem who then declared they both would be travelling to Israel and he would make an announcement personally from the courtyard of the new temple. His statement would be delivered on the eve of the following Sabbath; Friday evening about 5.30pm Jerusalem time. Max's interest soared as he heard the date on the evening news. He checked back to when the El-Hashem Jerusalem Accord was signed and it was about three and a half years but how many days exactly? Max counted them carefully – three and a half years. He read the verse in Daniel 9:27 again *"And he shall make a strong covenant with many for one week, and for half of the week he shall put an end to sacrifice and offering."* [ESV] Since Max knew the 'week' meant seven years, the middle of the 'week' was three and a half years. "We can expect fireworks this weekend," Max announced to Hazel that night. "Fireworks could prove a slight understatement if your predictions prove correct," Hazel answered wryly.

*(**Disclaimer;** All characters mentioned in this chapter particularly are fictitious and any resemblance of persons past or present is purely coincidental. The events, however, are loosely based on the reality of Bible prophecy.)*

*"Choose the bread of Life
or you are toast"*

Chapter 14
The Harpazo of the Saints

El-Hashem and his entourage arrived in Tel Aviv, Israel, and his motorcade paraded the seventy kilometres up to Jerusalem with much fanfare. A full legion of 1000 heavily armed Manticore protection squad accompanied the convoy and the world's press streamed the entire event live, desperate to capture every second of a potential unfolding drama. As the motorcade approached the Manticore troops quickly relieved the Israeli IDF as agreed and assumed an overwhelming show of force around the small Jewish temple standing to the East of the Temple Mount on Mount Moriah, opposite the Mount of Olives. The religious significance of the location was plain for all to see. Three gleaming limousines pulled up directly outside the temple steps and El-Hashem alighted from one, the Pope from another and an unnamed dignitary from the third. All three slowly climbed the steps to the temple forecourt in unison and approached the waiting temple priests. More than fifty Levitical priests had aligned themselves arm-in-arm blocking the entrance to the sacred alters and the holy tabernacle beyond.

The temple priests stood their ground as did El-Hashem and the Pope. The unnamed and unknown dignitary took two steps forward and proclaimed in a voice, earth-shatteringly clear and loud, "Make way for People's Man – In the name of God." The priests didn't budge but chanted back in unison Yahweh is our God. The unnamed man repeated his command twice more with the same priestly result. "I will show you who is god," he proclaimed loudly, "Unless you move out of the way let fire consume you, immediately." Barely had the words left his lips than a massive fireball descended from the sky and engulfed the protesting priests. Ignoring the screaming humanity being consumed by the fire in front of him the man walked forward two paces and flippantly swept the burning mass aside, clearing the way with a wave of his hand. He then stepped aside and majestically beckoned to El-Hashem to come forward and issue his decree.

The thronging crowds, the world's press and the millions watching around the world stood in shock and awe at what they'd just witnessed. The commentators scrambled to identify the unknown dignitary with these god-like powers. It was none other than El-Hashem's deputy who simply went by the title Haremakhet. Apparently so named after the Egyptian High Priest of Amun, who was a renowned holy man from about 600 BC. Max already had his Bible out and was reading in Revelation

13:11-13 *"Then I saw another beast rising out of the earth. It had two horns like a lamb and it spoke like a dragon. It exercises all the authority of the first beast in its presence, and makes the earth and its inhabitants worship the first beast, whose mortal wound was healed. It performs great signs, even making fire come down from heaven to earth in front of people,"* [ESV]. This is it Max shouted to anyone who would listen, but he was quickly distracted by the events being relayed through his TV screen.

El-Hashem marched right past the sacred alters, flung open the curtain door of the Holy Tabernacle and stood in the middle of the small room known as the 'Holy of Holies.' Via his pre-wired sound system he declared he had an entirely new message to the world, so listen up. "I am the long awaited Messiah. I am bringing peace to the earth and from this moment am in complete control of all things. There would be no more animal sacrifices in this temple as it was now the world headquarters of the Manticore. I, Haremakhet and the Pope will be permanently stationed in Jerusalem. Right at this moment Manticore troops are taking control of all Israeli Government facilities as you can hear from the helicopters overhead." The TV cameras immediately panned in unison towards the Israeli Knesset. The sky was darkened with hundreds of helicopters streaming in from the Mediterranean Coast and heavily armed troops could be seen abseiling down to the Knesset and other important government buildings. The IDF, momentarily distracted by being rightly focused on the spectacular events unfolding at the temple were caught completely unawares and never fired a shot. El-Hashem continued on for a further ten minutes dictating the facts as he saw them, maintaining he had absolute authority and was, in fact, god incarnate.

Max read a little more in Revelation 13, this time verses 2-6. *"And to it the dragon gave his power and his throne and great authority. One of its heads seemed to have a mortal wound, but its mortal wound was healed, and the whole earth marvelled as they followed the beast. And they worshiped the dragon, for he had given his authority to the beast, and they worshiped the beast, saying, "Who is like the beast, and who can fight against it?"*

And the beast was given a mouth uttering haughty and blasphemous words, and it was allowed to exercise authority for forty-two months. It opened its mouth to utter blasphemies against God, blaspheming his name and his dwelling, that is, those who dwell in heaven." [ESV] How incredibly accurate Max marvelled. He was certainly spewing haughty and blasphemous words. This man was no Messiah.

Max also recalled what Jesus had spoken in Matthew 24:15-21 *""So when you see the abomination of desolation spoken of by the prophet Daniel, standing in the holy place (let the reader understand), then let those who are in Judea flee to the mountains. Let the one who is on the housetop not go down to take what is in his house, and let the one who is in the field not turn back to take his cloak. And alas for women who are pregnant and for those who are nursing infants in those days! Pray that your flight may not be in winter or on a Sabbath. For then there will be great tribulation, such as has not been from the beginning of the world until now, no, and never will be."* [ESV] Max understood that only the priests were ever allowed into the Holy Place in accordance with God's Law and then only when they had been rigorously cleansed and sanctified. Anything else entering that place is rightly considered an abomination. El-Hashem was most certainly standing blatantly and defiantly in the most holy place, Max observed. Everything was revealed now, this unholy trio were a counterfeit trinity out to deceive every possible human that this was the real Messiah returned. Obey or be killed. Max prayed for many hours that night.

Unsurprisingly, the vast majority of the world governments weren't overly impressed to see an independent nation, even if it was just Israel, overrun so effortlessly. Mass protests erupted against the Manticore. Even if he was the Messiah he had been given no authority to assume the government of a sovereign state. El-Hashem, however, was prepared and immediately decreed that effective immediately no Government, corporation or individual would be able to access their e-Dollars by any means unless they first received a tiny electronic chip. This chip which was to be specific to every individual and must be implanted in either their right hand or on the forehead to fully identify a specific individual at any time. This chip would be loaded with all the individuals' details including health, education and tax information. No access to any service or many locations would be granted without it.

Incredible planning had obviously foregone the announcement as was quickly discovered. Every town and city around the world miraculously found they had an abundant supply of chips. The chips were about the size of a grain of rice, and since every individual's details were already available via cloud computer servers this could be easily downloaded onto the chip in seconds before it was inserted. Max read in Revelation 13:16-17, *"Also it causes all, both small and great, both rich and poor, both free and slave, to be marked on the right hand or the forehead, so that no one can buy or sell unless he has the mark, that is, the name of the beast or the number of its name."* [ESV] Max phoned Austin, Levi and Maxine and told them to get down to Timaru with their families immediately as times were going to get real tough. Max reckoned it would be less stressful for everyone if the whole family stayed together. Miraculously they all managed to get flights before the chip's ban took full effect.

The Manticore was now in complete control throughout the world. By simply controlling the flow of e-Dollars all dissent rapidly evaporated. Not a dissenting voice was heard, in public at least. The Pope encouraged all believers - Christian, Muslins or Jews to follow their messiah. Failure to do so would only bring starvation and death. This was God's way to bring order to the world, he exhorted.

The two raggedly dressed prophets who had been wandering the streets of Jerusalem for the past three and a half years were ordered shot. El-Hashem declared there would be no tolerance for negative voices and death was the only way to silence them. Once dead he ordered their bodies to remain in the streets and that news organisation broadcast their demise continuously as a warning to others. For three days the people of the planet had the grizzly sight beamed into their living rooms at frequent intervals. After three days, however, the broadcast stopped abruptly. No official explanation was provided but word soon broke that the two beggars, after lying there for three days, had risen to their feet, walked around for a short time then flew off to the heavens. Plenty of ridicule and sarcasm was attached to the report but Max knew the prophecy about the two witnesses well. Revelation 11:7-12 *"And when they have finished their testimony, the beast that rises from the bottomless pit will make war on them and conquer them and kill them, and their dead bodies will lie in the street of the great city that symbolically is called Sodom and Egypt, where their Lord was crucified. For three and a half days some from the peoples and tribes and languages and nations will gaze at their dead bodies and refuse to let them be placed in a tomb, and those who dwell on the earth will rejoice over them and make merry and exchange presents, because these two prophets had been a torment to those who dwell on the earth. But after the three and a half days a breath of life from God entered them, and they stood up on their feet, and great fear fell on those who saw them. Then they heard a loud voice from heaven saying to them, "Come up here!" And they went up to heaven in a cloud, and their enemies watched them."* [ESV]

Haremakhet, on the other hand, was intent on demonstrating the confirmation of the revelation of the king of the world. He excelled in extraordinary signs and wonders. Calling down fireballs was his personal favourite; it seemed, given its frequent use. He built a robotic replica of the Manticore and through some clever computer programming he'd created a form of artificial intelligence which made the replica appeared to have a life of its own. Its primary function was to monitor all financial activity simultaneously, which it handled with ease regardless of its location, connections or the time of day. Its symbol was 666 and every person throughout the world receiving the chip was required to pledge allegiance to the Manticore by physically bowing down to its image. Once an acceptable allegiance was made it was video recorded and added to the public report. Privacy was no longer relevant as the Manticore was the controller of everything anyway. Max understood the truth as he read Revelation 13:15-18, *"And it was allowed to give breath to the image of the beast, so that the image of the beast might even speak and might cause those who would not worship the image of the beast to be slain. Also it causes all, both small and great, both rich and poor, both free and slave, to be marked on the right hand or the forehead, so that no one can buy or sell unless he has the mark, that is, the name of the beast or the number of its name. This calls for wisdom: let the one who has understanding calculate the number of the beast, for it is the number of a man, and his number is 666."* [ESV]

The power of the Manticore was now complete. By economic stealth they had obtained control over the economies and governments of every nation on earth. Dissenting voices could not be tolerated and the chosen method to silence those voices was death. Jerusalem was the epicentre of everything. El-Hashem, Haremakhet and the Pope each severally and jointly ruled from their hastily built, lush private offices in the now disused Jewish temple.

Mass riots broke out on the streets of Jerusalem. These were led by the religious Jews, devastated to see their new temple so quickly desecrated but also strongly supported by the Jewish population stunned at their instant loss of democracy. The result was a bloodbath. The Manticore troops were ordered to meet all dissension with direct gunfire – no exceptions. There could be no place for any rebellious voice anywhere throughout the land of Israel and the soldiers of the Manticore scoured the land searching for any religious Jews who refused allegiance. Thousands were found and slaughtered where they stood. Revelation 13:7 *"Also it was allowed to make war on the saints and to conquer them."* [ESV]

Neighbouring Jordan, however, rode a fine line between acceptance of the Manticore and help for its distressed neighbour. They quietly offered temporary asylum to any person of Jewish descent who wished to take refuge in the ancient remains of Petra and its surrounding canyons. Hidden from sight more than a million fled and took sanctuary in the region. Jordan simply claimed these were displaced Palestinians seeking to distinguish their difference from the Jews in order to escape their fate. Strangely, the Manticore accepted their explanation and left Jordan alone. Max read the account of this in Matthew 24:15-16, *"So when you see the abomination of desolation spoken of by the prophet Daniel, standing in the holy place (let the reader understand), then let those who are in Judea flee to the mountains."* [ESV]

In addition to the very vocal outcry from the religious Jews in Israel, many strong believers in Jesus around the world joined the chorus and expressed their ardent opposition to the Manticore and the fake messiah. Unfortunately, vast numbers of Christians did not. They saw the miraculous signs of Haremakhet and heard the words of El-Hashem and asked, "Will Jesus do more signs than these when he comes?" This was the principal message from the Pope who stood strongly by the side of the other two declaring; "This is God's time on His earth. Regardless if you are Muslim, Jew or Christian now is the time to accept his rule or be slain. Revelation 13:8, *"and all who dwell on earth will worship it, everyone whose name has not been written before the foundation of the world in the book of life of the Lamb who was slain."* [ESV]

The true believers in Jesus, those that really knew Jesus, clearly saw the truth. Max and his family were firmly in that camp as he remembered the experiences from his life; it was all about knowing Jesus in an experiential way, not just the understanding of him intellectually. Unfortunately, many Christians had been told that either the rapture was going to come before the Anti-Christ was revealed or that the Church was going to influence governments to such an extent that they would become one and the same. Since the rapture had not come then these saw the position of the Pope and numerous other Christians close to him as a clear sign of the fulfilment of their understanding. Many intellectual Pastors who had long ago discarded genuine reading of their Bibles strongly preached the theme that now was the time when the Church was to take over the governments of this world and rule with the messiah.

The ones that had come along to church all those years just to get recharged and re-blessed by their giving God had quickly fallen in line. They of course still did church but only under the official sanctions of the Manticore. The teaching of the churches remained the same, just ask Jesus, (the now living messiah,) into your life and you'll live a full and gratifying life. Indeed, all those in these officially sanctioned churches continued with a plentiful life. They paid their allegiance regularly to the Manticore and in return received the full protection of the law.

Max and his family, however, saw no part in such a system and stopped attending. He quickly heard from many others who felt the same and they met together almost daily wherever they could to pray and worship the Lord. The move of the Holy Spirit during these times was astounding. The raw power of God ebbed and flowed through the service like the surf rolling up the shoreline. Healings were abundant as were words of knowledge. They knew exactly who to trust and what the next attack against them would be.

Timaru, well down in the lower half of New Zealand, wasn't exactly an extreme hotbed of Manticore activity but its presence was there and great care had to be taken. The Manticore once it had silenced all dissent in Israel had issued a new order stating that only officially sanctioned religious gatherings were allowed. The decree stated that the Manticore was the order and all worship was to be directed to it. God was no longer mysterious or hidden, he had now been revealed within the Manticore. Whatever your impression of god was previously, – Allah, Jesus, Yahweh, Buddha etc. – there was only one god now and only single worship is allowed. The penalty for non-observance was death. Most religions quickly fell in line with the edict but many true Christians worldwide did not. The Manticore quickly set to its task to quell rebellion and dispatched its troops to known hot-spots, hopeful that an example made of some would bring the remainder into line. Max had expected this as he'd read the verse in Revelation 12:17, "*Then the dragon became furious with the woman and went off to make war on the rest of her offspring, on those who keep the commandments of God and hold to the testimony of Jesus.*" [ESV] Max knew the woman referred to Israel and he also knew that he and his family definitely were among the ones who held to the testimony of Jesus.

Max shuddered as he heard the report. "Dear God," he cried, "Please provide for all those faithful to you." Max felt the calming power of the Holy Spirit within him and he knew that whatever the immediate outcome the long-term result was going to be just fine. Fortunately, Timaru saw little of the religious death squads but it would be fair to say that life was tough for the true Christian believers. Strangely the majority of this came not from the local authorities but from their so-called fellow Christians. People whom Max and his family had gone to church with for years would phone Max, begging him to save his life and return to the official church. When Max politely refused the abuse ran hot. Max was informed in no uncertain terms that his actions would bring disgrace on their gatherings and cause massive loss of life. Curses rained freely when Max in return stated that the serious disgrace would come for them when they were not found written in the Book of Life at the final judgement because they had pledged allegiance to the Anti-Christ.

Chapter 14
The Harpazo of the Saints

The stage had been set and while Max and his family kept to themselves the animosity of the cursers increased to fever pitch. Loud music was set up outside his house to prevent sleep in the household. Fortunately, this action was short lived thanks to the active and immediate complaints of Max's neighbours. Paint bombs and bricks were thrown at the house and before long it was dangerous for anyone to venture far outside. Even a trip to the clothesline was a combat mission.

Food quickly became an issue for the extended White family but somehow there was always enough to eat. Maybe not to the plentiful quantities the family was accustomed to but more than enough to adequately sustain life. Gathering with the other believers became impossible but the White family with little else to fill their day spent hours in prayer and praise and worship to their Lord and Saviour – Jesus Christ. The atmosphere within was one of celebration, the day of the Lord was at hand.

A few days passed when Max received a note, ironically tied to a brick tossed through a window. It was from his old friend Sam who lived on a small acreage at the other end of town. Sam gave the brick with the note attached to a secular worker who'd been doing some work for him that day as a favour. The worker enthusiastically embraced the task and quickly delivered it with gusto, happy in the knowledge his public stance was clear – he too distained those Christians. Austin was first to notice the note and read it allowed for all to hear.

Sam had numerous outbuildings on his land and he was inviting the entire White family to come and hold out in one of them. They'd be safer there than where they were and besides he had a garden and some animals for food.

Following the notes instructions the White family quickly packed a few belongings, convinced they were leaving the family home for the last time. Under the cover of darkness they scrambled over a fence in the back yard and scurried down a walking track toward a nearby children's playground. Max, Hazel, Austin with his wife and two children, Levi with his wife and three children, Maxine with her husband and two children all sat quietly in the shadows near the edge of the park. The last of the available food had been given to the children to help them remain as content as possible under the circumstances. None of the adults however felt like eating, this was a very dangerous mission. If one thug had discovered the little Christian group huddled in the park that night the end would certainly be swift and final. Most of the city residents were just concerned with getting on with their lives but mob rule prevailed and frequently if one wasn't seen to protest against the Christians they could quickly be branded as one and receive the same fate.

After what seemed like an eternity, a large van pulled into the park entrance and flashed its lights twice. Austin ventured out to ensure the way was safe while the family remained concealed. He needn't have bothered as Sam leapt from his van and called out Max's name as if he was attending a Sunday picnic. Not keen of a further summons the White family raced from the bushes and dove into the van on mass. "What's the panic?" Sam asked. Before Maxine could sarcastically answer, "Darrrr" Sam continued. "You know I asked the Lord to make this mission invisible to everyone but Him and he's done exactly that." Max noticed a couple walking their dog on the other side of the street and despite the commotion of fifteen people frantically scrambling into a van they hadn't even turned a casual glance their way. "Praise the Lord!" Max exclaimed.

Upon reaching Sam's compound the Whites were met by close to one hundred others that Sam had brought together on his little farm. The living was communal but amazingly everyone had their personal space and the Whites were quickly welcomed and escorted to their private quarters. The Lord was thanked for their safe recovery and the food was blessed. Someone had made a large pot of lamb stew over the open fire which the White adults devoured with gusto as their anxieties rapidly evaporated. For the first night in weeks the family slept soundly.

The days at Sam's village, as it quickly became known, soon became routine. Gathering and cooking food was the primary task and each took turns. Where all the food came from nobody knew. Some days there'd be a few sheep in the field or additional hens in the coop. The group woke one morning to find half a dozen milking cows wandering down the driveway, despite the road gate being chained shut. Boxes of fruit and vegetables appeared at the gate from unknown donors. The verse in Hebrews 13:5 was quoted often, *"Keep your life free from love of money, and be content with what you have, for he has said, "I will never leave you nor forsake you."* [ESV] Strangely, despite the large number of people living at the farm and the fact that each day more arrived, the authorities left the place alone. The occasional abuse was heard but mostly it was as if the place was shrouded in an invisible bubble.

Most days began with a time of personal and collective prayer followed by a praise and worship time. The worship, Max noticed, was very intense and very personal. Each soul present, truly enjoying the presence of God, worshiping Him in spirit and truth. Afternoons were a time for a Bible study and various topics were shared but most encouraged the group to remain faithful until the end. The collective echo was "Come Lord Jesus."

It was during one of these studies that the Feasts of the LORD were discussed. Passover was understood clearly as fulfilled when Jesus died on the cross on the actual day as the redemptive lamb. The feast of Unleavened Bread was fulfilled when He lay in the tomb and the First Fruits when He rose from the dead on the first day of the week. Pentecost was fulfilled when the Holy Spirit was poured out, also on the exact day.

The fall feasts, so named because they come in the autumn of the Jewish year, are all yet to be fulfilled. The very next one is the Feast of Trumpets. The clear leading of the Holy Spirit was that the fulfilling of the Feast of Trumpets would be at the time of the rapture or the Harpazo of the Saints as it calls it in 1 Thessalonians 4:17 *"Then we who are alive, who are left, will be caught up together with them in the clouds to meet the Lord in the air, and so we will always be with the Lord."* [ESV] Max knew that the original Greek word translated caught up was 'Harpazo'. The Apostle Paul talks about the last trump and at the celebrated Feast of Trumpets one hundred trumpet blasts are made but always the last blast is the longest and loudest.

The little gathering was excited to talk of the clear approach of the pending day. "But we already know the day that feast falls on," Someone asked, "and were told that no one knows that day or hour?" Another however quickly explained that we may know the month but in what year? "Nobody knows the year, but we certainly know it's close."

The September Feast of Trumpets date was much anticipated but, much to the disappointment of all, it passed without event. The gathering, however, strengthened themselves in the Lord and determined to make the year that followed one of desperately seeking the Lord in true repentance so that each one would be ready without one spot or wrinkle. The praise and worship times were intense and very powerful, even the young children present were fully caught up in the glory of the Lord. The joy of each person dialled to the maximum. The presence of the Holy Spirit was such that it could almost be felt. Max believed he was witnessing the fact of Revelation 3:4, *"The bride has made herself ready"* [ESV]

It had been almost two years now since the Manticore had taken over and while the news reaching Sam's village was sparse, enough got through to paint a terrible picture of world events under its control. Millions and millions of Christians around the world had been systematically slaughtered, particularly in the United States. New edicts to eliminate any potential challenge to the power of the Manticore were issued almost daily and all who challenged them were swiftly dealt to. "If this is the time of tribulation that Jesus spoke of in Mark," Hazel declared to the group one afternoon, "I'd sure hate to be on earth when God's pours out His wrath." Mark 13:19 *"For in those days there will be such tribulation as has not been from the beginning of the creation that God created until now, and never will be."* [ESV] "Yes, imagine that's just what man can do," Sam answered. "God's wrath is clearly explained when the angels are told to go and pour out God's wrath in Revelation 16. That will be truly frightening." *"Then I heard a loud voice from the temple telling the seven angels, "Go and pour out on the earth the seven bowls of the wrath of God."* [ESV]

Despite all this, the gospel of the Kingdom of redemption through the blood of Jesus Christ was widely proclaimed. Somehow the true gospel of Jesus filtered through. Many in the mainstream churches saw the light and broke ranks, declaring that Jesus is the only way to eternal salvation. Most of these were quickly 'terminated' as a reminder to others, but still they came. Many unbelievers, too, gave their lives to Jesus.

Max's sons Austin and Levi, along with several others from Sam's village, frequently made the dangerous trek into the local shopping areas primarily to witness to souls in distress, bringing many to the Lord. In addition, they learned that several groups similar to Sam's had sprung around the area but that the local authorities were becoming increasingly concerned. A raid was planned when sufficient troops were eventually allocated to the area. Much prayer was lifted from Sam's village to foil the plans of the devil and provide protection to those who truly loved Jesus.

It was new moon in early September and at dusk of that day the young men returned from town with a report they'd just seen a convoy of blue military trucks heading out towards the river on the other side of the city. Everyone knew there was a large camp out there. What was also clear was that once that was eliminated then Sam's village would be next. It was a very sober group that stood before the Lord that evening, crying out for their brothers and sisters by the river and for their own protection. With the prayer session over most quickly retired to their sleeping quarters but Max decided to sit out under the stars to linger in the presence of the Lord. For all of his eighty years the Holy Spirit had been faithful to him and Max never had tired of it. Soaking in Him was a favourite pastime. Besides, the Feast of Trumpets was approaching, with the onset of the new moon.

Max had barely sat down when a most deafening roar of a mighty trumpet broke the night air. Without the slightest chance to react Max found himself with millions of others standing in the presence of Jesus in the clouds above the earth. No longer was his body a frail one with eighty plus years of wear, it was youthful, vibrant and absolutely bubbling with life. Max surveyed the multitude and saw many he recognised; many to, long since dead but now very much alive and energetic. All his family were there as was his wife Hazel. This was it! Now we're forever with the Lord.

Jesus looked around and smiled at each one individually then with a wave of His hand said comfortingly, "Come with me."

As they all followed, Max recalled the scripture in 1 Thessalonians 4:15-18. *"For this we say unto you by the word of the Lord, that we which are alive and remain unto the coming of the Lord shall not prevent them which are asleep. For the Lord himself shall descend from heaven with a shout, with the voice of the archangel, and with the trump of God: and the dead in Christ shall rise first: then we which are alive and remain shall be caught up together with them in the clouds, to meet the Lord in the air: and so shall we ever be with the Lord. Wherefore comfort one another with these words."* [ESV]

*"Without the Bread of Life
you are toast"*

Authors Note

This book is a work of fiction but the events detailed either actually happened or are about to happen. While the later part of the book relates completely to the future and clearly I have embellished these with substantial fiction never-the-less the actual happenings are certain as they are clearly described prophetically in the Bible. My intent is to demonstrate how even a simple life with all its ups and downs can achieve righteousness acceptable to God most high. As demonstrated though the only way such righteousness is possible is if you surrender your life completely to the Lord Jesus Christ by acknowledging you are a sinner and through repentance asking Him to be the Lord of your life. If you do this He will redeem your soul and restore it back to the relationship God intended for you at creation. Jesus will make you fully righteous, placing you in perfect right standing with God for all eternity. You will be spared from the wrath of God soon coming upon this entire earth and be rewarded with eternal life, living and reigning with Jesus for ever. What amazing grace.

It is impossible to achieve this life by human endeavours as the first part of this book demonstrates. The Bible tells us that man's very best efforts are but filthy rags, totally unacceptable to Him. The Bible also tells us in Acts 4:12 that *"And there is salvation in no one else, for there is no other name under heaven given among men by which we must be saved."* [ESV] That name is Jesus Christ who died in our stead as a blood sacrifice for our sinful state. This is the same Jesus who rose from the dead on the third day thereby breaking the power of sin and death. Jesus has descended to heaven and currently sits at the right hand of the Father God. The Holy Spirit of God is given to those redeemed by Jesus to enable them to understand His word in the Bible and empower them to live a righteous life until Jesus returns. Jesus Christ is returning physically very soon to snatch away all those that are true to him while God pours out His wrath on the unrighteous remaining on this earth.

Where will you stand when He returns or when you are called to your life's end? Will you stand with the righteous or the unrighteous? There are only two possible states, Righteous or unrighteous and only the righteous obtain eternal life. There is no other way to that life except through Jesus Christ.

Perhaps you've never actually accepted Jesus as your Lord and saviour and don't like the sound of being subject to God's wrath, especially when the alternative is not onerous. If that's you I would like you to stop for a moment and intentionally recite this little prayer, aloud to confess with your mouth.

"Dear Lord Jesus,

I admit that I am a sinner, in need of you and your forgiveness. I turn now from my sinful past and make you the Lord, the King, the Boss of my life. I believe with all my heart and confess with my mouth that you are the Lord Jesus Christ and that you died on the cross in my stead for all my sins, you were buried and rose again to life. I thank you for the Father's gift of eternal life through faith and I believe in you alone. I surrender every part of my life to you Lord Jesus, forever and ever. Thank you for the gift of your Holy Spirit which I receive from you now."

Just saying those words doesn't bring salvation. It is only if you truly make Jesus the Lord of your life that you are born again thereby receiving eternal life. It must come from your heart. Only then are guaranteed to be spared from God's judgement through Jesus.

God bless you if you've just genuinely prayed that prayer, you have begun your journey towards God. I recommend you find a church, if you don't already have one, pray and read your Bible every day and talk to your Pastor about getting baptised. Praise the Lord!

If you have been helped by this please also drop me an email and let me know as it's encouraging to hear of God's work in others.

God bless.

About the Author

Robert (Bob) Cottle has been a scholar of the Bible for over 60 years having read, studied and analyzed God's word extensively during his lifetime. The discipline of reading his Bible was instilled in him at an early age. At first, this was a burdensome chore but later it developed into a perfunctory habit. As the years progressed, however, the habit matured into a pleasurable pastime exploring the detail of the God he loves and serves.

Bob has been actively involved in church life from a young age and served as a lay preacher for several years and also as a church elder for a time.

Married for 40 years Bob and his wife Julie live in Nelson, New Zealand and have three adult children and three grandchildren – to date. In his secular life Bob trained and worked in professional engineering then later in senior business management but is now retired from full-time employment and enjoys writing Christian books.

Blessed with a natural aptitude to portray verbal and/or written word pictures. In retirement Bob has focused his abundant free time to the study and understanding of God's Word in the Bible which combined with his previous writing skills has enabled him to develop and author his interesting books.

Bob has five books commercially published, and he is confident with the subject matter particularly given his extensive knowledge of the Bible. His desire is to pass on a little of this understanding for the aid of other fellow Christians for the furtherance of God's work.

Feel free to follow or contact Robert (Bob) on;

Robert J Cottle Author,

@bobcottle,

robertjcottle@gmail.com

Books by Robert J Cottle

- ➤ The Bible, True, Relevant or a Fairy Tale. (Non-fiction)

- ➤ Fifty Shades of White, one man's quest for righteousness. (A novel, fiction)

- ➤ The Gospel of the Kingdom, not the Gospel of the Church. (Non-fiction)

- ➤ Not Many Fathers, why Othniel became a Judge. (A novel, fiction.)

- ➤ Eschatology 101, What the Bible says about the end of time. (Non-fiction)

9 781738 615100